AMERICAN SAVAGE

AMERICAN SAVAGE

MATT WHYMAN

HOT
KEY
BOOKS

First published in Great Britain in 2014 by Hot Key Books
Northburgh House, 10 Northburgh Street, London EC1V 0AT

A CIP catalogue record for this book is available from the British Library.

ISBN: 978-1-4714-0069-8

1

This book is typeset in 10.5 Berling LT Std using Atomik ePublisher

Printed and bound by Clays Ltd, St Ives Plc

FSC

Hot Key Books supports the Forest Stewardship Council (FSC),
the leading international forest certification organisation, and is
committed to printing only on Greenpeace-approved FSC-certified paper.

www.hotkeybooks.com

Hot Key Books is part of the Bonnier Publishing Group
www.bonnierpublishing.com

For Emma, as ever

APERITIF

Titus Savage waited for his tenant to answer the door with one eye on the alligator.

He had spotted it as soon as he climbed out of his pickup truck. The creature was basking on the lawn that fronted the apartment complex. It hadn't moved when he approached the building and made his presence known. Even so, Titus knew that it was watching him closely.

'Does nobody read the signs?' he muttered to himself, wondering what was taking the guy so long.

It was the barbeque area around the back that attracted the reptiles. The smell of charring meat led them to crawl out of the waterway that bordered the property. Normally, they would watch from the undergrowth and wait for everyone to leave before seeing what they could scavenge. What made them a regular feature in the grounds lately was the fact that one or two idiots had decided it would be fun to toss them chicken bones. OK, so the gators around here were only a couple of feet long. They weren't as big or aggressive as the ones found upriver. Those beasts would strike at a splash. Still, they possessed a killer instinct, and that deserved respect.

Shaking his head at what he faced here, Titus made a mental note to call the wildlife removal company. It would be another cost at his expense, of course, and that only served to sour his mood when his tenant finally appeared behind the fly screen.

'You?' growled the guy in question, a bulky-looking man who sounded like he hadn't used his voice all day. 'You can't beat at the door making out you're a cop. I got rights!'

From inside the apartment, Titus could hear a television chat show coming through an impressive-sounding speaker system. His tenant was registered in the contract as Harvey Gulcher. He had come to the door in his vest and boxers, and was clearly irritated. This came as no surprise to Titus, who had attempted to reach him on his cell phone on several occasions. It was kind of rude, he thought, seeing as the man had been at home each time he called and was clearly just pretending not to be there. Titus knew this for sure as he had been discreetly watching him from his pickup throughout the past few days. Pretending to be a policeman on his porch had seemed like a sure-fire way to get Harvey's attention. No doubt it broke some law, but it was nothing compared to what Titus had in store.

'I've come about the rent,' he told Harvey, his voice calm and friendly. 'It's been two weeks now. I'm sad that you've gone quiet on me.'

Titus knew that in a certain light, with his bald dome and broad shoulders, he could appear somewhat formidable. His blue eyes had a hardened and penetrating quality, which is why he reminded himself to keep blinking and beaming.

'I've had cash-flow issues,' reasoned Harvey, which Titus knew to be true. Earlier in the week, he had been parked in the street waiting for the man to return from the grocery store when the delivery truck pulled up with the home entertainment system. Titus had even used the master key to let them leave the box in the hallway, and what thanks had he received in return?

'I appreciate times are tough,' said Titus with a smile that tightened. 'But I have to feed my family.'

From behind the screen, Harvey casually bit at his thumbnail cuticle as if to indicate that his landlord would have to do much better than that. Titus judged the man's body mass index to be close to thirty. No doubt Harvey considered himself to be bearlike or chunky. According to the numbers, however, he had arrived in the realm of the obese. In his late twenties, Harvey was a contract computer hardware technician with no significant others in his life. Titus tended to favour individuals such as this when it came to renting out his single-occupancy apartments. In total, he owned seven in the same complex. It was his father who had once joked that what his son had here was a battery farm, but Titus failed to see the funny side. His tenants were free to come and go as they pleased, and could count on him as a responsible and courteous property management agent. As long as they kept to the terms of their agreement, and were polite if they called him out for maintenance and repair tasks, chances were they'd live long and fulfilling lives.

'I wouldn't stick around out there,' warned Harvey just then, who had briefly switched his attention to the gator on the lawn. Titus turned to see that the beast had crept towards him by a couple of feet. He looked back at the tenant, who grinned at him. 'You don't want to end up as lunch.'

'So, may I come in to discuss the situation?'

Harvey considered Titus through the screen for a moment longer, the TV still blaring, before scratching at his chest and opening the door.

'The last thing I want is bloodshed on my doorstep,' he grumbled. 'Let's make it quick.'

'Oh, I intend to.' Titus was already reaching for his back pocket as Harvey led him through to the living room.

Like most of the tenants so carefully vetted by Titus before he handed over the keys, Harvey wasn't the kind of person who liked to socialise. One glance at the unwashed socks on the hallway floor assured Titus that the guy hadn't entertained in quite a while. As for the speakers sitting astride the widescreen TV, in Titus's opinion it was all too big for the space. Still, he gave it only a brief glance before stepping up behind Harvey and looping the wire garrotte around his neck. Harvey gasped in surprise, but even as his hands snapped upwards it was too late to escape from the clutches of his landlord. Just as Titus had promised, pulling tight upon the handles, he didn't take up too much of the man's time. In fact, it would've been over for him much sooner had Titus's son picked another moment to call.

'*Am I too late?*' was the first thing Ivan asked, once Titus had managed to pinch the cell phone between his ear and his shoulder. It was a struggle to hold onto the garrotte with one hand as he did so, but he could never ignore the boy's ringtone. It was the same if any other member of his family called. Whenever they tried to reach him, it never went to answer machine.

'Ivan, you were supposed to be here twenty minutes ago,'

4

grunted Titus, as the man struggling in his clutches finally sank to the floor. 'This apprenticeship is never going to work if you can't keep good time.'

The silence down the line was in contrast to the sound of strangled gargling as saliva collected in the dying man's throat. It provided Titus with just enough time to assure his victim that his memory would be treated with respect in the same way as his body. Then it was all over for Harvey as a tenant, and just the beginning of his journey to the table.

'*Something came up, Dad,*' said Ivan eventually. '*But I promise I'll be home in time for supper.*'

FIRST COURSE

1

As a precaution, the Savage family ate with the blinds closed.

In the dining room, as the tea lights began to expire, the dessert stage was proving to be quite a trial. There was no problem with the way the food tasted. It was the sheer volume that challenged their stomach capacity.

'That's me done,' said Ivan, who pushed his plate away. The boy had been unusually quiet since returning home from high school, and so this declaration of defeat drew attention from around the table. 'I'm stuffed,' he added, sitting back with his hands pressed to his T-shirt.

Seated across from him, behind the carcass on the roasting tray and the remains from previous courses that surrounded it, a gamine young woman peered across at him.

'I'm not surprised,' she said under her breath, but just loud enough to be heard by everyone. 'All that finger food earlier.'

'So? I was hungry!' At fifteen, but with an intensity that exceeded his years, Ivan levelled his gaze over the leftovers. 'Anyway, who put you in charge? You're not even a *Savage*.'

'That's enough!' The man at one end of the table glared at his son. Titus had opted not to push Ivan for an explanation as to why he'd failed to show at the apartment complex. The kid had a lot on at school. Everyone knew that. Even so, as head of the household, Titus Savage made no exceptions when it came to bad manners at the table. 'Amanda is one of us now,' he said, switching his gaze to their lodger, 'if not in name then in heart and soul.'

Amanda kept her hair cropped elegantly, which highlighted both her angular face and striking self-confidence. Titus was disappointed to find her smirking into her plate, but chose not to pursue it. In a way, Amanda simply filled the space vacated by their eldest daughter. With Sasha in her first year at university, wisely studying criminology and forensic science, Titus was pleased that every seat around the table was still taken. Inevitably, such a thought drew his attention to the centenarian sitting alongside him. At 103, it was a miracle that his father Oleg was still here at all. Titus observed the old man draw his dessert through a straw. He did so with a slurp, the thick fluid rising towards lips concealed by a long, white, whiskery beard, and then sighed with satisfaction. Through Titus's eyes, a meal like this was what invigorated them all. It was, he felt sure, the secret behind such a long and eventful life.

'If there are scraps left on Ivan's plate,' Oleg said, having run a tongue across his gums to clean them, 'just put it all through the blender and I'll finish up for him.'

Ivan and Amanda exchanged a look, each wrinkling their noses, which Titus didn't approve of one little bit. This was a feast, after all – a special occasion, with no place for bickering or disrespect. Everyone knew full well the lengths involved in laying on such a spread. As ever, sourcing the main ingredient had fallen to Titus, as did the entrapment and slaughter. It was a shame that Ivan hadn't been there to assist him and learn on this occasion, but the real hard work – the magic, even – was down to one bewitching and very talented woman. Extending his gaze to the far end of the table, Titus observed his dear wife clearing her bowl. Even Angelica's apple pie tasted like no other. It was the shortcrust pastry that he savoured most, made with lard that she had rendered herself from the meat joints. Yes, you could buy a more conventional kind of thing in the stores, but it didn't come close in taste or satisfaction. For the Savage family, there was no substitute.

'Yet again, you've triumphed,' Titus told her, and prepared to find space for one more mouthful.

'It's all for you.'

She rarely smiled, his wife, and yet Titus could judge her mood just by gazing into her eyes. Right now, Angelica looked quietly satisfied that she had delivered another unforgettable spread. Titus lifted the spoon to his mouth. Sensing his shirt pull tight across his belly as he did so, the slightest hint of self-loathing soured the mouthful. There was no denying that he had put on a few pounds lately. Ever since the family had moved here, in fact, he found himself climbing onto the scales with a heavy heart, but what could he do about it? He had always taken pride in locally sourcing food for their feasts, and it was inevitable that the meat from these parts would carry a little extra fat. There also tended to be a lot more of it on the bone, and the Savages never left anything to waste.

Titus was as surprised as everyone else when his meal repeated on him. Just as he swallowed the last mouthful of pie, the noise commanded everyone's attention.

'Pardon *me*!' he declared, much to the delight of the youngest family member. Little Katya giggled at her father, looking like a princess in her plastic tiara and dressing-up gown.

'You belched,' she said, in an accent that sounded more naturalised by the day. 'Daddy belched.'

'We say "burped", honey pie,' her mother stressed to correct her. 'Don't be vulgar.'

As everyone settled back to finishing their food, Titus observed his wife once more. Since their arrival, Angelica had embraced the gym, and how that showed in her figure! She was naturally slim, with a swan-like neck on poised shoulders, but had come to possess a lean and firm quality in her physique. Unlike Titus, she could enjoy a feast without piling on the pounds. Even the younger ones could get away with it, but not him. Still, Titus had more pressing concerns, and all of them were gathered at the table before him. This was his calling, and what a great source of pride it was to him. Looking around at his brood, he felt much better about the situation. If he could no longer look down naked and see his kneecaps then so be it.

Family came first, after all, no matter what got in the way.

2

As a culinary concept, cannibalism was not something Titus expected to break into the mainstream any time soon.

People didn't know what they were missing, in his opinion, but the practice was just too tied up in taboos to be something the general populace would embrace. For one thing, everyone still clung to an outdated concept of what it all involved. That kind of human meat eater, with a bone through his nose, a dance for the rain gods and an appetite for missionaries, well, it belonged to the history books. It was a damn shame, Titus believed. In a day and age when everyone fretted about the quality of the meat that went into their mouths, unknowingly gobbling up horse and Lord knows what else in their ready meals, here was a source of nourishment that wasn't just fresh but free-range and in bountiful supply. With a little groundwork, you knew exactly where it had come from and what condition it was in before it arrived in the kitchen. As for the moral considerations, it was perfectly possible to select someone for the table who basically deserved nothing less. Even when the purpose of their existence left a lot to be desired, Titus always set out to ensure the kill was humane. Harvey was a classic example. Causing the man to fear for his life for a prolonged period wasn't kind. It would also result in a surge of adrenaline – a hormonal rush that only tainted the taste of the meat.

Tonight's dinner had taken some preparation. In transforming his tenant into a tasty treat, every step of the process had required care and attention from Titus and his family. As he had hoped to show his son, had football not kept Ivan from the kill, the flavour always improved through hanging the carcass for a short time. With the air conditioning in the apartment switched off, it allowed the bodily enzymes to break down quickly along with the evaporation of excess moisture. So, as Titus owned the place, he had permitted Harvey to remain there a while longer – strapped by his ankles from the roof joist. Then, as the gases that bloated the body worked their way free, and just before the smell threatened to upset the neighbours, Titus had enlisted Ivan to help move him out at dusk. It was a start for the boy, he believed, though there was still a long way to go. Later, in the family kitchen, and with great pride and expectation, he had watched his wife transform the corpse into a spread of culinary delights. There was something just so incomparably life-affirming about the consumption of your own kind. It was like a fuel injection into the bloodstream. A supercharging of the soul. Once you'd tasted such a thing, there could be no going back.

To eat a feast was a treat, but the Savage family could not afford to leave a trace behind. Fortunately, Titus had selected a food source where people often took off without a sign. In the rental sector, tenants were forever defaulting and then

14

disappearing with their belongings. So as long as he continued to take on the kind of recluse who wouldn't be much missed – which tended to boil down to bachelors from the IT sector – he always had a door to knock upon whenever the occasion for a feast arose. As a result of such diligence, all that remained of Harvey after they'd eaten was the paperwork, as well as the odd juice speck upon the table. So, once everyone had finished their meal, and before Titus retired to his study, the washing-up operation commenced. Everything needed to be scrubbed and sterilised, from the crockery and cutlery to the kitchen surfaces and the cooking equipment, including the oven and the extractor fan over the hob. It was a deep clean that took care of everything from drops of grease right down to the DNA. It demanded patience and commitment, which is why Angelica was quick to suggest that Ivan should be the one to escort Oleg back to his home.

'But why?' asked Ivan. 'His mobility scooter is outside.'

'Because you're his grandson,' she told him, mindful that the old man was in earshot – not that he heard a great deal nowadays – 'and it's the right thing to do.'

Angelica tightened her lips as Ivan shrugged and turned to fetch his baseball cap. There was no doubt that he'd become a little sullen lately. Then again, it came as little surprise from a boy of his age. Angelica supposed she should be grateful that she didn't have a teenage son smoking weed in the back seat of a stolen car. Instead, he spent a great deal of his time at home and never missed a meal. Nevertheless, she didn't take kindly to the attitude.

'Ivan,' said Titus, who had witnessed the exchange, 'what

15

do you say to your mother?'

The boy slotted his cap on, bill facing backwards, and seemed confused about his response for a moment.

'Oh, yeah,' he said finally. 'Thanks for cooking, Mum. It was a good one.'

'It was *spectacular*,' said Oleg, as Titus helped the old man to his feet. 'At my age I have to assume it might be my last, but I enjoyed every mouthful.'

'That's good to hear.' Angelica stepped back to let Amanda cross between them with the plates. 'You'll always have a place at our table.'

'And no doubt there'll be many more feasts to come,' said Titus, before escorting Oleg across the tiled floor. Prompted by a nod from his father, Ivan opened the front door. With all the blinds still closed, the intense sunshine that flooded inside was in marked contrast to the gloom in which they'd dined. Oleg followed his grandson outside, squinting as he peered up at the sky.

'It's a shame we can never dine *al fresco*,' he observed. 'A barbeque would be wonderful.'

'Think of the breeze,' Titus cautioned, and then gestured with his eyes at the neighbouring villas.

In his lifelong experience as a modern-day consumer of human beings, Titus Savage had made few mistakes. He was a conscientious hunter, always going to great lengths to cover his tracks. Only once had the family's appetite for people been uncovered, which is why they'd had to leave England in a hurry three years earlier.

Naturally, Titus had planned for this eventuality. To overcome the arrest warrants, he'd had fake passports prepared for everyone. As Amanda was not a suspect at that time, having only dined with them as a guest on that one fateful occasion, she was free to flee under her own identity, before joining the family at a later date. Wanted for the murder and consumption of a man, and possibly many others, Titus was well aware that only another planet could provide a safe haven. It was a notion that prompted him to think hard about where the family should relocate. In hindsight, Panama had been a mistake. The kids just complained about the humidity and erratic internet access, which is when he had set his sights on Jupiter. It would seem like light years away from their former lives in London, as he pitched it to them all, but not as alien as they first feared. When Titus had unfolded a map of America and explained that Jupiter was in fact a sleepy coastal town in the country's Sunshine State, he just knew that this was a golden opportunity for the Savages to start afresh and thrive.

'Four hundred years ago,' Titus had said, in a bid to seal the deal, 'the earliest English settlers arrived on the country's shores at Jamestown. Only the promised land was a little short on something central to their survival.'

'Videogames?' Ivan had suggested.

'Food,' his father pressed on, having pretended not to hear. 'So, as the cruellest of winters set in, those poor souls were forced to dig up the corpses of the fallen and eat them just to stay alive. We're talking about America's ancestral heritage here. They might not feast on human flesh any more, but it's in their genes! In my view, that makes it our spiritual home.

17

We can live among these people and instinctively nobody will suspect anything out of the ordinary.'

'As long as the climate is good where we're going,' Angelica had said. 'Warm, with good shopping.'

A northernmost suburb of Miami, divided by a broad water inlet and shot through with creeks, Jupiter was a world away from the skyscrapers way down in Florida's most famous metropolis. Unlike the outgoing spirit of the city, the people of Jupiter liked to keep themselves to themselves. With a waterside villa in a sought-after spur community, and false documentation that completely severed all links with their former existence, the Savage family were no exception. Every residence on the loop road was screened by careful landscaping, and featured private jetties out back to make the most of the tidal waters. It was a quiet, affluent but uneventful pocket of the county where palm trees sliced up the skyline everywhere you looked, pelicans roosted on porches and the rise and fall of the sun set the sky ablaze. Outsiders often said that the town's attractive, clean and tidy appearance was just a front that hid the more desperate aspects of life. You only had to venture behind the local parade of stores, where freshly watered flower baskets hung from the awnings, to find vagabonds and crack addicts in the shadows of the alley. In many ways, this tendency to pretend that bad things didn't happen suited the Savages just fine.

'People only see what they want to around here,' Titus once told his son on a drive across town. 'That's what helps us blend in.'

They had just passed a traffic accident of some description, marked by hastily erected screens and all the cops who waved them on. From the passenger seat, Ivan had strained for a better glimpse.

'If only that was true,' he had muttered to himself on facing the front once more.

For a centenarian like Oleg Savage, Jupiter's pleasant climate and peaceful neighbourhood offered a new lease of life. The regular feasts helped, of course, but by and large the old man felt at home here. He had settled in nicely, drawing no attention to himself, just like his son and daughter-in-law. As for the grandkids, while little Katya had practically grown up native, it was Ivan who continued to stick out, despite his best efforts. Just then, as the boy accompanied his grandfather home, Oleg was forced to slow his mobility scooter to a crawl just to stay level with him.

'My dad,' asked Ivan, who walked with a pained-looking swagger as if he had some eggs in the seat of his pants and was trying not to break them, 'was he always this controlling?'

Oleg looked across at the boy, with his clip-on sunglasses flipped down and the scooter whining. He didn't think it helped that Ivan had belted his shorts so they hung around his thighs. Another inch lower and the boy risked falling flat on his face.

'Your father does the best he can under difficult circumstances,' he told him. 'You should only ever think of him as caring.'

A moment later, a car with tinted windows crawled along the road. Rap blared from the speakers. Ivan looked nervous. As it passed, he flinched behind his grandfather's scooter.

'Will you relax?' said Oleg, shaking his head. 'This is hardly a gangland.'

Ivan turned to check that the car had really gone.

'I wasn't scared,' he said, sounding thoroughly unconvincing. 'A Savage isn't scared of anything!'

As the boy resumed his swagger along the road, leaving his grandfather behind this time, Oleg reached for the accelerator dial on his scooter. With safety in mind, Titus had applied a strip of tape to indicate that the old man should never exceed half-speed. Just then, Oleg barely turned the dial by a notch before he found himself closing in on his grandson once more.

'It's quite a walk you have there,' he observed finally. 'I'm guessing it doesn't come naturally.'

Ivan glanced over his shoulder at the family elder humming along just behind him. Oleg was wearing a flannel shirt tucked into his slacks, while the old man's mirrored shades offered the boy a clear picture of himself.

'It's got to be done,' he told his grandfather. 'This is the U S of A.'

Oleg thought better of telling Ivan that his centre of gravity looked all wrong. It seemed to him like he had an invisible thread affixed between his shoulder blades, tugging on him as he moved. He also opted not to inform the boy that someone had penned the words 'kick me' across the back of his shirt. He'd find out for himself as soon as he took it off, which had to be marginally less humiliating than having it pointed out by his grandfather. Instead, as they approached the junction that led from the inlet community to the main road, the old man wondered what he could do to help him integrate better.

'How is school?' he asked.

'The same,' said Ivan.

What with the shirt, Oleg took this to mean that after all this time the boy had yet to make any friends.

'Your mum says you've joined the football team,' he pressed on, looking for a bright side. 'That's great news. What position do you play?'

'Bench,' said Ivan.

Oleg appeared baffled by the response, but chose not to pursue it. If anything, he had to admire him for taking up the national sport. For Ivan wasn't involved in the kind of football that used jumpers for goalposts, as it did in Oleg's day. This was American football – a completely different ball game with rules that flummoxed the old man. He just hoped the lad's young mind made it easy for him to embrace.

'Well, bench sounds promising,' he told his grandson regardless. 'It's certainly a start.'

As he trundled across the junction, with Ivan still strutting awkwardly alongside him, Oleg focused on the sign on the lawn for the whitewashed complex up ahead. When the Savages first moved to Jupiter, it had been his idea to move to the Fallen Pine Nursing Home. At Oleg's time of life, it was just easier all round. The home had lovely staff, with no stairs for him to negotiate, while the company of other people also in their winter years came as a comfort to him. With his son's family just around the corner and a place at the table whenever a feast was served, the home suited his needs in every way. In fact, when one occupant passed on in the room across the corridor, and another one moved in, Oleg had encountered a renewed zest – one that he believed he had left behind in his teenage years. Negotiating the ramp towards the main doors, he looked across at the window to the communal room and saw her sitting there, as she always did when he was out, waiting in the sunny spot for his return.

'Priscilla looks pleased to see you,' noted Ivan.

Oleg Savage nudged the scooter into the park position on the porch. 'That's my girl,' he said, with a wink in the old lady's direction, and then began the slow, painful process of dismounting from his steed.

3

'Now, be good,' said Angelica, as she hung Katya's coat on her pre-school peg. 'No biting other children today, understood?'

'OK, Mommy.'

'Promise?'

The little girl looked up with an air of such innocence and purity that Angelica found it hard to accept that she had now been warned twice for leaving tooth marks in her classmates. On the last occasion, the indentation was close to going beyond play that had got out of hand. Angelica had been forced to put on quite a performance to appease the teacher, and really didn't relish the prospect of being called in again.

'I promise not to taste them any more, Mommy,' Katya replied.

'Good girl,' said Angelica. 'And it's pronounced "muh-mi",' she added. 'As I keep telling you.'

Katya nodded, and then puckered her lips with her eyes scrunched in readiness for her traditional kiss goodbye. She really was a sweetheart, as Titus kept repeating to anyone who would listen, with honey-coloured ringlets spilling over her shoulders, shining blue eyes and a little mouth in the shape of a perfect bow. Angelica watched her skipping off into the busy playground, and quietly hoped she really did recognise that friends should not be considered food.

When the family had first arrived in Jupiter, baby Kat was still crawling and knew just a handful of words. She had since spent more than half her life here, and so it came as no surprise to her parents that she should sound so naturalised. Angelica was careful that she didn't go too far, though she herself had come to love life in Florida. If the family didn't already possess false documentation to support their citizenship, Angelica would've been first in the application queue. Yes, Ivan still nursed some issues settling in, but she felt sure that in time he would fall into the American way.

Driving out to the gym with the top down, this toned, tanned mother and housewife relished the warm breeze on her face and gave no thought whatsoever to her former life. Jupiter offered the family everything, and that included a plentiful supply of people that nobody missed whenever the time arose for a feast. Maybe it was the year-round sunshine that had brought out the best in her, for Angelica had come to complement her love of cooking with a passion for keeping fit. In particular, she liked to train in the open air, and so her mood got even better on pulling into the gym car park, where her personal trainer was busy stretching his hamstrings.

'Good morning, Joaquín,' she said, on killing the engine. 'I hope you're not going to push me too far today.'

The young man awaiting her arrival was dressed in a vest that exposed his broad shoulder blades and running shorts accentuating his tight waist. His wavy black hair was waxed back to the nape of his neck, while Angelica often joked that she could strike a match on his stubble. Joaquín Mendez was a twenty-one-year-old Argentinian with strong beliefs. The cross around his neck symbolised his deep religious commitment, while the absence of trainers on his feet marked his passion for the soulful art of barefoot running.

'If I didn't push you, Mrs Savage,' he said, in his rich South American accent, 'I would not be doing my job to the best of my abilities.'

Angelica climbed out of the open-top and shut the driver's door while facing him. 'My husband hates to see people suffer,' she said. 'You're so different from him in lots of ways.'

Titus Savage had arrived early at the apartment in order to prepare the place for a new occupant. With a viewing lined up that morning, he needed it to be clean, tidy and smelling of fresh coffee rather than the corpse he had recently allowed to mature in the front room.

Sitting in the kitchenette, having flung open the windows, he found himself thinking ahead to lunch. No doubt Angelica would bring something nice back from the deli, as she always did after a workout. Some bagels, perhaps, or the sourdough bread that he liked so much – especially when it was still warm from the baker's oven. You couldn't live on human flesh alone. Like any diet, it was important to keep things healthy and balanced. He dwelled on this over the large latte he had picked up on the way over. With the plastic travel lid in place designed for sipping on the move but which never seemed to work, it was inevitable that he'd slop several drops onto his tropical shirt. Peering down at the wet spots where his stomach sloped outwards, Titus was reminded that one aspect of his eating habits really needed to be addressed.

'This must be what they call a midriff crisis,' he half joked with himself. It wasn't that long ago when a spilled drink like this would've had a clear drop to the floor. Nowadays, Titus often found he had to brush crumbs from his belly. Setting the latte on the kitchen counter, he hopped off the stool and stretched. Then, out of curiosity, he attempted to touch his toes, but got no further than his upper thighs. Standing tall once more, he shook his head and sighed. 'You've let yourself go,' he declared, addressing his reflection in the oven door. 'What are you? A Savage or a slob?'

Titus felt a tinge of shame. As head of the family, especially one with such a noble tradition to uphold, was it not essential that he led them like a warrior? He took a long look at himself in the darkened glass and then let his shoulders sag. As a second-generation Russian, born in the UK but with the pride of the motherland in his heart, blood and bones, what had happened to him out here? Florida was a wonderful place to be in lots of ways, but the temptations had taken their toll. Titus only had to look at so many of the citizens to know what was responsible for his increasing weight. There was no denying that such fatty food had caught up with him. Despite what he faced in the glass, however, Titus couldn't allow himself to go to seed like this. Angelica had taken steps to look after herself, and Amanda seemed able to eat pretty much anything without putting on weight, but that wasn't the point. Take his son, Ivan. The boy looked up to him, and a father who broke a sweat while carving wasn't setting much of an example. Titus resolved to do something about it. For one thing, he told himself, there was no need to drive to the apartment complex as he had just now. It was a short walk from the Savage residence, just three blocks beyond his father's nursing home. The next time he came out here, he decided, the keys to the pickup would stay in the villa.

It was the sound of the door buzzer that prompted Titus to stop gazing disapprovingly at his stomach. He glanced at his watch. The potential tenant was precisely on time, which was impressive. Turning to answer the call, he hoped this meant he would be renting to someone who wouldn't cross him for a while. For Titus resolved just then that he needed to get in trim before the family could enjoy another feast.

4

Amanda Dias had a particular taste in men. The slight but determined twenty-one-year-old could look back on a healthy number of dates since arriving in Florida. None of them had ended well, however. The guys who asked her out came from all walks of life. What they all lacked was the backbone to develop a relationship with a girl who had such strong views about food. Amanda didn't chew them up in the physical sense. That aspect of her diet wasn't something she'd ever share. Still, each one was quickly forced to recognise that they were dining with someone who possessed uncompromising convictions.

'Have you chosen?' she asked the young man sitting opposite her that lunchtime while consulting the menu in her hands. 'I like the sound of the corn and blueberry salad.'

Only recently, Amanda had been forced to cut short an evening out when the junior lifeguard on her arm had spotted a burger joint on their way back from the pictures and declared himself to be ravenous. On this occasion, Amanda had cautiously accepted an invitation to a beachside bistro overlooking the breakers because the chef was known to do fabulous things with seasonal fruit. Unlike the lifeguard, whose idea of making an effort went no further than a red vest, surf shorts and flip-flops, the young fund manager who had invited her here had dressed carefully for their date. With a jumper arranged casually over his shoulders and a pastel polo shirt, Nate Dunlop looked both confident and relaxed as he folded his menu and beamed at his date.

'There's only one choice for me,' he said. 'The tuna with avocado and kiwi salsa.'

Amanda Dias flattened her lips, trying hard not to look crushingly disappointed. She'd had such high hopes, after all. Nate had first struck up a conversation with her under a hotel awning during an unexpected tropical storm, and then hailed her a cab home when the downpour worsened. This date had been something she'd been looking forward to, and now it was ruined.

'The salsa sounds good,' she said with a sigh, and considered her menu once more. 'The tuna not so much.'

'You don't eat fish?' Nate sipped at his mineral water.

'I play no part in the rape of the oceans.'

Coughing only slightly as he swallowed, Nate set down his glass.

'OK, so maybe I won't have the fish.'

'How about the meat?' Amanda looked over the top of the menu, her eyes narrowing.

Nate looked like he really could do with moistening his mouth with another slug from his glass.

'I sense I may be about to give you the wrong answer.' He offered a nervous smile. 'What can I say? I'm a sucker for a steak.'

The blinds behind Nate were set to counter the glare of the

sun. When Amanda sat back in her seat to fully assess her date, it caused harsh bars of light and shadow to cut across her face.

'There is *no* justification for eating defenceless animals in any shape or form,' she declared. 'The same goes for the fish.'

'I see,' said Nate, who had begun to look a little amused. 'A vegetarian, right?'

'Vegan,' she told him proudly. 'I don't do half measures.'

Nate responded by breaking into a broad smile. Amanda knew that would vanish if she revealed just how much further down the culinary road she had travelled with her surrogate family. A chance encounter with the Savages at the table had marked the beginning of her journey from a university undergraduate who rejected all animal-based products to the young woman she had become with an appetite for people. Instead of being horrified at the sight of a family consuming a human being, Amanda considered it a revelation. This was the ultimate in progressive eating, she had concluded. Nobody was preying on another species, but simply turning on their own kind in an overpopulated and resource-starved world. In her mind, dining on human flesh in no way contradicted her beliefs. In between feasts, she continued to pursue a way of life that spared all animal suffering. As for people, they perpetrated so many crimes against the creatures of the earth that this occasional, secret indulgence was her way of biting back.

'You know what?' Nate said next. 'You strike me as quite a man eater.'

Amanda cocked one eyebrow. A rare glimmer of amusement played across her face.

'That's very observant of you,' she replied. 'So, I'm

disappointed that you can't see beyond the prospect of a juicy T-bone and recognise the suffering behind it.'

'Don't you ever give up?' Nate addressed her with some exasperation, only to raise his hands as if to apologise. 'OK,' he said, now grasping for a conversation beyond the tense small talk they had shared so far. 'Convince me.'

'Really?' Amanda emerged from the shadows and leaned in on her elbows. It wasn't just the sun on her face that brightened her expression. 'Very well,' she began. 'Imagine if the meat eaters were presented with a choice.'

'I'd say medium,' said Nate. 'Rare can be risky and anything more is overcooked.'

'I'm talking about the choice between life and death,' she pressed on, quietly irritated by the interruption. 'One day the grazers will rise against your kind for the centuries of misery and bloodletting you have brought upon the animal kingdom. Time is running out, Nate. We are gathering in number, massing in ranks and becoming radicalised in the face of so much cruelty and suffering just so people like you can be served cheap cuts of meat. Well, enough is enough,' she added, and banged her fist on the table. 'A food revolution is in the air, and come that day you'll know how it feels to be hunted, scared and *butchered with your heart still beating!*'

Nate Dunlop had listened with growing alarm to what sounded like a murderous manifesto – one that had started calmly but ended with people at the neighbouring tables turning to see what had possessed this young lady now glaring balefully at him. He glanced around, drumming his fingers on the table as he did so.

'Well, it was nice meeting you,' he said finally, and rose prematurely to his feet.

Amanda sighed to herself. 'Not again,' she muttered, following him with her eyes.

Nate fished his wallet from his pocket. He dropped twenty bucks on the table for the drinks.

'It's not you,' he told her, 'it's me.'

'Really?'

'If I was half as crazy as you,' he said, with some irritation in his voice, 'then perhaps we'd be close to having a connection.'

It was only as Nate took his man bag by the strap from the back of his chair that she met his gaze for a moment.

'Paying for the drinks won't spare you,' she told him.

Nate glared back at her. Then a hint of pity came into his eyes.

'Listen, you're a nice girl,' he told her, before slinging his bag over his shoulder, 'but all this talk is nuts.'

With that, he left Amanda facing the chair. A moment later, she twisted around to see him easing through the throng towards the door.

'Hey!' she called out angrily, which caused yet more heads to turn. 'There's nothing wrong with nuts!'

Ivan Savage returned to his position on the bench and sat hunched over in his shoulder pads. With his cheeks flushed, and his hair in a tangle having just popped off his helmet, he willed himself to stay calm. After-school football practice had begun over an hour ago. So far, he'd been given three opportunities on the pitch. Each one had lasted no more than a minute before the coach opted to take him off again.

'It's for your own safety,' he told the boy. 'Even with protective gear, you're in danger of sustaining a head injury.'

'Give me a chance, boss. It's all I ask.'

'Ivan, you're playing with big boys here. Yes, it's a game, but it's not a *game*. There's a difference.'

Reflecting on the exchange, Ivan sat there with his helmet in his hands, as if it was a skull in need of crushing.

'Damn them all,' he muttered, with his own team in mind. 'Those guys should just learn to pass properly.'

Was it his fault that his teammates deliberately hurled the ball at him, knowing he lacked their handling skills? OK, so he was smaller and slighter than the other players out there, but nobody gave him a chance, and that included the coach. Ivan could barely break into a trot without being whistled off and placed on water-boy duties. Then there was the opposition. Just what was the point of slamming him to the ground like that? It was asking for payback. The boy sat there, stewing, and tried to take his mind off things by making another stab at understanding how the hell this game was supposed to be played.

If only Ivan could get his head around the rules. American football remained his perfect path to being accepted at high school. It was the country's national sport, after all. Embracing it as an outsider would earn him lasting friendships, or so he had believed at first. Nobody at school knew Ivan's true origins, of course. His father had ensured that their cover story was foolproof. Even so, he had expected his classmates to show a little more willingness to engage, rather than teasing him about his accent and calling him an oddball. Ivan had arrived at school eager to integrate as he knew best. Unfortunately, unspeakably sick jokes and magic tricks involving pins and razor blades that tended to result in minor injuries for his volunteers failed to bring him respect, admiration or friendship. Instead, it had earned him several visits to the high-school principal's office. On calling in the boy's parents, and tabling the prospect of expulsion, he had been assured by Titus and Angelica that Ivan was simply a determined soul. Everything he had done, despite being misguided, was driven by his need for acceptance. That's when the principal had suggested that a team sport might be the way forward, with no concept whatsoever that as the school years progressed it would be his undoing.

'C'mon, coach,' Ivan grumbled, as the man in the Miami Dolphins jersey gravitated up and down the touchline. 'Give me a break here!'

'I can't do that,' the coach replied, with his back to the boy. 'It would be negligent on my part.'

'But how am I going to learn?' pleaded Ivan. 'All I do is sit here for session after session!'

The coach turned, looking pained.

'Ivan, I understand your frustration and appreciate your enthusiasm, but why don't you think about a non-contact sport? Something solo, perhaps, like . . . distance running.'

Ivan listened to his coach's advice, while quietly assessing the cords in the man's neck. He looked kind of chewy in the boy's opinion, which wasn't all bad with the right cooking technique. A stew, perhaps, or cooked with chopped onion, jalapeño peppers and spices for a tasty burrito filling.

'I'm good at football,' he said after a moment. 'You need me on side, coach. You just don't know it yet.'

5

Titus Savage had returned to the villa in good time for lunch. It was now heading towards late afternoon. He had tried reaching his wife on her cell phone, left a message and a text, but she had yet to respond. It was Amanda who found him in the kitchen, fixing up a snack.

'You really should consider going vegan in between feasts,' she said, and gestured to the salami on the counter. 'Those poor animals.'

'I make up for my bad habits,' he told her with his mouth full. 'Since we've been here, all the people we've chosen for the table have been carnivores. Amanda, if it helps, I'm making the world a safer place for the cows, pigs and sheep. We're thinning out the meat eaters in the food chain.'

'I can swallow that,' she said, grinning despite herself. 'But what about the fat content?'

Titus looked at the bread roll in his hands, crammed with meat, mayo and pickled onion slices, and cringed. Were the extra pounds that noticeable to everyone else?

'So, how was your date?' he asked, in a bid to shift the subject.

'Same as ever.' Amanda opened the door to the cupboard

where the family kept the canned drinks and cordials. 'Another gastronomic mismatch. I like a challenge, but not a lost cause.'

Tearing off a bite from his bread roll, Titus considered his lodger as she filled a glass with fruit juice. It had been at a family discussion, during the heart of a feast, that the Savage family elected to invite Amanda Dias into the fold. Every one of them was well aware of her fiery and unyielding nature. Still, as she had walked in on their secret and promptly converted as though it was something missing from her life since birth, Titus had decided that it was better to keep her with them so he could keep an eye on her.

With her place at the table assured, Amanda had gone on to embrace the concept of feeding on human meat with the same alarming passion she displayed for veganism. Convinced that people who ate animals deserved to be consumed themselves, Amanda would've happily dined on someone every day. As that was a shortcut to being caught, however, Titus had convinced her to restrict it to a special treat, while she continued to pursue her vegan ways in between feasts. He knew she didn't like the fact that her adoptive family enjoyed a midweek spaghetti bolognaise, or eggs over easy on a Sunday. Then again, the Savages had transformed her eating habits. So, Amanda simply learned to tolerate it while rustling up a tofu salad for herself. Over time, and with the Savages' eldest daughter, Sasha, now studying in New York, Amanda had become a welcome member of the household. One that Titus worried about as much as he did everyone else, for his lodger's convictions didn't just compromise her love life.

'Maybe you should be more open-minded about meat eaters,'

he suggested, having swallowed his mouthful. 'It might even help your career prospects.'

Amanda returned the juice bottle to the shelf and faced him.

'Does a good cop turn a blind eye to a terrible crime?' she asked him. 'It just isn't me.'

Whenever Amanda found work, mostly as a waitress in diners, her opinions didn't take long to find a voice, and they were usually directed at the customers. Only recently she had been asked to leave her last job with immediate effect, which came as no surprise to Titus in view of all the American breakfasts she was serving.

'Amanda, you can't tell paying customers that they're cold-blooded murderers,' he told her, well aware that she had yet to forget her grounds for dismissal. 'You can see how it would rub some people up the wrong way . . . '

'I held out for three months in that joint,' Amanda replied defensively. 'That's twelve weeks smelling of bacon.'

Titus prepared to bite into his roll once more.

'I guess it got into your pores.'

Amanda pulled a face, nodding all the same. 'My dream job is out there,' she said. 'I just haven't found it yet. Until then, I have the rent to pay.'

'Amanda, you're family.' This time, Titus addressed her with his mouth full. The point he had to make was too important for him to wait. 'There's no need to take on dead-end jobs. You'll always have a place at the table and time to work out what you really want to do with your life.'

'You're very kind,' she said, and then levelled her gaze at him. 'But I'm not a charity case. I *always* pay my way.'

Having cut all contact with her papa and three older brothers back in England – who regrettably considered her missing in the worst possible sense – Amanda Dias looked up to Titus as a father figure. As a matter of principle, she had rejected his offer of living at the villa rent-free. She was an independent young woman, after all, and held onto high hopes of finding employment that wouldn't conflict with her values. Amanda chose not to tell Titus that she had an interview lined up already. If she got the post, she wanted it to come as a nice surprise. Besides, at the sound of the front door opening, Amanda knew that in moments she would no longer have his full attention.

Eight miles. That's how far Joaquín Mendez had taken Angelica on a run that day. It was further than he had ever ventured with her before, but she had placed every ounce of her trust in him. They had headed out on the coastal route, along the beach and the boardwalks, heading south towards Boca Raton. Joaquín had run without training shoes, the soles of his feet looking toughened and tanned to Angelica's eye, while his rhythmic, loping strides had seemed completely in tune with the terrain. She had followed close behind, in her cross trainers and white ankle socks, both of which he had asked her to remove when they reached the halfway point and prepared to turn around.

'I want you to feel at one with the ground beneath your feet,' Joaquín had told her, before tying the laces of her trainers together, stuffing both socks inside and then slipping them around his neck. 'Do you feel the connection now?' he asked, and held her gently by the wrists. 'Run with me. Run as nature intended.'

Now, having completed the session and the drive home to the villa, Angelica felt elated. Her ankles ached like mad, but Joaquín had said that was because she'd used muscles and tendons she never knew she possessed. When it came to meat for a feast, Angelica had plenty of experience in assessing quality by squeezing and tweaking such components, yet it surprised her to feel these things at work inside her own body.

Leaving the open-top in the drive with the hood still folded back, Angelica inched her way painfully towards the front door. Then she hobbled all the way back again when little Kat called out to her from the booster seat in the car. She knew it had been one hell of a workout as soon as she had stopped off at kindergarten to collect her youngest daughter. If she wasn't going to expire from exhaustion then she needed to eat.

'You look fit to drop,' observed Titus, when Angelica followed their youngest daughter into the kitchen. She found her husband in the kitchen with the lodger at the window finishing a juice. 'Are you OK, honey?' Titus found her a seat before she could reply.

'Joaquín,' she said weakly, as if that would explain everything.

'What has he done to you this time?' Amanda enquired disapprovingly before setting her glass in the sink. 'Every time that guy puts you through your paces you return home half dead.'

'I'll be fine.' Angelica waved away her concern. 'I feel good, really I do. At least, I will in a minute.'

As Katya reached up to the counter and helped herself to the last of the salami, Titus fetched his wife a glass of water. Angelica sunk it in seconds. She noted the remains of her husband's roll on the plate. Despite not eating since breakfast and having burned what felt like every last calorie in her body, she opted not to finish it on account of all the mayo.

'You can have too much of a good thing,' Titus told her with great concern. 'Are you sure you're not taking this workout thing too far?'

'In Florida, you have a choice,' said Angelica, grimacing as she lifted one Lycra-clad leg over the other. 'You stay fit or die lardy.'

'Well, just take it easy for the rest of the day,' mumbled Titus, having taken a step away from his wife. 'I can handle supper.'

'Excellent,' said a voice from behind them. 'I'm always hungry after training! And Dad serves up big portions.'

Angelica turned to see Ivan drop his sports bag at the kitchen door. He was still wearing much of his football kit, which looked as clean as when his mother had last washed it for him.

'How was it?' asked Amanda. 'Did you pack a cushion for the bench?'

'I saw some action,' he told her testily.

'From the sidelines,' she said under her breath, and headed for her room.

Amanda's comment left an uneasy silence in the kitchen for a second.

'So, what was the score?' asked Angelica, keen to move on.

'I'm not sure.' Ivan shrugged and set his helmet on the table. 'I don't even know which side won.'

'Never mind,' said Angelica. 'It's the taking part that counts.'

'Your mother is right,' Titus added. 'You'll get the hang of the rules in time.'

Angelica didn't like to point out that their son had been playing American football for nearly two school years now. Yes, the game could seem complicated to an outsider, but Ivan had many hours of training under his belt. It was just one more reason for Angelica to worry that her boy would never fit in. Titus shared her anxiety. It was evident in the way he looked at his son so uneasily.

'How about we go outside and throw the ball for a bit?' he suggested. 'The practice might help.'

'I'm good,' he replied.

Angelica watched Ivan assess his father dismissively, which prompted Titus to haul in his paunch.

'It might benefit you both,' she offered quietly, and then shrugged when Titus shot her a look. 'I'm only thinking of his happiness . . . and your health.'

'Well, you don't have to worry on that count,' Titus told her. 'I have a plan to get into shape, and that starts tomorrow. Until then,' he said, offering Ivan a supportive wink, 'who's up for a post-training takeaway?'

6

Oleg Savage liked to dress for the day in front of the mirror in his room. This simply served to remind him that he still had a physical presence in the world. At his age, it was easy to feel like a ghost-in-waiting. Oleg buttoned his collarless shirt to the neck, and then made sure the strands of his beard weren't caught in any of the buttons. He studied his reflection, looking deep into his eyes. They had seen so many things over a century, both heavenly and abominable. Despite fading in colour, they still had the capacity to twinkle at times, and forever in the name of love.

'Look at you,' he muttered playfully to himself. 'Always the fool.'

As a younger man, many decades earlier, Oleg Savage had gone to hell and back for the woman he considered his soulmate. He could still remember how he looked back then; completely different from now in size and frame, proud and upright in his army uniform, but with the very same glimmer in his gaze around someone so very special to him.

Born and raised in Russia, Oleg and his new bride had found themselves caught up in one of the most appalling events of World War Two. When the Nazis laid siege to Leningrad, blockading the city and cutting off food and medical supplies, the citizens suffered for 900 long days. Many thousands died of starvation, or succumbed to the bitter winters. As despair hung over the city like a fog, survival demanded increasingly desperate measures. For Oleg, who had learned to force down weeds and wallpaper paste, it meant reluctantly crossing a line laid down by God. In an act of desperation, when all other options ran out, he had sustained himself and his new wife with flesh cut from corpses. Even then, Oleg knew it was an act that could never be forgotten, let alone forgiven.

The revulsion and self-loathing was intense, just as he had imagined, and yet he found that there was also something supremely restorative about human meat. It didn't just swell the belly but the spirit, too, while the very act of eating transported the mind from the horrors of a conflict that would otherwise have consumed them. It was a revelation – something no other food source could achieve – and one Oleg longed to share with others. If people knew how much stronger and more positive they would feel if they dined on their own kind, he decided, the world would be a better place. Even so, he chose not to speak about it when the siege came to an end. The practice had brought Oleg and his wife enlightenment, but he knew that spreading the word would earn him nothing but damnation.

Instead, having fled to England with his wife after the war, Oleg elected to introduce their only child to what was becoming a regular event. When Titus passed it on to Angelica and the kids, Oleg even felt some pride in what he had started. Over time, what had begun in a moment of great hardship became something of a refined ritual for the Savages. The old man smiled at himself, thinking fondly of Titus and his belief that a family who ate people together stayed together. Without a doubt, the occasional feast served to unite everyone at the table. The tradition had outlasted Oleg's dear wife, who had left this world many years earlier, and would no doubt continue long after he joined her. For now, however, as the memory of his younger self faded in the mirror to a reflection of the man he had become, Oleg smoothed back what was left of his hair. It was enough to turn the old man's thoughts to the special lady who had prompted him to pay more attention than usual to his appearance lately. They were due to meet on the shaded terrace overlooking the inlet at any time, for coffee, cake and simple companionship.

A knock at the door signalled to him that the moment had arrived. Oleg made his way across the room, allowing his joints the chance to assemble some kind of rhythm, and opened the door. Before him stood a portly male nurse in a capped white shirt and with a purple plug in each earlobe.

'Ready to roll, big guy?' Vince was the name of the nurse, who always seemed a little breathless to Oleg, and gestured at the wheelchair awaiting him. 'If there's one woman you don't want to keep waiting, it's Priscilla.'

It came as no surprise to Ivan when the first scrunched-up paper ball of the lesson struck his head. It happened so regularly that he could even tell who had thrown it. Although everyone was reluctant to be his friend in case they attracted ridicule and grief, it always came down to one of three boys: Ryan, Chad or

Bryce. The ball had hit on the left temple. This told Ivan that Chad was responsible, given that he sat across from him, while the hissed comment from behind could only be from Bryce.

'Hey, new girl! I heard you been sitting on that bench for so long it's gonna have a plaque with your name on it!'

This trio of alpha jocks had made it their mission to leave Ivan feeling as low and isolated as possible. All three were physically bigger than him, with the kind of buzz-cut hairstyles that suggested they shared the same barber. Even though Ivan had been attending the school for several years, they insisted on reminding him that he was still the last to join, and always referred to him in the feminine as if it was the funniest insult in the world. Ivan turned to the boy who had thrown the paper projectile, scowling so sharply that a groove formed between his eyebrows.

'I keep telling you to leave me alone,' he growled. 'One day you'll be sorry.'

Both Chad and Bryce pulled the same face, mocking the boy by pretending to be scared, while Ryan at the back just shook his head in pity.

'All you got to do is quit the team,' he whispered, having waited for the teacher to begin writing on the whiteboard. 'It's embarrassing with a nutsack like you on the gridiron. Makes us look like pussies, rather than the best this county has to offer.'

'I'm entitled to be in the squad,' replied Ivan, facing the front once more. 'Even if I am on the sidelines.'

'Give it up,' growled Ryan, who was well aware that the teacher was about to turn. Ivan watched the boy lower his brow like a bull. 'Show your face at one more training session,' he added, jabbing a finger at him, 'and we'll tear you limb from limb.'

Ivan said nothing in response, if only because the teacher had just spun around and was now scouring the class for the pupils behind all the whispering. Instead, in the wake of the threat, he opened his exercise book and smiled to himself contentedly.

On their arrival in Florida, Ivan had been the most enthusiastic of all the family to embrace the American way. His father had seemed so proud of the effort he made to get to grips with the culture. It was just a shame that Ivan fell short in every area. It wasn't his fault if people failed to understand a word he said when he put on a southern accent, and what was with the grief he got when he rocked into school with his shorts slung gangster-style? People just didn't click with him, and it had been just the same in England.

Despite the name-calling that had begun pretty much on his first day in school, Ivan soldiered on. He had immersed himself in hip hop and plastered his room with posters of the legends: Snoop, Tupac, Vanilla Ice and MC Hammer. When that did little to stop the ridicule, his interest in American football had started to flower. It had been hard to avoid. Every time he surfed the TV channels he'd come across a game, while kids in their inlet community were forever tossing a ball in the street. After the inexplicably negative reaction towards his pranks and magic tricks, Ivan saw it as a way to earn attention for all the right reasons. Despite his struggle to understand the rules, he had signed up with the school squad and hadn't missed a session since.

All Ivan Savage ever wanted to do was to make a friend. Instead, his experience only served to harden his sense of injustice. It also left the boy determined not to give in.

Hopping off the bus in downtown Jupiter, Amanda Dias braced herself for the stink of diesel fuel and dead fish. It always happened this close to the harbour, but she had grown used to it over the years. On this occasion, she wasn't here to stage a protest or upend a crate of striped bass into the water. That had got her banned from the wharf some time ago. No, Amanda had arrived with just one goal in mind, and that was to return to the villa with a job.

The man who answered Amanda's phone call – the bar manager, so he'd said – had confirmed that the vacancy was still open. He'd been a little cagey about the precise requirements, and the advert hadn't given much away, but it was work and Amanda was committed to making her contribution to the Savage household.

The Crankbait Sports Saloon was located on the waterside road close to the boat ramps. Sandwiched between a motorbike repair shop and an empty, weed-stricken lot, the most notable aspects of this single-storey building were the red and blue neon piping and front windows covered by security mesh. Amanda stopped before the porch steps and studied the sign. It had seen better days, for sure, but no doubt shone brightly after dark. She hoped that she could say the same for the man in the vest and sweatpants who answered the door. It had taken him a moment to open up after she rang the bell on account of all the sliding bolts. Rolan was his name. He had dark eyes under bushy slugs, and a chip in his teeth she found hard to ignore. He waited for her to meet his gaze once more before apologising for his appearance. It was early, for him, he said, and he'd grown used to people rocking up and having second thoughts about an interview. Amanda had barely drawn breath to stress that it wasn't a problem before he offered her the position.

'Is that it?' asked Amanda. 'I'm in?'

Rolan nodded, adjusting the crotch of his sweatpants without taking his eyes off her.

'You're welcome to take a look around,' he said. 'But you won't find any surprises.'

Amanda peered over his shoulder, seeing little in the gloom. She wasn't at all concerned for her safety. Having witnessed the lengths that Titus went to in pursuit of a feast fit for the family, she was quite capable of handling herself. What mattered here was the possibility of a wage.

'One thing,' she asked. 'The advert said nothing about serving food.'

Rolan adopted a look of quiet amusement.

'Guys don't come here for the food,' he told her. 'Unless you're talking about the potato chips that go with the beer.'

'What flavour chips?' she asked, and placed her hands on her hips.

'Plain salted,' Rolan said with a shrug. 'We don't do fancy here.'

'So, when do I start?' asked Amanda, before promising not to let him down.

7

The grounds to the rear of the Fallen Pine Nursing Home sloped gently to the shore of the inlet. From the terrace, looking across the broad expanse of water, Oleg was able to locate his son's villa by the boat moored beside the jetty.

'Do you see it?' he asked his breakfast companion, and handed over the binoculars with the sticker restricting use to the terrace only. 'Titus has a wonderful family. He'll stop at nothing to create a loving and stable environment over there. It makes me so proud.'

The elderly lady sitting across from him was wearing a plastic visor tinted pink to counter the subtropical sunshine. In her white dress and oyster shawl, Priscilla looked as pretty as a dewdrop, which was exactly how Oleg had put it when he first shuffled out to meet her. Just then, holding out the binoculars, he noted that Priscilla had also applied lipstick. Only recently, she had shown him photographs of her glamorous past, married as she had been to a NASA executive from the Kennedy Space Centre up at Cape Canaveral. Even though her frame had long since contracted, she still possessed a refined beauty that was as evident now as it was in those sepia pictures.

'I'm going to have to take your word for it,' she said, with a trace of a smile and both hands clasped in her lap. 'I couldn't possibly see that far, even with assistance.'

Oleg waited a moment before speaking. He watched her gaze out across the inlet, the sky above just a different hue of the brightest blue, and wondered if she was simply consulting her imagination.

'Cataracts?'

Priscilla nodded, looking content all the same. 'It isn't just memories that fade at our time of life.'

'It doesn't have to be that way.' Oleg returned the binoculars to the table and collected his glass of orange juice. 'I see everything, and feel good, too.'

'Everyone feels good in Jupiter,' said Priscilla. 'Living here soothes the bones as much as the soul.'

Oleg knew just what she meant, and yet it was his firm conviction that the climate wasn't wholly responsible. He just wished that he could reveal what he believed to be the true secret to his long life. Titus shared his view that their chosen diet kept the years at bay. Angelica had once delicately pointed out that it hadn't worked for Oleg's late wife, but both he and Titus pretended not to hear. The benefits of eating your own kind outweighed any drawbacks, they maintained. It stood to reason that nutritionally the flesh contained everything another human being required to stay fit and healthy. As for a spiritual level, it took you places that even living in a nice environment just couldn't match. It was a shame, in Oleg's view, that nobody was prepared to lift the blinkers from the standard meat on their plates. As he saw things, most people just couldn't let

50

go of the belief that poultry, pork, lamb and beef was the way to continue, despite the industry that engulfed it. The factory farming turned his stomach, from the confined conditions to the artificial hormones and that awful journey to the abattoir ... the whole *hideous* production line. That was inhuman, in his view. Unlike the calves and the piglets, the chickens and the sheep, the people his family picked off had no idea what was coming to them. Thanks to the swift, respectful slaughter methods he had passed on to Titus, their approach to eating sat well in both the belly and conscience. What's more, with the world population heaving at the seams, wasn't this the ultimate in environmental responsibility?

Oleg liked to think so. He just didn't want to spoil things with Priscilla by admitting to it.

'The sea air is certainly restorative,' he said instead, having taken a couple of long, slow breaths to stay calm.

'I adore it here,' said Priscilla. 'When Larry died I feared I might be all alone, but I've made some great friends. Truly special,' she added, and faced him with some deliberation.

All of a sudden, Oleg felt his neck begin to prickle. With just the briefest lick of her lips, there was something suddenly suggestive in the way that Priscilla regarded him. It seemed entirely inappropriate, and yet Oleg found himself raising his bushy white eyebrows in response.

'I think we've both been very lucky to have found the loves of our lives in this world,' he said after a moment focusing on the patio stones in a bid to compose himself. 'But even though they've moved on, we're entitled to be happy in our final years, aren't we?'

He looked across at Priscilla and found that she had closed her eyes. This happened a lot among the residents, Oleg included. Short but frequent naps were what got everyone through each day. Just as he settled down to admire her at rest, a smile crept across her face and she nodded in agreement.

'You're a good man, Oleg,' she said, and opened her eyes once more. 'You know, just lately I've been feeling like a teenager all over again.'

'Me too,' said Oleg, with a flash of teeth that were a little too white to be his own. 'I sense a rebellion coming on.'

Priscilla chuckled like a contented hen and placed her hands on the armrest of her chair. 'Well, just say the word and I'm there.'

Oleg held his juice aloft and waited for her to do the same thing. 'Here's to Jupiter,' he said, by way of a toast, and smiled as they clinked glasses. 'And here's to us.'

'I'll drink to that.'

Oleg savoured the moment, only for concern to creep into his expression when Priscilla returned the glass to the table.

'Don't forget your medication,' he said, and gestured to the plate of pills that her nurse had counted out for her.

Priscilla tutted, as if reality had just intruded on the moment.

'Oleg, you're the only man at Fallen Pine who isn't propped up on these things.' She switched her attention from the pills back to him. 'Are you sure it's just the warm weather that keeps you looking so young?'

'Well, it helps that I have something to live for,' he told her, with a twinkle in his eye and the memory of his last feast in mind.

'This bar,' said Titus Savage, who had picked up a call from Amanda to be greeted by a screech of delight. 'Tell me they don't serve food.' He smiled and nodded to himself at her response. 'Then it sounds like a job for life! When do you start?'

The last to leave the villa for the day, Titus was alone when his cell phone had rung. While Amanda explained that she could be working five evening shifts a week if everything worked out, he took himself to the kitchen window overlooking the rear garden and the inlet beyond. Titus had a boat down there. It was a handsome-looking outboard moored alongside the jetty that he'd picked up shortly after they'd moved in and then barely boarded. That the tarpaulin covering the vessel was still dotted with leaves from the previous season spoke volumes about his commitment to providing for his loved ones. Titus had forged a life here that many could only dream about, only to find himself entirely focused on keeping the roof over their heads, the bills paid and the larder stocked. Despite it all, however, it seemed to him that the really important things in life, the people surrounding him, were somehow slipping away.

'A midnight finish is kind of late to be out,' he told Amanda when she had finished bringing him up to speed. 'I should drive you home at that hour.'

Amanda assured him that she would be fine. She could take care of herself, she said, before telling him she had a bus to catch.

And I know how to take care of family, Titus thought, but chose not to share it with her. Instead, as she closed the call, he found himself focused on the boat and wondering if he could afford to take it out for a day on the water. Then he thought about the effort involved, and all the maintenance tasks that needed undertaking at the apartment complex.

As a compromise, and because Angelica insisted that it was good to spend time with people occasionally rather than slaughter them, Titus headed out that morning with his golf bag on his shoulder and a secret wish that the stupid game had never been invented.

Ivan sat alone in the canteen at lunchtime. Ignoring the orange peel that landed on his tray from afar, he wondered what it would take before people paid attention properly.

'All I want is some respect,' he muttered to himself, and dabbed his shirt with a paper napkin when a boiled potato plopped squarely into his bowl. 'You'll see, one day. Nobody messes with a Savage. *Nobody*.'

Ivan often talked to himself during school hours, which didn't help his cause. Having finished his meal, he made his way towards the corridor, ignoring the names and the looks of amusement. This he did by imagining what each and every pupil responsible would look like served up on a roasting dish, their cooked limbs tucked tight against the torso with string and an apple wedged inside their jaws. Ivan was so lost in thoughts of cooking as a form of justice that he failed to notice the girl on the other side of the door until he had pushed it into her face.

'Oh, God, sorry!' he said, coming to his senses.

He had seen her before. She was in his year, with curly auburn hair and creamy skin that made him wonder if she'd taste like milk. He wasn't aware of her name, just the trickle of blood that snaked from her nose where the door had hit her.

'It's OK,' she said, sounding muffled on account of the fact that she was attempting to staunch the flow with both hands. 'I'm not dead.'

'Tip your head back,' Ivan suggested, allowing the door to the canteen to shut behind him. 'Pinch the bridge of your nose and wait for the blood to clot. It should only take a few seconds, unless you're a haemophiliac or type B negative. That stuff can take a little longer.'

'Oh,' said the girl, with her neck craned now. 'I don't know what blood group I am.'

'Type B can taste a little bitter on the back of the tongue,' said Ivan earnestly, and then stopped himself. He glanced over his shoulder, worried that this incident would surely lead to someone accusing him of doing it deliberately. Ivan knew the girl wasn't one of the most popular, but she had friends, which was more than he could say. 'It was an accident,' he said quietly, producing a tissue he had used several times that day to blow his nose. 'Will this help?'

'I'm good,' she told him, still facing the ceiling. 'I've been better, but I'll survive.'

'That's what it's all about in this school,' Ivan said, mostly to himself.

Carefully, the girl glanced down. Her eyes crinkled a little, which suggested to Ivan for just one moment that she might be smiling. Then she removed her fingers from the bridge of her nose. Blood glistened on her upper lip, with a streak that ran to her chin, but the breach had stopped.

'I'm Crystal,' she said, and then glanced anxiously through the door window into the canteen. Ivan didn't need to turn to know that the scraping of chairs meant people were gravitating towards the scene. 'And I think perhaps for your own safety you should make yourself scarce.'

At the gym, in front of his locker, Joaquín Mendez accessed the diary on his cell phone. As he examined his schedule for the afternoon, he dug one hand inside his shorts to scratch himself. Working out under the Florida sun meant jock itch was a hazard of his job. Certainly when the coastal breeze dropped it could become quite uncomfortable. On seeing the first name on the list, however, Joaquín stopped what he was doing and raked the same hand through his hair.

He boasted a long list of middle-aged women in need of a workout, but only one who could quicken his heartbeat. Angelica. The elegant siren who seemed to defy the years she had lived. Joaquín had no idea what her secret could be. Angelica had come to him to keep her waistline in trim, so she had said, but in truth she already looked like she had ingested some miracle pills.

'OK, Mrs Savage,' he said to himself, slotting his cell phone into the pouch strapped around his bicep. 'Today maybe we push things to the next level.'

Joaquín was not the kind of personal trainer who set out to seduce his married female clients. Far from it. He knew plenty of guys in the business who took advantage of their free time and low self-esteem, but not him. The crucifix around his muscular shoulders ensured that he did not stray at times of temptation – and there had been opportunities. Instead, his work was his greatest passion. Turning to head for the gym lobby, which attracted several appreciative glances, Joaquín's sculpted body was a living advertisement for his drive and determination. He'd experienced his fair share of passes from women, but ultimately he was a good boy who was still blessed with the support of his mother back in Buenos Aires.

Then Angelica Savage had walked into his world, and increasingly he could not stop thinking about her.

This wasn't just a physical thing. There was a spiritual spark between them. He could feel it in his aching heart at the end of each workout, in a way that had little to do with press-ups or spin cycles. What made it especially tough for the young Latino was that he couldn't fathom whether Angelica shared his feelings. The lady possessed an armour-plated exterior. Whenever she made eye contact during a session and let it linger, Joaquín had no idea what lay behind it. Was something stirring within her, as it was within him, or could it simply be her way of prompting him for further instruction? Well, in due course he would find out. Joaquín wasn't sure how, exactly, not without the risk of turning Angelica against him, but with each session in her company his feelings only intensified.

On reaching the door to the stairs, having glimpsed who was waiting for him in the reception area, Joaquín paused and quickly headed back to his locker. There, Jupiter's most popular personal trainer opened the metal door, faced the laminated picture of the Virgin Mary and quietly asked for her forgiveness in advance.

8

Titus Savage only played golf under pressure. This came in the form of gentle but persistent challenges from the two friends that he had made since settling in Jupiter. Just then, both men were watching from the lip of the bunker where he'd found his ball trapped.

'Let me do this my own way,' muttered Titus, dismissing their advice. 'I didn't get this far in life from people telling me how to play the game.'

For the third time in succession, Titus swept his club towards the ball only to chip it uselessly into the bank of sand. With sweat pricking the crown of his head, he peered up at the pair.

'I'm prepared to look the other way,' said one. 'We could miss our reservation at the clubhouse restaurant if this goes on.'

'It seems like your son isn't the only family member to struggle with sport,' the other man observed under his breath, and was first to back off so that Titus could toss the ball onto the fairway.

On their journey to Florida, the Savages had gone through several identities. Even so, Titus remained close to his roots. He had never visited Russia, but the few friends he allowed himself in Jupiter included two expats from the motherland. Just then, the pair waited impatiently for Titus to clamber out of the bunker. Lev and Kiril had made a killing shortly after the fall of communism, buying tractor plants from the state at a knock-down rate and then selling for a profit to foreign investors. They had relocated to Florida when the Russian mafia moved in on their market and happily let their lives turn fallow in the years that passed. Facing up to the men now, Titus found some solace in the fact that he did at least have a purpose to his days beyond making the most of his golf membership. Lev and Kiril still maintained a healthy income stream, but didn't appear to work hard for it. Titus never pressed them on the subject, of course. When it came to keeping some things behind closed doors, such a code of conduct suited him just fine.

'My boy is committed to the football team,' he told Kiril, having overheard his comment. 'Mark my words, by the end of this season his name will be on everyone's lips.'

All three men wore tropical shirts, slacks and shades. While Titus favoured a repeating pattern of desert islands and blue seas, Kiril sported a floral combination of white kukui blossom and pink roses. Lev, the stockier of the two friends, preferred more restrained pastels for his palm trees, but this was no reflection of his voice, which travelled across the golf course when he chuckled.

'There speaks a proud father,' he said.

'Deluded, but proud,' Kiril added.

'I stand behind every member of my family,' said Titus, who declined his hand in scrambling out of the bunker. 'It's what I do.'

'You need to give your son some space,' said Lev, as the trio

59

began to make their way along the fairway. 'Let him make his own mistakes. Don't be such a helicopter father.'

Titus looked across at his friend, and then swapped a smirk with Kiril.

'For a man who made his money dealing with the Siberian underworld,' he said to Lev, 'you're surprisingly sensitive towards modern parenting concepts.'

A square-set man whose grey sideburns were at odds with his dyed black hair, Lev shrugged like they could tease him all they wanted.

'My boy is all grown up now,' he told them. 'I like to think he earned his place in the world because his dad knew when to back off.'

Kiril sniggered at this, sounding like a dog with kennel cough. The man had a whip-thin frame, receding hair and high, funereal cheekbones. He also sported a paunch, which from the side made him look as if he was in the early stages of a miracle pregnancy.

'Lev heard it on daytime TV,' he said, pretending to whisper. 'He loves to watch those shows where the families can't cope with the kids and call for expert help.'

'So it's a guilty pleasure,' said Lev with a shrug. 'Just let me know when you guys are ready to admit some secrets.'

For the next hour, Titus fought to keep up with his friends. While it appeared as if their golf balls were being drawn towards each hole in turn by some kind of tractor beam, Titus struggled to stay out of the rough.

'I'm thinking of joining a gym,' he told them later in the clubhouse, where the *maître d'* had made a big show of the fact that they were late for the table. This was something that instantly ceased to be a problem when Lev slipped forty bucks into the man's shirt pocket. 'It's time I got buff.'

'Really?' Kiril looked as surprised as Lev. 'What's wrong with loosening your belt by a notch at our time of life?'

'It isn't healthy,' said Titus, helping himself to bread from the basket.

'Nor is it fun,' Kiril pointed out, who had already tucked into a roll. 'You can't give up on us, Titus. We're the guys, you know? It's how we roll out here. Mixing business with pleasure.'

It was true that Kiril had been the one to suggest to Titus that he consider the property business when the family first settled in Jupiter. Keen to establish a reliable source of income, Titus came to value their nose for profit ever since he had rented out his first apartment in the complex. With encouragement from the pair, he had gone on to purchase more units as they became available. Unbeknown to his Russian friends, of course, Titus also considered the place to be a convenient pickup for one vital ingredient whenever a feast was on the cards.

'Getting into shape is top of my list,' he told them now, mindful of Angelica's example. He turned to the menu in front of him. 'So, what are you guys having? The special looks good today.'

For her first shift in the new job, Amanda Dias elected to dress conservatively. Knowing that she would be on her feet serving drinks, she opted for pumps to go with her black jeans and white vest top. As soon as she arrived at the Crankbait Sports Saloon, however – twenty minutes early in order to settle in – it became quite clear to her that flat-soled shoes would not be appropriate.

'Here,' said Rolan, having crouched in front of an alcove under the bar. 'You need these.'

Amanda didn't take in what had just landed in her arms until she looked down.

'Roller skates?' She faced him again with a start. The lighting in the bar was minimal; mostly neon piping that weaved around the interior walls. Amanda noticed that the poles ringing the dance floor were also well illuminated, but for now her focus was on Rolan. 'You want me to wear skates?'

'If you still want the job,' he said abruptly, and returned to unloading the glasses washer.

As he spoke, several girls could be heard chattering and laughing in a back room. Amanda looked around and saw a door in the gloom with a sign on it that read 'KITCHEN'.

'You told me food wasn't on offer here,' she said. 'Just potato chips.'

'Potato chips and eye candy. That goes without saying.' Rolan rubbed the back of his neck. 'The girls use that space to pretty themselves so they look a million dollars whether they're serving drinks or dancing.' He paused there and drew her attention to the poles under the spotlights. 'Or both, if you're looking to make a little extra dough.'

Judging by the way Rolan's eyebrows wagged as he said this, Amanda knew exactly what he was proposing. For a split second she considered just turning right around and leaving. Then she reminded herself of the money, and her pledge to pay her way in the Savage household.

'You're the boss,' she said, in a way that made it sound as if only a total jerk could earn that status. 'But I'll dance over your dead body.'

Half an hour later, as the bar steadily filled, Amanda began her first shift serving drinks to the tables. This was no easy task, given her new footwear, but some experience on wheels as a little girl ensured she delivered each tray without spilling more than a few drops. Most of the men were glued to the baseball game going out live on the big screen behind the dance floor. Those who did make eye contact, she found, only did so fleetingly, before dropping their gaze to her chest. Amanda didn't like it one bit, and yet she reminded herself that it had to be better than delivering animal flesh to their tables. Ultimately, it was her choice to be here, even if it did put her in a caustic mood. This was evident when she set a beer in front of a guy with a double chin and cigarette breath who promptly asked for pork cracklings to go with it.

'We don't have those,' she said immediately. 'Never have and never will.'

'Oh, really?' said the man. 'But I'm asking nicely.'

Amanda didn't blink.

'I'll get you some potato chips,' she told him.

Making her way to the bar, with Rolan looking on disapprovingly, Amanda willed herself once more not to unstrap her skates and walk out. Just then it felt as if her feelings about meat were close to being overshadowed by her distrust of men. Only Titus had her complete confidence. He had he shown her that it was perfectly possible to be a carnivore who made

63

a valuable contribution to the world. What's more, he was a gentleman at heart who placed his family first.

'What's the problem?' asked Rolan, as Amanda stopped herself by bumping the fronts of her skates into the bar. He gestured at the customer waiting at the table. 'He looks unhappy.'

Amanda glanced over her shoulder.

'He's hungry is all,' she told him, and asked for a bowl of potato chips.

'Hungry for what?' asked Rolan, and purposely looked her up and down. 'You know, a dance wouldn't kill you. It's what the customers expect.'

'I thought they came here for the sport,' she said.

'They do.'

Amanda waited without word for the chips, drumming her fingers on the bar counter with military precision.

'I'll make sure he doesn't forget me,' she told her boss when he came back with the bowl, and forced a smile that seemed to satisfy him.

The customer was already halfway through his beer when Amanda returned with the chips. He looked unimpressed as she approached, having seen what she was carrying. Still, she hoped that if the encounter reduced the demand for pork cracklings by the bag then it would've been worth her while.

'Thank you, sweet meat,' said the man, as she placed the bowl in front of him. 'I sure hope something tastes good here.'

At the same time, Amanda felt the palm of his hand cup her buttock. She stood up straight and glared at him. The guy caught her eye and seemed surprised when her scowl softened to a smile. It was as if she had experienced a sudden change of heart, which aroused his interest all the more. Then, without invitation, she gestured at him to move across so that she could share the booth. He did so without hesitation, and even extended his arm along the headrest. Amanda responded by nuzzling his ear with her lips. In this dimly lit, crowded sports bar, with music blaring and girls working the poles, nobody paid them any attention whatsoever.

'Taste means everything to me, too,' Amanda whispered, before nuzzling his earlobe.

'Oh, right there,' purred the man, who was clearly surprised by such forward behaviour but also enjoying it. 'Is this gonna cost me?'

Amanda responded by taking the very edge of the man's earlobe between her central incisors and then biting down by a millimetre. She did so with such finesse that the slither of flesh that came away could've been cut by a surgeon's scalpel. The man gasped. She pulled back and found him looking utterly shocked.

'The salt in your blood gives it body,' she said, and pinched the slither from her tongue in order to inspect it. 'In the oven, at a high temperature, this would be so much more rewarding than those miserable cracklings you ordered.'

The man touched his ear, stunned by the stinging sensation and the drop of blood on his fingertips. He looked back at this crazy woman, lost for words. Amanda patted his knee before leaving him alone with his drink and the snack, both of which remained untouched when she glanced back a moment later to find that he had made a hasty exit.

9

Later that week, Titus Savage set off on his run, having first checked that no neighbours were cleaning their cars or watering the plants. He reached the junction out of the inlet community at speed, anxious not to be seen in the gear he'd picked up from the fitness store that morning. The shorts were OK – a little high cut for his liking – but it seemed that size medium for a vest was no longer a comfortable fit. Waiting for the lights to turn, Titus stood with his shoulders slumped, panting heavily. Looking down, even his new trainers seemed out of character on him.

'You can't give up,' he grumbled to himself. 'You owe this to your family.'

Across the junction, Titus attempted to get into some kind of trot. What distracted him was the unpleasant sensation caused by his stomach rocking up and down in perfect synchronicity with his moobs. It brought his physical shape into raw focus. Jogging along the sidewalk, ignoring any pedestrian who so much as glanced in his direction, Titus was determined to turn the tide. He was a Savage, after all, and it was his duty to present himself to his family as leader of the pack. The kind of formidable hunter who was capable of bringing home a kill slung over his shoulder without risk of a coronary.

With his pace dropping by the block, Titus lumbered past the nursing home that housed his father. As a boy, when first introduced to the pleasures of eating human flesh, he had looked up to his old man as someone who existed above and beyond the law. Oleg was a god through his young eyes. A culinary pioneer who had seen the light while others relied solely on whatever processed meats the food industry chose to force upon them. All those years ago, Titus had considered it a great honour to be initiated into the ritual sourcing and slaughter of the next feast, and was determined that his children should look upon him in the same way.

Mulling over how far they had come as a family gave Titus all the more reason to pick up the pace. His face was flushed as he stumbled past the drug store, his forehead needling with sweat and his lungs threatening to shut down with every gulp of air. The will to get in shape was there, without a doubt, but not the stamina. Approaching the boat rental with the sandwich board on the sidewalk, Titus felt both ashamed and a little shocked at his lack of fitness.

'I've become what I eat,' he muttered to himself. 'A bloater.'

For too long now, Titus realised, he'd been picking off people who packed a few extra pounds. He only had himself to blame, having deliberately favoured a particular type of tenant. Those solitary tech heads lived in front of their computers, grazing on a steady diet of instant noodles and oven chips, and that was beginning to take its toll on Titus. If he wanted to regain his figure then pounding the tarmac in this way just wasn't enough. Titus would have to become more selective, not just with his day-to-day food intake, but with the feasts, too. Yes, American-raised belly tasted good, especially when Angelica roasted it for several hours basted in garlic and cracked coriander seeds, but when that became a regular treat, all the fat just transferred to his arteries and waistline.

Up ahead, Titus spotted a stop sign. Not fifteen minutes into his run, with his heart kicking like a mule, he read it as a personal message that had nothing to do with the cars at the lights. He slowed to a halt, panting hard, and placed his hands on his knees. One glance at his watch told him that he couldn't go home just yet. Even if it was just a neighbour who spotted him, Titus had no desire to carry the shame inside. Instead, at walking pace, he followed the corner onto the beach road. Down there, in between the dunes, Titus knew of a little coffee stop. He could just pull up on a plastic chair there for a while, enjoy the sunshine and some light refreshment. They also did great pastries, he remembered. A moment later, Titus willed himself towards his destination at a trot, because that way he'd have earned a sugar hit.

When Amanda surfaced from her room, she took one look at the kitchen clock and found another reason to dislike her new job. It was early afternoon and she had only just climbed out of bed. Not only did her shift end late, it was also exhausting having to constantly fend off advances from the saloon clientele. What was it with those guys that they felt they could disrespect a woman in that way? She had set each one straight without hesitation, and though they always left quickly, still more kept on coming. In Amanda's view, it was like dealing with a testosterone-fuelled zombie horde. At one point, she had complained to Rolan about the manhandling. He had just shrugged in response, before suggesting that dancing for them might satisfy their needs while bringing in more tips.

Amanda Dias considered her principles to be embedded in her genes. She couldn't simply switch them off. Despite the heavy hints from Rolan, there was no way she was going to perform for those punks at the saloon. Instead, whenever they ordered a meat-based snack, she would cuddle up beside them, find their ear or take their hand and suggestively slot a finger in her mouth. A moment later, Amanda Dias would come away with a butter curl of flesh pinched victoriously between her teeth. It meant if they hurried back to their wives with a minor wound and second thoughts about their first choice of food then her job was done.

'Well, good morning and good afternoon. That's quite a lie-in you've had today.'

Amanda turned to see Angelica at the kitchen door. Little Katya hung back in the lobby, cooing at a box on the floor that was covered by a tea cloth.

'I'm on shift time,' Amanda said by way of explanation. 'I don't suppose you want to join me for a very late breakfast?'

Angelica smiled and placed her car keys on the counter. Then she peeled the sweatband from her head and breathed out long and hard. In her Lycra top and leggings, looking like a superhero without her cape, she gave Amanda no reason to ask where she'd been before picking up Katya from kindergarten.

'All I need right now is a rest,' Angelica said. 'I'm beginning

69

to think that Joaquín's made it his mission in life to get me to the peak of fitness. He's such a driven young man.'

'That's good to hear.'

Amanda turned to the fridge. The only thing she'd been driven to lately was distraction by all the slimeballs at the saloon. For a moment, she considered confiding in Angelica about what the job really involved. What stopped her was the belief that this was something she could handle on her own terms. So, instead of moaning about Rolan, she reached for a carton of chocolate-flavoured soya milk. Amanda had a shelf reserved just for her. It was completely meat free, in direct contrast to the other shelves. The sausages and the mince didn't disgust her here as it might elsewhere. In the Savage household, she was prepared to make this concession given how they had shown her the way forward when it came to feasts.

'Is Ivan home from classes yet?' asked Angelica.

Amanda detected the note of concern in Mrs Savage's voice straight away. She turned with the carton in hand to see Angelica straining to see if anyone was down by the jetty.

'It's just me here,' said Amanda. 'Titus is out jogging.'

This was enough to command Angelica's full attention, but she chose not to pursue it. Instead, having glanced back at little Katya in the lobby, she leaned across the counter and addressed Amanda in hushed tones.

'Kat has brought home the class gerbil. Tinky Dinks is with us for the week.'

'Oh, that's sweet!' Amanda poured herself a glass from the carton. 'We had a hamster at our school. A little pet like that is a great way of teaching responsibility.'

70

Angelica didn't look like she disagreed. Even so, she appeared pained.

'Ivan is having a tough time at school,' she said, still keeping her voice low, as if her son might somehow be listening. 'You know what he can be like when he's stressed.'

Amanda was well aware of Angelica's concerns. Ivan's unwitting disregard for the welfare of other people was a constant source of concern to his parents. Looking at Angelica now, Amanda figured she was worried that the boy might extend the same thing to small, furry creatures.

'He wouldn't,' she said. 'Would he?'

'I'd sooner not put it to the test.' Angelica glanced over her shoulder. Her youngest daughter was on her hands and knees, peering into the box at the new arrival. 'It's best that Ivan knows nothing about this.'

Amanda lengthened her gaze to the lobby. In her view, any abuse of an animal's welfare was punishable by death. As an exception, she recognised that Ivan's seemingly cruel streak was an unforeseen result of his upbringing, rather than the instinct of an idiot. He was an impressionable boy, eager to please, who was being raised to compartmentalise his sense of compassion where necessary to become the ultimate hunter. He was bound to struggle with boundaries at this stage of his apprenticeship, but this wasn't one that she felt happy for him to test. As she had come to like Ivan – and not just because she shared his commitment to the consumption of human flesh – Amanda agreed it was in everyone's best interests that the gerbil stayed under wraps throughout its stay in the villa.

10

What sounded like an incoming tsunami filled Ivan's ears just a moment before water flooded into his nostrils. With his head forced low into the toilet pan, this was the second flush in a matter of seconds that the boy had endured. He found it no more comfortable than the first one.

'Stop it!' he cried, coughing and struggling against the hand that clamped the back of his neck. 'Let me go!'

'What did we say about showing up for training?'

The boy snarling over him was Ryan, while Chad held him down and Bryce prepared to pull the chain again just as soon as the cistern had refilled. Ivan had watched a documentary only recently about waterboarding torture. This felt like the high-school equivalent of that kind of hell.

'You heard us good,' snarled Ryan, after Chad had followed up the initial question by asking whether Ivan was deaf or something. 'And yet still we find you here in the changing rooms!'

'What's the matter, dude?' asked Bryce. 'You have a problem respecting us?'

Ivan was too busy coughing still to answer, which was Chad's cue to haul him upright.

'All I want to do is be a team player!' the boy in their grip gasped. 'Give me a break, guys!'

Ryan repeated Ivan's plea, having adopted the voice of a little girl. A little girl speaking the Queen's English.

'You can't play,' Bryce told him. 'It's not in your blood. You're good for nothing but that stupid game you Brit fairies play with a bat.'

'Baseball?' asked Chad, looking across at his friend.

'Like that but lazier,' said Bryce. 'Less running.'

'You mean cricket,' said Ivan, which earned him a third dip in the bowl. The next time the trio dragged him upright, they did so with such force that his spine slammed against the inside of the cubicle door. Before the boy had a chance to slump, Bryce gripped him by his throat with one hand and then jabbed him hard in the stomach with the other.

'This is your final warning,' he snarled, as all the air left Ivan's lungs in a pitiful bark. 'You're not on the team. You'll never be a player. Now go home, new girl, and stay out of our way! You don't fit in here, OK?'

It was Bryce who shot the bolt free, Chad who snatched open the cubicle door and Ryan who thrust the boy out. Ivan stumbled backwards onto the tiles, causing the small crowd of squad members who had been drawn to the commotion to step hastily from his path. Ivan looked around, on the floor now, his hair dripping wet and his cheeks hot with tears. Nobody met his gaze.

'You'll be sorry,' he croaked, struggling to keep a sob at bay. 'Every last one of you will regret messing with me!'

'Get outta here,' growled Chad. 'Beat it!'

Picking himself up, Ivan looked around as if each boy was shining a flashlight in his face. Then, having turned full circle, he scrambled for the door.

'Way to go!' cried Ryan from behind him.

'Now that's what I call a home run,' crowed Bryce. 'All the way back to Mommy!'

Oleg Savage had elected not to notify his nurse that he was popping out to pick up some things from the store. Vince would only ask questions. Given his taste in meat, the old man had plenty of experience in concealing the truth. On this occasion, however, he figured it was purely the grin on his face that would give everything away.

Zipping along the sidewalk on his mobility scooter, on his way back to the nursing home, he reflected on his time with Priscilla. She was such good company, and the frequent naps weren't unwelcome. It gave him time to reflect on what a lucky man he was to be feeling this way at his age. It was late afternoon, but the sun still dazzled. A gentle sea breeze kept the heat at bay. It brought a salty tang to the air, which felt good on Oleg's gum line when he ran his tongue inside his top lip. The old man relished the feeling, especially with the accelerator dial turned several notches beyond the cautionary mark made by his son. Even Angelica kept saying he really ought to be wearing a protective helmet, gloves and elbow pads, but the advice fell on deaf ears. Oleg wasn't some kid fresh on a bike. He'd been on this earth through two world wars and had only surrendered his driving licence eighteen years earlier. In his white vest and mirror shades, he grasped the handlebars and imagined himself to be on a Harley Davidson, living the American Dream.

'Hey! Wait a minute! *Slow down!*'

Oleg normally ignored such calls from pedestrians, and they happened frequently. On recognising the voice this time, he opened his eyes, guiltily turned the dial down to zero and waited for Titus to catch up.

'You're in jogging gear,' Oleg observed. 'Is this a dare?'

For a moment, Titus was too breathless to reply. He just stood there with one hand on the back of Oleg's scooter, gasping for breath.

'It's a fitness drive,' he said eventually, before standing straight. 'You know, it isn't safe to be riding this thing at speed. What if you knocked someone over?'

Oleg glanced at his son's new trainers and shrugged. 'Do you remember that time as a kid when we took you on a driving holiday across the Highlands? That hiker crossed the road out of nowhere. She left me with nowhere to go.'

'I remember,' said Titus, but sounded as if he wish he hadn't. 'At least her suffering was brief at the speed you were travelling.'

Oleg considered him for a second.

'Well, we didn't let her go to waste,' he said. 'In fact, you declared that roadkill tasted better than any meat you'd eaten before.'

Immediately, Titus checked nobody was within earshot.

'I was just a boy back then,' he told him quietly. 'And let's not forget that we're in this country under false documentation. That's fine, so long as everyone is careful.'

75

'I am careful,' Oleg grumbled, affronted that Titus would even call this into question.

'Careering along the sidewalk at full tilt on a mobility scooter isn't careful. It could earn you a ticket for reckless driving, and then where would you be? At 103, you need to slow down in more ways than one.'

Oleg sighed to himself and looked wistfully at the way ahead.

'I don't feel old,' he said quietly.

He didn't need to spell out to Titus exactly why he felt younger than his years. That Oleg's late wife had passed on at a natural age wasn't something he liked to dwell on. If he could turn back time, he would've insisted that she had extra helpings of human flesh each time they enjoyed a feast. Something was behind his long life, after all. Oleg couldn't say for certain whether his diet meant he might live for an eternity, but it often felt that way. He drew breath to remind Titus that, whatever the case, as his senior, he deserved a little respect. Instead, he watched his son's attention turn to the brown paper bag in the scooter's front basket.

'What's this?' asked Titus, grabbing it without waiting to be invited. He opened the top of the bag and peered inside. A moment later, he looked up at Oleg as if the old man should've known better. 'A four-pack of beer? Really?'

'It's just a thing,' said Oleg, sounding a little embarrassed. 'I'm planning a picnic with a friend.'

'A friend.' Titus placed his hands on his waist. 'Ivan has told me all about Priscilla. Are you sure you're not leading an old lady astray?'

Oleg shrugged, feeling a little under fire.

'We're not breaking any laws here,' he said quietly. 'When you reach my age, would you want Ivan to be the guardian of your fun?'

Titus considered his father. Then, with a sigh and the sweat on his face still glistening, he nodded in agreement.

'I'll walk with you,' he said next, and gestured for Oleg to crank the dial by no more than a notch. 'Just don't make me break into a jog, OK? I'm struggling here.'

'So it seems,' said Oleg, grinning, and set off as directed. 'So, what's with the need to get fit?'

'Just something that has to be done,' Titus replied, with his wife in mind. 'Even if it kills me.'

11

In the days that followed a feast, Angelica liked to eat lean. She also served herself controlled portions, as if to counter the excessive intake that came with finishing off a human being. Even as a family, it was a huge quantity to put away, especially since their move to the Sunshine State. Something just took over when they ate. The appetite was extraordinary, with no sense of feeling full for quite some time. Despite the extra calories that came with sourcing locally, she was well aware that it enriched the spirit like no other meat.

Angelica only had to look at her youngest daughter for proof. That week, little Katya had been brimming with more joy and laughter than usual. The feast had undoubtedly left her invigorated, though the presence of the gerbil clearly contributed.

'Tinky Dinks will be quite safe while you're at school,' she assured her. 'You don't need to worry.'

Together with her daughter, Angelica had created a space for the gerbil's cage on the floor of Katya's wardrobe. To ease her concerns, Angelica had even used some shoeboxes to create a wall in front of the cage. As a result, were someone to open up the doors, it wouldn't attract the eye. Even so, little Kat continued to look worried.

'But what about Ivan?' she asked. 'Tinky Dinks sure won't like him. Tinky Dinks is scared of boys like my brother.'

'He won't even know that Tinky Dinks is here,' Angelica assured her.

Katya stood before her mother in her pre-school uniform, blinking like a fawn.

'But you know what he did to my dollies,' she said.

Angelica didn't need to be reminded. It had taken some time for the oven to stop smelling of burned plastic, which is where she had found Kat's beloved collection some weeks ago, melting on a baking tray.

'Ivan tells us he was only trying to change the shape of their faces a little,' she said, stroking her daughter's hair and then clasping her cheek to maintain eye contact. 'He's just going through a difficult phase at the moment, but he'll soon settle in. Now, go say goodbye to Tinky Dinks and then get ready for school.'

Minutes later, the pair headed out to the car. As soon as Katya was strapped into the back seat, she appeared to forget all about Ivan and started singing to herself, which made Angelica smile. Driving out towards the pre-school, on her way to the gym, she knew there was no reason to fret. She would be home from her workout that day long before her son returned from school. It was a shame that they had to be so cautious about Ivan. Deep down, despite his difficulties, Angelica knew that her son had a good soul. The poor lad didn't seem to be making much progress, but things would settle in time. Until then, it was her responsibility as the mother of a Savage to make sure that he didn't express his frustration by harming innocents.

Ivan Savage had been in plenty of time for school that morning. Before setting off, he had shared a plate of pancakes and bacon with his father and then grabbed his bag as usual. It was a fifteen-minute walk to the school gates, but the boy never made it that far. Instead, at the junction from the community inlet, he had ducked down to the beach, sat on his bag in the dunes and watched life passing by on the boardwalk.

After the incident in the changing rooms, Ivan just couldn't face seeing Bryce, Chad and Ryan. He felt humiliated and ashamed, and well aware that by now the whole school would know that he had fled from them in tears.

'You don't mess with a Savage,' he grumbled, clawing at the long grass so hard that it came out in clumps. 'You just *don't.*'

Ivan wasn't quite sure how he would teach them a lesson. Ideally, he wanted to prove it on the pitch. If he could just find the skills to make an impact on the playing field, rather than muff every catch and kick, the boy knew he would earn the respect he deserved. As he never had the chance to practise, confined as he was to the bench, all hope of proving himself was a dead ball. The very thought saw him bury his fingers into the sand up to the knuckles. Not that he was aware of his actions. Instead, with his eyes and mouth pinched, he felt only sadness and resentment that his efforts to integrate into the American way of life had ended so badly. As far as Ivan was concerned, his baseball cap could stay on its hook from here on out. He'd put the way he walked behind him and the hip hop could go to hell. It didn't matter how hard he tried, some people would not let him settle.

Just then, knowing that his parents would have left for the day, Ivan planned to hole up at home and use the time to plot his revenge.

As he pondered the fate of his three tormentors, a battered brown estate car pulled up in the parking bay in front of the boardwalk. Ivan noticed the tarpaulin on the rear seat. Even before the man stepped out of the vehicle, the boy had marked him down as a kidnapper. Hacking away into his fist as he made his way round to the trunk, the guy certainly looked like someone whose front room housed a pit to contain a couple of captives. Ivan watched with interest when he fished out a jacket striped like a squeeze of toothpaste and a straw boater studded with smiley-face badges. He looked completely different once he'd buttoned himself up and tipped the hat to a jaunty angle on his head. It all made sense when Ivan observed him climb onto the boardwalk and make his way towards a shuttered stall. Within minutes, beaming broadly behind the counter, the ice-cream seller had already attracted several customers.

Ivan watched with interest as a young mother approached with a buggy and a miniature dog. The dog was pulling sideways, yapping at the gulls, while the kid spotted the stall and flung out her arms. The seller smiled and rubbed his hands together, which only served to stoke up the child's pleas. The mother pushed onwards, grim-faced and with the dog still barking at the birds. When the kid wailed, she slowed and then came to a standstill. The poor woman looked utterly defeated, thought Ivan, who rose to his feet for a clearer view.

81

'Wow,' he said to himself, as she drew the buggy back to the stall. With his eyes locked on the scene, Ivan watched as the guy served the kid. He handed down a single scoop of strawberry ripple, which put an end to the howling, and then waited for the mother to hand over two dollar bills. 'That's it!'

What he had just witnessed came as a revelation to the boy. Had that mother seen the man before he transformed his appearance, she would've pressed on by without hesitation, and maybe even picked up her pace. There was no way she'd have bought an ice cream from anyone who looked that rough around the edges, let alone fed it to her infant daughter. It could've contained just about anything, the boy realised, thinking razor blades not raspberry ripple. Ivan had no doubt that there was nothing in it that could harm her, but the fact remained that she'd taken it without question. Quite simply, the guy had played a part in the right place and time to deliver a treat the kid could not resist. With three soccer jocks in mind, Ivan realised exactly the same approach could work for him. At last, his plan had fallen into place.

Knowing that Angelica Savage would be his second client of the day, Joaquín Mendez had used the time between sessions to shower and change his vest. As soon as he saw her open-top pull into the parking bay outside, he headed down to the lobby hoping for a welcome hug. Then Angelica breezed in with her hair tied back and her cell phone clamped to her ear, which meant Joaquín was forced to spend an awkward couple of minutes pretending not to listen.

'Can this wait until later?' she had hissed into the phone

at one point, and made a vague effort to turn away from her personal trainer. 'It's just too early for me to think about what we should eat for supper.'

In the midst of what sounded like a quiet domestic with her other half, Joaquín decided to check his feet. He took his time, assessing the roadworthiness of each toe so he had something to look at other than Angelica becoming increasingly clipped. Finally, on hearing her sign off, he sprung upright and spread his hands as if he'd just become aware of her presence.

'And how are we today?' he asked, with some hope that she might just walk into his embrace. Instead, with her thoughts clearly elsewhere, she simply stared at him. 'Mrs Savage?' he added after a moment, and began to wish he had waited for her upstairs in the gym.

Angelica blinked, focused on Joaquín and finally acknowledged him. He had hoped she might do so with a smile. Instead, she practically pinned him to the wall with her gaze.

'I hope you're going to bring me out in a sweat today.'

'Really?' Joaquín blinked and sensed his Adam's apple bob up and down.

'This is time out just for me,' she told him. 'I intend to make the most of it.'

Joaquín did his level best to hold Angelica's gaze, but saw no hint of whether she was deliberately being suggestive with him. For weeks now, this client had been steadily invading his thoughts and refusing to leave. Yes, he was a professional, but there was an aura so entrancing surrounding Angelica that he could not ignore it. Even when she was being frosty, Joaquín sensed his emotional temperature rise. It was something he had never encountered in all his tender years.

'You know, you're a difficult lady to fathom,' he confessed, almost blurting out the words. 'I find it hard to read your mind.'

Angelica looked puzzled, as if she had missed something here, and then glanced at the clock behind the reception desk.

'You're a personal trainer, Joaquín, not a psychic,' she said, in a way that left him feeling like a small boy. 'Let's get on with the workout.'

In his experience, some clients liked to talk. Others preferred to exercise in silence. On this occasion, having started the session on what felt like the wrong foot, Joaquín Mendez opted not to attempt to kick-start a conversation with Angelica. Instead, running on bare soles, he chose to lead the way through the first few miles in the hope that she would burn off her mood. It was only as they approached the sand bar separating the beach from the sound and the mainland that he dared to break the silence.

'The sun is climbing,' he said, and slowed to a halt. 'We should rehydrate.'

Angelica pulled up behind him, breathless but mindful to stretch as he had taught her so as to avoid any muscle strains. Joaquín unclipped the water bottle from his running belt and offered it across. He caught her eye as she accepted it, looking for some sign that she had softened.

'It's good to be out,' she said between small swigs. 'It beats fretting about what to feed the family.'

'Whatever it is, I'm sure it'll taste good,' said Joaquín. 'Your husband is a lucky man.'

'Titus is on a health drive right now,' she told him, and turned to face the ocean. 'All of a sudden, he needs to know how many calories are in each serving.'

'Well, that's a positive outlook.'

'Not when he's looking over my shoulder every time I prepare a meal,' said Angelica, with her focus fixed on the horizon now. In the distance, so far away it looked like a pencil sketch against the sky, a tanker inched across the horizon. 'OK,' she said next. 'Where do we go from here?'

Joaquín sensed the crucifix around his neck, warming in the sunshine. He closed his eyes for a second, wishing he had stowed it in the locker, before grimacing slightly at an impulse that took root in his mind. A moment later, he found himself clasping his client gently by the wrist.

'Forgive me,' he murmured, and took Angelica's other hand as she turned from the sea with a start. 'I can't help myself any longer.'

Angelica caught her breath, staying that way when her personal trainer leaned in to kiss her on the lips. She blinked as he found her gaze again, this woman who had come to devour his heart, and awaited some sign that she felt the same way.

12

On his return to the villa, Ivan knew that he wouldn't be home alone. Ever since Amanda had started working late shifts at the sports saloon, she was rarely seen before sundown. It was beginning to feel more like they had a vampire in the spare room than a lodger. Still, as the boy let himself in and clicked the front door shut, he reminded himself that the shifts worked in his favour. Amanda was rarely up at the same time as him, and when she did rise he stayed out of her way. They had a shared bond with one another over the feasts that graced the table. At any other time, however, she was here as a guest of the family. In many ways, Ivan thought, it was no different from having his big sister, Sasha, at home.

'A snack,' he said to himself, and made his way to the kitchen. When it came to issuing payback to your tormentors, in a way that they would never forget, it was important to plot the precise means on a full stomach. Opening the fridge door, Ivan pulled a face at the sight of all the vegan food on Amanda's shelf. He wondered why she bothered with the soya cheese slices and stuff, given her passion for human flesh every once in a while, but then Ivan's father had taught him not to judge. *Our taste in meat makes us more of a minority group than the vegans*, he had said. *Which is why it's so important that we stick together.*

The salt-beef sandwich that Ivan constructed involved four different layers of rye bread. With nobody around to take him to task, it was also crammed with gherkins and mustard, which dripped onto his plate as he headed upstairs to his bedroom. Having awoken that day feeling so hollow about school and then brooded in the dunes about his lot in life, this was the first time he felt an upswing in his spirits. Ryan, Bryce and Chad? Those jerks could burn in hell, and they would do so to a crisp if he had his moment in the sun. Just thinking about them again caused Ivan to press his back molars together. He hated feeling this way. All he wanted was to be treated normally, like any other kid. Instead, he'd become an outcast, and yet they had no idea what he was really like. If they knew that sometimes he looked at them not as sports jocks but as tender cuts, they'd shut the hell up once and for all. Well, it was too late for them to make amends, he told himself, on passing his kid sister's bedroom. Soon they'd pay the ultimate price for crossing swords with a Savage. He was on a war footing now, and nothing could stop him.

Ivan's mind was in a maelstrom as he reached for his door handle. Even so, all the thoughts raging within couldn't distract from the sudden scuttling sound. It was over as quickly as it had begun, but appealed to his senses as if he were on a hunting trip with his father.

'What is that?' The boy looked up and around, hearing the same thing again. 'Do we have a pest problem?'

With the plate in his hand still, Ivan held his breath, with both ears primed to pick up the slightest sound. Rats would be great, he thought. It would be a chance for him to hone his trapping skills. A raccoon in the loft space would be even better. The kind of challenge that would make his dad proud. When the further pattering of tiny paws broke the silence, Ivan turned his attention to Katya's bedroom door. It was coming from in there, he felt sure.

'Come out, come out,' he whispered, and retraced his steps as quietly as he could. '*Whatever* you are.'

In view of their advanced age, Oleg Savage had decided that a lunch date with Priscilla would be better than a night out. Like everyone at the Fallen Pine, both he and Priscilla always retired to their rooms by half past eight. If Oleg booked a table any time beyond that, there was a distinct danger that one or even both of them would be found face down in the soup.

'So, where are you taking me?' Priscilla asked, travelling alongside his scooter on a smaller, pink model fitted with a sun umbrella. 'This is so exciting!'

'Just enjoy the ride,' said Oleg, beaming across at her. 'There's nothing like a road trip to make you feel alive! Well, almost nothing . . . '

Following the sidewalk and stopping only for the crossing before the highway bridge, the pair had travelled out towards the old lighthouse. It stood proud upon an elevation overlooking the inlet, a red-brick structure on oyster-shell foundations, surrounded by parkland and banyan trees. In Oleg's opinion, as they trundled through the main gates, it was the perfect place to dine with someone special.

'I used to come here as a little girl,' Priscilla told him. 'My family would bring a picnic and watch the boats go by.'

Oleg smiled to himself as they followed the sloping contours of the parkland.

'Your family sound like my kind of people,' he said, and pulled up to wait for her. 'I just hope I can live up to their standards.'

When Priscilla drew alongside, Oleg pointed towards a bench on the shady side of the treeline. He watched her peer ahead, then squint for focus, before her face illuminated in surprise and delight. For there stood Vince, the Fallen Pine's nurse with the stretched earlobes. He faced them with his arms folded in front of a rug bearing a generous picnic spread.

'Is this for me?' asked Priscilla, and clasped her hands to her chest.

'For us,' said Oleg, and turned the dial on his scooter to complete the last few yards of their journey.

Everything had been carefully selected to appeal to Priscilla. Oleg knew how much she liked Cuban sandwiches with thin slices of ham, pork, cheese and pickles. He had also made sure the cherry cake slices were fresh from the bakery. Then there were the beers that he had bought for the occasion. As soon as Oleg had presented them to Vince as thanks for his help in arranging everything, the man took himself off to a bench overlooking the inlet and left the couple to dine in peace. Knowing that alcohol would only send them both to sleep, Oleg produced a bottle of lemonade for a toast.

'You're a prince,' sighed Priscilla, who had required some

help in seating herself on the rug. 'This is quite a feast!'

Oleg was filling a plastic cup when she said this. He only glanced up at her for a moment, but it was enough for the froth to spill over the edge.

'It's the next best thing,' he said under his breath. When Oleg offered her the drink, she smiled fondly. In that moment, as they touched the cups together in a toast, everything seemed just perfect to him. So it came as a surprise to the old man to see a tear streak down her cheek. 'What's wrong?' he asked, suddenly concerned.

'It's nothing.' Priscilla wiped the tear away and mustered a little chuckle as if to suggest she was just being silly. 'You really don't have to worry.'

'You can tell me,' insisted Oleg, and offered her a napkin to dry her eyes. 'All of a sudden, you look so sad.'

Priscilla accepted the napkin, brushing his hand as she did so.

'You're a kind man, Oleg. At my time, I couldn't ask for anything more.'

'Your time?' Oleg tipped his head to one side. 'You make it sound like it's running out.'

He had never seen her composure slip before, even for a moment. It came as a shock from someone who was so naturally sunny. Now, as he held Priscilla's gaze, awaiting an answer, Oleg sensed that what she was about to say was not something he wanted to hear.

'I saw my doctor recently,' she said, and dropped her gaze to the spread of food. 'So it's good that you're helping me make the most of what I have left.'

'I see.'

Oleg had no desire to press her for details. He knew what she meant, and felt numb. Here they were, late-life companions, and now the woman he held in such fond esteem had to go.

'These sandwiches are the best ever,' said Priscilla next. On taking a bite, she made a circling motion with her free hand as if to draw his attention to their wider surroundings. 'This is so beautiful, what you've done here, Oleg. I have butterflies and my heart hasn't beat this quickly in a long time! You make me feel so young. I've loved every moment in your company.'

Oleg blinked back into focus to see her eating with relish. It was almost as if the exchange had been a figment of his imagination. Priscilla gestured for him to take a sandwich. He reached out for one, only to hesitate and then withdraw his hand.

'I don't want you to leave me,' he said, with a catch in his voice. 'You can't . . . die.'

Oleg struggled with the last word. It barely made a sound on leaving his lips.

Priscilla took a second to swallow, and then smiled fondly at him.

'For years now, every day has been a surprise to me and a blessing,' she told him. 'What matters is that we make the most of what's left.'

'*No*,' said Oleg, so forcefully that Priscilla nearly dropped the rest of her sandwich. 'It doesn't have to be this way.'

'Oh, shush now.' Priscilla touched a finger to her lips. 'I'm sorry you had to hear that, but it's important that we have no secrets. Now, you need to eat,' she said sternly, and gestured once more to the sandwiches. 'Don't let this spoil, after all the effort you've made.'

'It's just a picnic,' said Oleg, waving at the plates dismissively. He glanced across to the bench. Vince was nursing a beer, enjoying the sunshine with his back turned to the couple. Just then, Oleg knew he had a confession for Priscilla and struggled to remind himself why he shouldn't share it. Ever since that first time, when he and his late wife forced down human flesh during the war, it had remained a secret that was never mentioned outside the family. Now, after decades of keeping it that way, Oleg considered breaking the silence. This centrepiece to his diet had kept him alive beyond his years, so he believed, so surely it would do the same for Priscilla? Looking at his dear companion once more, his heart bruising at the thought that she might depart, his reservations deserted him. 'There is something I'd like you to taste,' he said, leaning in across the blanket to find her ear. 'Something . . . restorative.'

'Ooh.' Priscilla turned to beam at him. 'Is it a chocolate?'

'An elixir,' he said, sounding as serious as he looked. 'The cure for everything.'

'So it *is* chocolate!'

Oleg shook his head, waiting for her to realise that he was being deadly serious here.

'All you have to do is let me make arrangements with my family,' he told her. 'I guarantee you won't regret it.'

Priscilla held Oleg's gaze for some time, as if waiting for him to crack.

'What are you hiding?' she asked curiously, before a sparkle in her eyes preceded a grin. 'You're a sweetheart, Oleg. I hope there's time for more dates, even if I do think there's a wicked streak inside you!'

13

Titus Savage cruised to a halt outside the Crankbait Sports Saloon. As he did so, the reflection from the neon piping gleamed across the bonnet of his pickup truck. He wound down the window and rested his elbow on the edge. It was a warm, close night, underscored by the sound of crickets in the scrub behind the building and a muffled but thumping beat from inside. Titus studied the frontage for a moment. In his hands, he thought idly, the grilles would have to go from the windows so it didn't look as if the place had something to hide. From experience, he knew the importance of outward appearances.

'What a dive,' he muttered to himself, and killed the engine. 'Why would anyone want to work here?'

Titus had just left the apartment complex when he decided to collect Amanda from her shift. It was only a short run down the freeway, and he could just sling her bicycle in the back of the truck. He had been working late on fixing a boiler. The new tenant was another software drone, but unusually this one possessed impeccable manners. The man had been deeply grateful to Titus, supplying him with cold drinks throughout the evening as he sought to restore the hot water. On his way out, Titus hoped his son might grow up to be that considerate. Certainly the guy would not be finding his way onto their dinner plates in a hurry.

Now that he'd arrived at Amanda's place of work, however, his sense of goodwill towards people began to crumble away. This became apparent when two dishevelled-looking figures tumbled from the main entrance and out into the night – one tall, the other squat, but both in the same state of inebriation. The pair could barely stand, observed Titus, and seemed overcome by some hilarious joke. What was with these idiots? Did they have no self-respect? Personally, Titus never touched alcohol outside the home, and even then it was limited to a fine vintage wine to wash down a feast. It was only when the two men turned to teeter down the steps that Titus realised with a jolt that they considered him to be their friend.

'Hey, man!' called out Kiril, on recognising the black-and-chrome pickup and the driver who'd been a moment too late to shield his face from them.

'What's a guy like you doing prowling the streets after dark?' asked Lev, as Titus's buddies from the golf course approached the truck. 'You'll earn yourself a reputation.'

'Fellas.' Titus nodded at them both, ignoring Lev's comment. 'I'm here to collect our lodger.'

'Right.' Lev shared a look of amusement with Kiril. 'Sure you are.'

'She works here.' Titus swapped his attention from one man to the other. 'Serving drinks.'

It was Lev who guffawed first, followed by his drinking buddy.

94

'Serving beers and then some,' said Kiril under his breath, which provoked yet more laughter.

'Am I missing something here?'

'The bar shuts in twenty minutes.' Lev grinned and slapped the top of the vehicle's cab. 'Go make the most of it, big guy!'

From the wing mirror, Titus watched them shuffling off into the night. Why they would want to be out at this time was beyond him. So long as work didn't draw him from the villa, all he wanted to do was enjoy supper with his family and then spend some downtime with them. Even if that meant watching Angelica's choice of makeover show on cable, while Ivan played videogames in his room and little Kat slept soundly, that was fine by him. Everyone was under the same roof, locked away from the world. Climbing out of the pickup, Titus wished Amanda would find herself a day job. One with regular hours so she could join her surrogate fold.

The noise when he opened the door to the saloon bar really wasn't pleasant on his ears. It was the kind of pumping techno that kids down on South Beach liked to blare from their car stereos. Titus was surprised to find the interior strikingly gloomy, with little more than the glare from the big screens and the neon to light the tables. It was also very busy, with clusters of men standing around expectantly with drinks in their hands. He looked around, hoping to spot Amanda, and that's when the first of the pole dancers swung into his line of sight. Wearing only a tiny pair of shorts and body glitter, the girl beamed at the new customer, who promptly dodged around her and hurried to the bar.

'What can I get you?' asked a man with a chipped tooth and thick eyebrows, before Titus had even reached him. 'If you want a private dance with your beer, that's forty bucks and the drink is on the house.'

Titus glanced over his shoulder. It just hadn't occurred to him that the Crankbait Sports Saloon would be host to this kind of gymnastics. More importantly, a girl he had taken under the family wing had found employment here. Had he known, Titus would've paid her *not* to take it.

'I'm looking for Amanda,' he said, scanning the booths and tables.

'Oh, her.' The barman glanced from one side to the other and then leaned in over the counter. 'You can try, but we don't do refunds.'

Titus held the man's gaze until he withdrew from the counter. Then he ordered a bottle of water from the cooler cabinet.

'Keep the change,' he growled, and flipped a twenty-dollar bill at him. 'The drink is all I want.'

'She'll bring it over.'

With a bad feeling rising in his guts, Titus cut back through the gloom. The TV screens showed a montage of shots from a basketball game, but few customers were watching. Most were on their feet, gathered around the girls as they twirled and gyrated for them. Titus ducked into the first available booth, sinking into the shadows. He'd barely settled, however, when a figure in silhouette rolled up to the table.

'Here's your drink, sir. Before you ask for anything else, that's restricted to potato-based snacks. You got a problem with that, have someone else serve you.'

The voice sounded bored, brittle and tired. Titus looked up with a start.

'Amanda?'

The young woman with the tray wheeled back on her skates, gasping in surprise.

'What are you doing here?' she hissed, setting the tray on the table.

'Look at these animals.' Titus gestured at the men gathered to eyeball the dancers. 'You think it's acceptable to be treated like a piece of *meat?*'

'I won't dance for them,' said Amanda, as if to clarify. 'It wasn't in the job description . . . at least, not until I started.'

Titus grimaced, closing his eyes for a moment.

'Who is in charge here?'

Amanda looked pained. She glanced nervously at Rolan, who was still behind the bar where he had served Titus.

'None of us are wild about the terms, but it's a wage,' she reasoned. 'At least it would be if we didn't have to hand over the tips.'

Titus considered her for a moment, his mouth flattening.

'Get your coat,' he said next, and gestured for her to move aside for him. 'Everyone is leaving.'

Rolan had been quietly watching the encounter from behind the bar. The new girl did a passable job waitressing, but her reluctance to work the floor like the others meant he'd have to get rid of her soon. He figured maybe the end of this shift was as good as any. On seeing the man with the shaved dome rise from the booth, Rolan wondered if Amanda had managed to offend by her dogged refusal to dance for him. He certainly had a grave look on his face as he approached, Rolan noted. But Rolan barely had time to step back before Titus vaulted over the counter, using one hand as a pivot and grabbing him by his shirt with the other as he came over the top.

'A word,' he growled, and shoved Rolan against the wall. 'This bar is closing with immediate effect.'

'Hey!' Rolan lifted his hands in protest at the assault, but found himself powerless.

'Not only do you brazenly parade these women, you don't even pay them properly,' snarled Titus. 'They're human beings, not cattle. Do you understand me?'

'Are you crazy? Get outta here!'

'First, I'm going to tell you something that might persuade *you* to leave,' snarled Titus. 'You see, I eat people like you for breakfast. That's right, *breakfast*.' Titus was now so close to Rolan's face that the barman would later swear that he could smell beef on the guy's breath. 'Now, if you're still here at daybreak, and my mood remains this bad, I'll be back to cut out your kidneys and force you to watch me frying them in a pan!'

As he outlined his plan, Titus jabbed deftly at the organs in question. Rolan responded by urinating a little into the fabric of his pants. There was no way of knowing if this psycho was bluffing, but the sheer purpose in the man's voice told him not to question it.

'Let me go,' he whispered, aware that the brute had scrunched the throat of his shirt and lifted him onto his toes.

'First, you promise to pay these ladies what you owe them,

98

plus three months extra to see them right while they find better employment.'

'Nobody is forcing them to dance,' Rolan protested, a little unwisely.

Titus responded by tightening his grip on the man's collar.

'Even when I'm slaughtering someone for the table,' he hissed, no longer blinking as he constricted Rolan's windpipe, 'I do it with *respect*.'

By now, the drama behind the bar had become the focus of the entire club. Through bulging, oxygen-starved eyes, Rolan was dimly aware that a lot of the customers were hurrying to leave, while the girls on stage just gawped in shock and amazement. None of them were paying any attention to the thumping music, nor did they react when Rolan's flailing foot swung into the CD rack behind him and brought silence to the club.

'I'll pay,' he croaked, just loud enough for Titus to hear him, before gasping for breath as his soles found the floor once more. Finding himself released in this way didn't stop him from crumpling, however, and balling up with his back to the stereo. 'Are you for real?' he asked in barely a whisper. '*Another* one?'

Titus heard him clearly, and immediately figured this wasn't the first time a customer had taken him to task for the operation going on in here.

'Don't make me mad by breathing a word about what I just told you,' he warned, as Amanda Dias appeared behind him with a murderous look in her eyes. 'All this grief has given me an appetite,' he added, 'and you *really* wouldn't like me when I'm hungry.'

SECOND COURSE

14

Alone in her bedroom, Katya Savage stood before her wardrobe and blinked. There had been no need for her to remove the shoeboxes concealing the gerbil cage. They had already been disturbed. As soon as she had opened the door, excited about providing breakfast for her new pet, the little girl's eyes began to glisten like rock pools.

'I knew it,' she whispered to herself, sounding choked as she drew breath, before rushing out to find her parents.

Kat could tell from the smell of frying bacon that she'd find them in the kitchen. At weekends, her dad enjoyed a traditional English breakfast. He couldn't understand why she preferred her rashers with waffles and maple syrup. Just then, however, his youngest daughter had no appetite whatsoever.

'Good morning, Kitty Kat!' said Angelica, who turned from the hob with a spatula in hand. 'Just in time.'

Her father sat at the breakfast bar, leafing through the *Miami Herald*, but it was her brother who commanded Katya's attention. Ivan glanced up at her, hunched over his bowl, and continued to scoop cereal into his mouth.

'Tinky Dinks is missing!' declared Kat with unbridled fury.

Angelica responded by sighing wearily. Titus closed the paper and joined her in staring at Ivan. The boy set down his spoon. Then he glanced at them in turn.

'What?' he asked defensively. 'I didn't torture him!'

In the silence that followed, his protest seemed to hang unsteadily in the air. A moment later, Angelica's cell phone on the counter signalled an incoming message. She picked it up to glance at the screen, looking tense and uncomfortable all of a sudden. Katya, meanwhile, just stared at her father expectantly. Titus drew breath to address the situation, only for his own phone to begin bleating. Frowning, he checked the name that had flashed up before answering.

'Hey,' he said, mouthing an apology to Katya as he moved away from the table to address the caller. 'What's up?'

With Ivan still glowering at her, stung by her accusation, Katya switched her attention to Angelica.

'But he's been a bad boy again . . . *Mommy!*'

It took a second for Angelica to lift her attention from the phone.

'What was that?' she asked distractedly. Behind her, the bacon continued to crackle unattended in the pan. 'Anyway, it's *Mummy*, Katya. How many times?'

The little girl's mouth quivered indignantly. She glanced at Ivan, but he had returned to his breakfast bowl as if the situation really wasn't a big deal. When Titus closed down his call, he looked helplessly at his youngest daughter.

'I have to go out, honey pie, but we can deal with this later.'

'Mommy!'

Angelica was hammering out a reply with her thumbs as

Kat focused on her. She hurried to press send as Titus collected the keys for the pickup, before waving away his apology for skipping breakfast.

'Everything OK?' Angelica asked him, and assembled a smile when she met his gaze.

'Business,' he told her. 'An emergency call-out.'

As he made his way to the lobby, Amanda appeared in her dressing gown. She took one step in, crinkled her nose at the smell of the cooking and backed right out again as if she might wretch. Katya paid her no attention, but continued to appeal to her mother to intervene. Instead, Angelica waited for the sound of the front door to open and close before pocketing her phone.

'Something has come up for me, too,' she said, twisting around to switch off the hob. 'Help yourselves, kids. Any problems, Amanda is in charge.'

Angelica hurried past her youngest daughter, who seemed several seconds behind what was going on. Katya had fully expected her parents to share her outrage at the missing gerbil. Instead, they had vanished in a matter of moments. Ivan pushed his empty bowl to one side just then, drawing her attention.

'So, do you want bacon?' he asked.

'I want Tinky Dinks!' Katya told him, on the verge of tears again.

Ivan considered her for a moment.

'If you like, I can help you look for him.'

Katya stared at him with an expression that hovered between disbelief and disgust.

'How can you be so cruel?' she demanded to know. 'Just

admit that it was you!'

Without waiting for Ivan to respond, Katya stormed for the stairs. She didn't slam the kitchen door behind her, but wished that she had on hearing her brother's parting words.

'Well, I guess that means all the more bacon for me.'

Joaquín Mendez was a young man in turmoil. Ever since Angelica Savage had left him on the beach path following that fateful attempt at a kiss, he had thought of nothing but her. In making that move on a married woman, the Argentinian fitness trainer had gone against his religious convictions and called his professional conduct into question. His mother back home would be thoroughly ashamed of him. He knew that. He could barely believe that he had been so bold, and yet his instinct had left him no option.

'I am wild about you,' he had breathed back then on the path, having pressed his lips to hers. 'I think about you day and night.'

In response, Angelica had simply stared at him for several seconds. As ever, it had proved impossible for Joaquín to fathom what she was thinking. He just could not see into her soul, despite being so close to her. It was as if she had assembled some invisible force field to protect her every thought and feeling.

'Joaquín,' she had said finally, and for a moment he thought she might fall into his arms. 'I think perhaps we have come far enough.'

It had taken him a moment to realise that Angelica was referring not to their relationship, but to the run. This was made apparent to him when she resumed the stretching exercises she had been undertaking before he had made the advance. Joaquín swallowed uncomfortably, took a step away to give her some space, and then embarked upon the most excruciating jog back to the gym with a client that he had ever experienced in his career.

Following the incident, Joaquín hadn't intended to bombard Angelica with text messages. The trouble was her silence. Not knowing how she felt was unbearable, and so he had continued to give into temptation in the hope that she would reply. It was only when he had reviewed his one-way correspondence the previous evening and found himself scrolling the screen that he realised he might be coming across as a little intense. That night, Angelica had weighed so heavily on his mind that Joaquín hardly slept. If anything, his feelings just fed upon themselves. Yes, she was considerably older, but he sensed a connection across the decades even if she had made no attempt to express the same thing. All those signs he believed she had given him? In hindsight, Joaquín accepted that he might've read a little too much into them, but until she told him directly, he just couldn't give up. When the young man finally received a response to the text he'd dispatched on waking that morning, his spirits had soared. Angelica's offer to meet him was all he could've asked for. As soon as her car swept into the parking lot outside the gym, he jogged over with bare feet to meet her.

'I'm so glad you came,' he beamed.

'Get in,' said Angelica, looking around warily. 'Before someone sees us.'

Joaquín was dressed in a fresh vest and black jogging bottoms, with a pair of sunglasses propped up on his head. As soon as he slid into the car beside her, he dropped the shades over his eyes as if that would help to soften her mood. Instead, Angelica gunned the engine and headed off at speed towards the freeway. Immediately, Joaquín sensed his heart pick up the pace. She drove with a purpose, he realised, noting how her knuckles had turned white where she gripped the wheel. Despite being such a difficult individual to read, it revealed something about her that surprised him. Angelica, it seemed to him just then, was a woman capable of extremes. In this case, he figured in his smitten, sleep-deprived mind, what she was doing here was leaving everything behind. Giving it all up, for him.

'This feels so right,' he told her after several blocks. 'Just me and you, going places at last!'

Angelica responded by squeezing the gas pedal by another degree. Joaquín felt the wind in his locks and made sure the seat belt was clipped in properly. This was turning out far better than expected, he thought, as they followed the signs for the main route out of town. Only an hour ago he had appealed to Angelica out of desperation in one last text, and now, all of a sudden, here she was, apparently taking him on the ride of his life. Joaquín felt no sense of doubt about what was happening here, though he wished he'd had time to pack a travel bag. He looked across at Angelica, facing her side-on. She glanced at him, just long enough for the young man to feel a hint of discomfort about the sudden lack of attention she was paying to her driving.

'You're a nice boy,' she said eventually, and promptly flipped the nearside indicator. 'But this is the end of the road.'

'What?'

He faced the front once more, unsure what this meant. The ramp onto the freeway was in sight, after all. With a straight run, they could be in Orlando by lunchtime. As if to spell it out for him, however, Angelica pulled off beside a stretch of wasteland. Judging by the rubble and the weeds, an industrial plant had been demolished here some time ago. A large hoarding had been set up in the middle, advertising the impending construction of luxury homes. It bore a picture montage featuring a family in a range of happy domestic situations.

'See that?' said Angelica, before killing the engine. 'What they're selling here is a fantasy. Nobody looks that content unless there's a cheque in it or they're on tranquillisers, but it doesn't stop people buying into it. They want to believe that's how life can be.'

'Right.' Joaquín nodded, unsure where this was heading.

Angelica turned to face him.

'I'm one of those people,' she told him, and paused there for a moment. 'My family mean everything to me, but we're not perfect by any stretch of the imagination. There are things that go on behind our front door that you'll never see on a billboard, just as there are in every household across the country. For all our faults, however, despite all the bad stuff, I still buy into that dream for the sake of my sanity, and I'm not prepared to throw it away for anyone. Now, I'm sorry if you got the wrong idea about me, Joaquín, but I'm not the one for you. Under the circumstances, for your sake as much as mine, it's only right that we go our separate ways from here. If you want to move on then you don't call, you don't text, you don't even *think* about me. Above all, if my husband found out about your intentions . . . well, let's just say he's a very protective man.'

As Angelica spelled out her position, the young trainer sensed his spirit deflate like a punctured medicine ball.

'Please,' he said, appealing to her to reconsider. 'I've never felt like this before.'

'You're young enough to be my son.'

'It could still work. Just let me prove it.'

'Trust me,' said Angelica calmly. 'I'd eat you alive.'

15

Titus Savage found Kiril and Lev at their usual table inside the golf clubhouse. The pair had ordered coffee, but nothing to eat. The second unusual thing that Titus noted was the air of tension and anxiety that greeted him when he took a seat. For two men in sunny tropical shirts, their mood was surprisingly gloomy. Despite his paunchy frame, Kiril seemed drawn, while his friend and business partner looked pallid, which wasn't helped by a head of freshly dyed black hair.

'So, where's the fire?' Titus asked Lev, who appeared puzzled by the question. Titus reached for the laminated menu. 'Your tone of voice when you called,' he explained. 'It sounded like you were set to lose everything in a blaze.'

'There is no fire,' said Kiril, whose hatchet face seemed deeper set than usual. 'But there's gonna be an inferno unless we do something fast.'

Titus frowned, ordered an espresso when the waitress approached and then returned his attention to the two men who had forced him to abandon his breakfast in such a hurry. He waited for them to speak, making a circling gesture with one finger as if to draw out an explanation.

'The Crankbait Sports Saloon,' said Lev, and cleared his throat. 'You shut it down.'

Titus shrugged. This wasn't news to him. Nor was he sorry for his actions. He had personally stayed to usher everyone out, and towered over Rolan as he shut off the power, padlocked the door and handed over the key.

'The place had no right to be there,' he said, 'taking advantage of the girls like that.'

'It was a service,' Kiril grumbled. 'Now it's history.'

Titus sat back for a moment, sizing up the two men.

'Are you telling me this as customers? You guys really should know better.'

Lev and Kiril glanced at one another.

'The bar was a business interest for us,' said Lev.

'We managed it for a . . . let's call him a client.'

The hesitation in Kiril's voice prompted Titus to lean forward once more. With his hands folded on the table, he furrowed his brow and considered his next question.

'No doubt your client is unhappy,' he said finally.

'That's an understatement.' Kiril gave a hollow laugh. 'He wants blood.'

'So who is he?' Titus remained quite composed, despite the fact that his two friends looked so haunted. 'Do I know him?'

'He's from the home country,' said Lev. 'An associate of ours, before times got tough.'

'You mean before the crooks moved in,' said Titus.

Kiril cringed and glanced over his shoulder.

'Will you keep your voice down, Titus? Anyone could hear us!'

112

'This crook,' Titus pressed on. 'Would I have heard of him?'

'If you keep an eye on Russian affairs,' said Kiril, whose voice had dropped close to a whisper.

Although Titus had never visited his father's place of birth, he wore his heritage with pride. Nowadays, this extended to lingering on the English-speaking news channel from Moscow whenever he was flicking through the TV schedules. It was Lev who beckoned Titus closer, having first looked one way and then the other.

'Nikolai Zolotov,' he said, nodding as he sat back, as if the name needed no other explanation.

Titus switched his attention between the two men.

'A politician?' he asked. 'A football club owner?'

'A cannibal,' said Kiril, with a note of disgust in his voice.

Titus caught his breath at the mention of the word. Not only did it secretly define his family, he realised with a start that he'd misunderstood the barman that night. Titus wasn't just another aggrieved customer, as he had thought. The man was referring to *another* human flesh eater. He'd never heard of the individual that the pair spoke about in such hushed and fearful tones, but already it felt too close to home. It meant that his next response was to dismiss the claim outright.

'Sounds like you guys have spooked yourselves,' he said with a chuckle.

Lev and Kiril showed no hint of amusement, which only left Titus more uncomfortable.

'Zolotov made his fortune smuggling goods into the country following the fall of communism,' said Lev.

'So did many people,' Titus pointed out. 'You guys weren't

exactly angels when the motherland was on her knees.'

Lev stretched out his fingers, signalling that he hadn't finished.

'The man served twenty-five years in a Siberian prison for the killing, dismemberment and consumption of a rival smuggler,' he continued. 'Nikolai Zolotov is believed to have slain two further cellmates during his sentence, and paid off the wardens who found him eating their body parts raw.'

This time Titus made a face, but only because there were very few cuts that tasted good uncooked.

'The man sounds like a beast,' he said.

'He's infamous in the underworld,' Lev continued. 'Ever since Zolotov's release, he's been ruthless in rebuilding his empire.'

'Anyone who gets in his way –' said Kiril, taking over. He then finished by making a cutting gesture across his neck. 'Killed and eaten as a warning to others.'

'He's easy to recognise on account of his teeth,' said Lev. 'Zolotov's molars were ruined by years on a poor prison diet. Nowadays, he wears metal implants and a diamond-studded grill to reinforce what's left.'

'They say it also helps him to chew more efficiently,' Kiril added solemnly. 'Bites through meat like butter.'

Titus listened to all this without a word.

'Can I ask a question?' he said eventually. 'You guys got out of the country decades ago. This is your life now, growing old, tanned and bald on the golf course. What are you doing mixing with a lunatic like this?'

'You can take the businessman out of Russia,' said Lev with a shrug, 'but he'll never turn his back on an opportunity.'

'Even if the paperwork isn't all there to back it up,' Kiril added, as if that was all that needed to be said.

'Zolotov deals in dollars,' Lev continued, 'but he needs to clean the cash so it can't be tracked back to him, and that's where we come in.'

'Money laundering,' said Titus, who didn't need to have it spelled out for him. 'You put the dirty dough behind the till at the saloon, and rinse it out into the wild, right?'

Lev spread his hands. 'It was easy work. Where's the harm? Nobody died.'

'Not yet.' Kiril continued to look hounded. 'Zolotov ships out monthly cash bundles on a freight ship. We pick up ours at the Port of Miami, but what are we gonna send back now you've shut down his bar and paid off the girls to find other work?'

Titus lifted the last of his coffee to his lips, checking the wall clock at the same time.

'You'll work something out. Now, I really have to be getting home . . .'

He moved to get up, but Kiril reached forward and grasped his wrist.

'That barman you chased out of town. It was Zolotov's nephew.'

Titus closed his eyes for a moment. All of this was keeping him from his breakfast.

'When Nikolai finds out, he won't let this go,' warned Lev. 'He goes in hard every time. In the past, when an associate let him down, they say the man hunted down every member of his family, killing them one by one, until the poor soul had nothing left in his life but an urge to suck on the muzzle of a gun.'

'But he won't just come after us.' Kiril flattened his lips. 'Titus, you'll be at the top of his hit list.'

'After your wife and children,' Lev said to correct his friend.

Titus switched his attention between the two men. Both looked like they were just waiting for the guy to storm in and chew off their faces.

'You worry too much,' he told them, and dismissed their claim with a wave of his hand. 'This Zolotov guy is way back home, thousands of miles away. He can threaten you as much as he likes, but you're safe from harm here. This is Florida. Relax. Enjoy the sunshine.'

'He's going to get mad,' said Lev.

'As in crazy mad,' Kiril stressed. 'Crazy, *brutal* mad.'

Titus toyed with the empty coffee cup, mulling over the dregs.

'Listen, I'm sorry I messed up your business arrangements,' he told them, 'but no doubt it's just one of many irons you guys have in the fire. In a way, you should thank me for shutting down something that could get you into trouble with the law.'

'Right now,' said Lev, as Titus rose from his seat to leave, 'the law is the least of our worries.'

Even before Oleg Savage knocked on the front door of his son's villa, he could tell that some kind of search was underway inside.

'So, what have you lost?' he asked the lodger when she opened up.

'Well, we could start with my job,' Amanda told the old man, 'but that's yesterday's news.'

Amanda Dias was wearing denim shorts and a 'Save the Manatee' T-shirt. She looked a little harassed. From somewhere on the first floor, Oleg could hear his youngest granddaughter calling repeatedly for something.

'So, what's today's headline?' he asked.

'Tinky Dinks is missing from his cage.' Amanda stepped aside for him. 'It's Kat's turn to take care of the school gerbil, which is a challenge seeing that he's vanished.'

Oleg had parked his scooter on the driveway and brought his walking stick with him. He eased himself into the lobby and peered up the stairs.

'Ivan?' he asked, feeling no need to spell out that they should probably fear the worst.

Amanda looked entirely unsurprised by the suggestion.

'I asked him earlier, but he just got cross.'

With both hands resting on his stick, and as Kat continued to call out for the missing creature upstairs, Oleg bowed his head and nodded to himself.

'A feast would lift her spirits,' he suggested hopefully, peering up at Amanda from under his wiry white brows.

'We've only had one recently.' Amanda rested her hands on her hips, grinning at him. 'We don't want to get greedy, Oleg. That's when mistakes are made. Besides, Titus is pretty happy with his tenants right now. We gorged on the last one who gave him grief.'

Oleg tried not to look frustrated. In the time that she had been lodging with his son's family, Amanda always proved the most enthusiastic of human meat eaters. He had hoped to gain her support before approaching Titus about his plan for Priscilla. Ever since she had confided in him about her dwindling health and effectively confirmed that she was dying, all he could think about was introducing her to the cure-all. It wasn't proven, of course, but human flesh had saved him as a young man during that barbaric siege, and sustained him to an age he never believed he would see. What harm would come from allowing Priscilla to share a meal with them? It was hardly going to kill her. That was how he planned to pitch it to his son. As much as he had a soft spot for Amanda, and banked on her fondness for another family gathering, he reminded himself that she didn't decide when they would sit together again.

'Well, let's hope Titus doesn't leave it too long, eh?' Oleg forced a chuckle, which did little to cover the tension in his voice. 'A feast is what keeps me alive!'

Amanda regarded him with a hint of amusement in her expression.

'How are things with your lady friend?' she asked, and raised one eyebrow by a notch. 'No doubt she takes years off you.'

Looking to the floor tiles, Oleg refused to play along. Amanda's observation was well intentioned, he had no doubt, but it lacked a little respect for a man of his age.

'I enjoy the company,' he told her after a moment. 'Just having someone to sit beside as the sun goes down is a comforting thing.'

Amanda smiled but seemed distracted by the fact that Kat's repeated calling for the gerbil was threatening to break into a wail of anguish.

'This search is futile,' she muttered to herself.

'It's just prolonging the misery,' Oleg agreed.

'Kat's so little, what else can I do?' Amanda sought to keep herself from being heard. 'But if I don't go through the motions, she'll know for sure that her brother killed it!'

'There is another way.' Oleg stopped there, turned and announced his presence to Katya. 'I know where we'll find Tinky Dinks!' he called up to her.

'Where?' Amanda whispered.

Little Kat appeared at the top of the stairs just then. It was quite clear to Oleg that she had been crying for some time, though he beamed broadly when she rushed down the steps to find out where they should look.

'The pet store,' he told Amanda under his breath, and opened his arms to greet his granddaughter.

16

Ivan Savage was wearily familiar with bad days at high school. On the first morning back the following week, he weathered teasing and intimidation right up until the lunch bell. The prospect of having his food tampered with persuaded him to stay away from the canteen. It meant that when the last lesson of the afternoon finished, the boy hurried from the classroom feeling famished and quietly furious.

'It's football practice tomorrow, new girl.'

'Don't forget to leave your kit at home!'

'Unless you want your hair washed in the can again.'

Well aware that the walk home might not be trouble free, Ivan scurried for the main gates in a bid to get ahead of Chad, Ryan and Bryce. He glanced over his shoulder on hearing their stupid dumb laughter as they emerged from the halls. To his ear, they sounded like cows lowing on their way to the dairy. He smirked at the thought, only for his heel to catch the kerb as he reached the sidewalk. Ivan had just enough time to fling out his hands before hitting the ground. It left the boy with his palms skinned and the contents of his bag fanned out in front of him.

'When is my luck going to change?' he muttered bitterly to himself.

Unwilling to be seen by his tormentors, Ivan scrambled to return his schoolbooks and pens to his bag. When a hand reached out to help, he looked up with a start.

'I'm beginning to think you're a walking disaster,' said Crystal, the girl with the dairy-white skin and the ginger hair. She grinned, looking fresh-faced without the nose bleed, and crouched beside the boy.

'I'm fine.' Ivan snatched the papers she'd just picked up for him. 'Thanks, but I have this under control.'

Next, he reached for a notebook, the pages fluttering in the breeze, but Crystal got there first.

'What's this?' she asked, holding it just out of his reach. 'Oh, wow! You can draw.'

Ivan watched her fearfully. He drew his bag closer to him, as if it was a comfort blanket.

'It's nothing serious,' he offered quietly. 'Just doodles.'

Crystal glanced across at him as if to say he'd have to come up with a better explanation.

'You're very talented,' she said, eyeing him side-on. 'Should I be scared of you?'

Throughout the last lesson, having had enough of the constant teasing and the put-downs, Ivan had vented his fury by putting pen to paper. Crystal flicked through the notebook, which he had filled with sketches of the three boys in various stages of dismemberment.

'I don't mean anything by it,' said Ivan, who collected the last of his stuff from the ground.

'Well, you should,' said Crystal. 'Those idiots make your life a misery.'

Behind them, the trio in question emerged from the halls. Ivan heard their voices, and picked himself off the ground.

'I need to get going.'

'I'll walk with you.' Crystal rose to her feet. 'Seeing as you're so accident-prone right now, someone needs to watch your back.'

'There's really no need,' said Ivan, but he didn't protest when she set off with him. 'My family watch out for me.'

For the first couple of blocks, Ivan replied to Crystal's questions about his life with some reluctance. Her full, round bottom and chubby midriff certainly appealed to the boy's taste buds. It was her enthusiastic nature that made him wary. She asked him about the movies he liked, questioned what insect he would be if he had to make a choice and whether he'd heard the rumour that the school caretaker had a criminal record in Arkansas for child molestation. Gradually, in spite of the constant queries, he began to warm to her company. Crystal was good at filling all the awkward silences, and despite relaxing in her company, Ivan created a lot. A case in point occurred as they passed the Fallen Pine Nursing Home. Having randomly shared his *Call of Duty* kill streak record, Ivan was pleased to point out that he had family there, simply to change the subject, only to snatch his eyes from the building and quicken his pace.

'Hey, what's the hurry?' Crystal jogged a couple of feet to catch up. 'Is it someone from school?'

She looked around, caught sight of a couple on the bench

in the porch of the old people's place and then stopped in her tracks.

'Oh, boy, check out those two,' she said, grinning. 'Do you think they remove their false teeth first?'

Ivan was well aware that Crystal had also spotted his grandfather making out with his new girlfriend. As soon as he'd seen them, his instinct was to pretend it wasn't happening. It still seemed so weird that Oleg had a love life going on. When the family learned that he was dating once again, Ivan just assumed it meant he'd found someone to finish the crossword with. Now, seeing them snogging like teenagers, with their sticks side by side against the wall and her leg hooked over his, the boy felt a sense of shock, horror and shame.

'I should be getting home,' he said, but Crystal remained entranced by the sight.

'What's going on now?' She narrowed her eyes. 'I think he just made it to second base.'

Ivan could barely bring himself to glance back at the porch. When he did so, it was enough to spur him onwards.

'It can't last,' he said, as Crystal reluctantly followed him. 'How can it?'

'Well, I think it's kind of sweet,' she replied, with one final look back at the porch. 'I guess at their age there's nothing more to be embarrassed about. If I get that old I hope I still have that lust for life.'

'A bucket of cold water is what Grandpa needs,' muttered Ivan out of earshot.

'Do you think they go all the way?' asked Crystal, who caught up with him just then. 'You never think of old people

123

having sex, do you?'

'*Never!*' said Ivan, who practically broke into a trot just then. What he had just witnessed left him reeling. Grandpa was just Grandpa. He'd lived his life. The boy just didn't expect him to behave in this way, especially as he had yet to experience anything like it.

'I imagine they need a whole lotta lubricant.'

'Crystal, can we change the subject?'

'But it's totally natural, when you think about it. Even seniors get horny, just like us.'

Ivan glanced across at her, and then immediately wished he hadn't. She had not only kept up his pace, but there was also something in the way Crystal looked at him that told the boy she wasn't only referring to the appalling scene they had just witnessed. It made him feel quite dizzy. As they approached the junction for the inlet community, the question of where she was heading became uppermost in his mind.

'I live over there,' he said, gesturing towards the far end of the private road. 'See you at school tomorrow, then.'

Crystal swapped her bag from one shoulder to the other.

'Aren't you going to ask me in?'

'No,' said Ivan, without thinking. 'I mean, did you want me to?'

Crystal shrugged, smiling in a way that made him feel odd given how he was coming to regard her.

'Got any food in the house?'

'Hope so,' Ivan replied. 'The school canteen is kind of out of bounds for me right now. I haven't eaten since breakfast.'

'Then what are we waiting for? Let's fix ourselves a *feast!*'

Ivan watched Crystal set off along the road and just stood there staring at her. He only came to his senses when she turned to face him.

'What do you mean by a feast?' he asked cautiously.

Crystal seemed surprised by the question.

'Well, let's see what you've got in the fridge,' she suggested. 'Maybe you can surprise me!'

On the drive home from pre-school, Angelica glanced in the rear-view mirror and prepared to choose her words carefully.

'So,' she said, on making eye contact with Katya in the back. 'Was your teacher pleased to see Tinky Dinks after his weekend away?'

'She's always pleased to see Tinky Dinks,' her daughter replied.

Pleased, and relieved no doubt, Angelica thought.

'And she didn't say there was anything . . . different about him?'

'Nope.' Katya shook her head, and switched her attention to the water as they drove across the bridge.

'Well, that's good,' said Angelica.

'Why would Tinky Dinks be different?'

'Oh, no reason,' she replied, and then switched on the radio to distract Kat from further conversation.

Angelica had Oleg to thank for saving the situation. First, he had invited his granddaughter to climb on board his scooter. Then he sold her a story that the plucky gerbil had gone on a shopping trip to the mall. By all accounts, Kat had completely fallen for it. She had even provided him with a good description of his appearance, so that Oleg knew just what to look for when they rode into the pet store. He'd always had a kind heart, Angelica reminded herself, and that had certainly been reflected in his actions since striking up his sweet, chaste little friendship with the old lady from the home. Just thinking about that made her smile briefly, until she reflected on Ivan's role in the episode. Angelica was still cross with her son, of course, mostly for continuing to deny any involvement in the original gerbil's disappearance. Killing a little creature like that was one thing, and goodness knows whether he'd learned anything from his father about making it humane. What really bothered her, however, was the dishonesty. How he could look into his mother's eye and swear that he had played no part in it was just so disappointing.

It meant that when she arrived home to find Ivan in the kitchen with a friend, Angelica was less than welcoming.

'This is Crystal,' said Ivan, speaking with his mouth full. 'She's just shown me how to make a *six*-decker sandwich.'

'And used up all the bread in the process.'

The pair were clutching their creations, layered with ham, rocket, tomatoes and mustard. In the wake of Angelica's comment, Crystal set hers down on the plate, her face reddening. Angelica hadn't intended to sound as snappy as she had, but the work surface was a mess and Ivan had spilled the orange juice he'd poured for them.

'My grandma will be wondering where I've got to,' said Crystal, hopping off the stool. 'It's nice to meet you all.'

Angelica forced a smile when Crystal caught her eye, but as she was standing there with her arms folded, it only served to hurry the girl from the kitchen.

'I'll see you tomorrow,' Ivan called out after her, and then looked sulkily at his mother at the sound of the front door closing. 'That's if she'll talk to me again.'

Angelica felt bad that her arrival had cooled the temperature this much. She hadn't meant to be so severe, but this thing about the gerbil still sat uncomfortably with her.

'Nobody at school realised that Tinky Dinks was a new model,' she told him, setting her bag on a stool. 'Thanks for your concern.'

Katya could be heard trotting up the stairs to her room as she said this, singing to herself as if nothing had happened.

'Well, that's a happy ending,' said Ivan, before taking another bite from his towering sandwich.

Angelica said nothing for a moment. She just observed her son eating and wondered where they had gone wrong.

'All you have to do is own up to it, Ivan, and then we can move on.'

Ivan swallowed his mouthful, but didn't even attempt to break from his mother's gaze.

'I didn't kill Tinky Dinks,' he said finally, as he had so many times over the weekend. 'I didn't touch the stupid thing!'

Angelica drew breath to suggest that Ivan might like to reconsider things in his room, only to watch him leave his stool and march off in that direction anyway. She breathed out long and hard as he left, aware of the mess he'd created, and crossed the floor to collect their plates. Normally, a workout in the gym would've helped her take a more relaxed approach to managing the household. It was a shame she'd had to let go of Joaquín, but she couldn't focus on her fitness regime with a personal trainer who'd let his emotions run unharnessed. Yes, it had been flattering, but family always came first. It had to, what with the tradition that bound them together.

As she wiped down the surfaces with an antibacterial spray, Angelica's thoughts turned to Titus. He'd always gone the extra mile to provide a comfortable life for them all, and put a feast on the table when they needed it most. Even so, it was clear to her that he'd lost his drive lately. The man was a hunter, but that was all too easy out here. Then there was the management, repair and maintenance of all those single-occupancy apartments. It took up a great deal of his time, but it was hardly a challenge for him. As for her husband's sudden desire to get in shape, that had to come from a sense of dissatisfaction within himself, just as it did for Angelica. Reaching for the rubber gloves in order to wash up, she wondered what she could do to help renew his zest for life. A moment later, the cell phone in her bag began to ring. She'd already snapped on one glove by the time she answered; pinning the phone between her ear and shoulder so she could slip her hand inside the other.

'Hello?' she said, and then fell quiet for a moment. What she heard next caused her to gasp and take a step backwards. It took another second for her to snatch the phone from her ear and stab a button to kill the connection.

'Cold call?' asked a voice from behind her. Angelica turned to find Amanda at the fridge. She was examining the contents of her shelf, unaware of the direct and menacing threat that Angelica had just received.

'Wrong number,' she told Amanda, still reeling from the

detail the caller had offered that left her in no doubt that it was meant for her.

Amanda returned her attention to the fridge, but only for a moment, because that's when the cell phone in her pocket began to bleat.

17

Locked inside his bedroom, sitting on his bed with his arms folded tight around his legs, Ivan Savage chose not to answer his phone when it rang.

'I didn't do it,' he muttered to himself. 'Why does everyone think it was me?'

It was unusual for Ivan not to come straight home from school and take out his frustrations through his videogame console. After a day of being teased and picked on by Chad, Bryce and Ryan, he would load up a first-person shooter and keep them in mind as his kill count gathered traction. On this occasion, when his phone finally fell silent, the boy stared at his socks and brooded. No matter how many times he had pleaded ignorance about the fate of the gerbil, everyone just gave him that look like he should know better than to lie to his family.

'It's just so unfair,' he grumbled, his mouth tightening, and then turned his thoughts to the girl who had shared a bite to eat with him.

Crystal was weird, he thought to himself. Frankly, anyone who wanted to spend time in his company, without worrying about what everybody else might think, had to be unusual. He still felt mortified at having come across his grandfather feeling up the old lady from the home. What troubled him more, however, was Crystal's fascination. That kind of intimacy just wasn't for him. Even a cuddle from his mother left him tense, and mercifully he'd only been in that situation a handful of times. Ivan figured he should probably distance himself from the girl. Not just for his sake, he decided, but for hers.

'What do I have to do to make a simple friend?' he asked out loud, before sighing long and hard.

It was another beautiful day outside. With his window open, Ivan could hear cruisers out on the waterway and the chatter of sparrows in the trees. Sunshine slanted onto the floor tiles, creating a square of light in the gloom. Ivan wasn't looking directly, but when something hurried across it he snapped upright in surprise.

'Hey,' he said aloud, and eased off the bed for a better look. At first he thought it was a cockroach, which prompted him to decide its days were numbered, only to spy the swish of a tail. Slowly, the boy dropped to his hands and knees. 'Don't be scared. Let me see you.'

Ivan held out his hand and stayed quite still. Then, from out of the shadows under his desk, a tiny whiskery snout emerged. When two black beady eyes caught the light, he knew exactly what he was facing.

'Tinky Dinks!' he declared under his breath. 'So this is where you've been hiding all along!'

The boy hadn't lied when he said he'd played no part in the gerbil's disappearance. Yes, he had opened up Kat's wardrobe, searching for the source of the scrabbling. OK, so they'd gone

131

to some lengths to hide it from him with the shoeboxes, but he'd had better things to do than pull it limb from limb. At the time, Ivan had bunked off school in order to plot how to get back at the three boys making his life a misery, and that's exactly what he'd done. If anyone had left the cage open, Katya would've done so later that day, but nobody ever had a bad word to say about her.

'It's OK,' he said, as the gerbil crept closer. Slowly, he got down on his knees. 'You can trust me to take care of you.'

Ivan glanced at his bedroom door as a thought entered his mind. As far as Kat's pre-school was concerned, she had returned Tinky Dinks from his weekend away. It would only complicate matters, he decided, if he produced the original. No doubt his mother would think he'd stashed the creature away as a means of tormenting his kid sister, which would only earn him more trouble.

'That's it. Come to Ivan,' he whispered, before carefully shooting out both hands to catch Tinky Dinks before he could turn. 'Oh, my pretty,' he said, and created a gap between his thumbs for a peep at the captive creature. 'What fun you'll have with me!'

Titus Savage had spent his morning viewing apartments in a new condominium complex. He'd gone with a view to putting in an offer on one, hoping to build up his property business, and left feeling as empty as the rooms he had inspected. What made things worse was the number of mirrors that had been fitted. There had just been no escaping from himself and the extra pounds he'd started packing.

All in all it had been a low moment, and yet Titus decided to park his mood on pulling up outside the villa. Unlike Lev and Kiril, he didn't feel the need to share his problems.

'Where have you been?' asked Angelica, before Titus had even closed the front door behind him. She was at the breakfast bar with Amanda, who looked equally rattled. 'I've been trying to reach you!'

Titus checked his cell phone. He'd missed four calls from his wife, which was down to the fact that he'd set it to mute before viewing the apartment and then forgotten to restore the volume.

'Did anyone else contact you?' asked Amanda.

'Nobody.' Titus looked up from the screen. 'What's the emergency?'

It was unusual for him to see his wife this unsettled. In all the years of their marriage, she had always maintained calm in the face of a crisis. That time when he had delivered a body for a feast and the damn thing had started to twitch and groan? Angelica had simply tutted and reached for the meat cleaver without hesitation.

'Titus,' she said, and slipped from the stool to take a step towards him. 'Who is Nikolai Zolotov?'

Blinking once on hearing the name, Titus took a moment to compose a response.

'Has he left a message for me?' he asked quietly.

'You could say that.' Amanda held her phone out accusingly. 'Whoever this whack job is, he plans to make a meal of our entrails.'

'Starting with your youngest daughter,' said Angelica,

sounding fragile all of a sudden.

'And then working his way up through the family, including me, and finishing with you.' Amanda glared accusingly at Titus. 'Is this some kind of sick joke? I'm thinking it can't be a genuine threat, because entrails are only good for a stock.'

Titus drew breath to deny all knowledge, only to let the air from his lungs in a long sigh.

'I didn't tell you because I saw no reason to be concerned,' he said eventually. 'This changes the situation a little.'

'A little?' Angelica invited her husband to sit with them at the breakfast bar. 'We don't keep secrets in this house, Titus.'

'We *are* the secret,' Amanda added.

'So,' Angelica continued. 'This man . . . '

Even as he shared what he knew, Titus was at pains to stress that they shouldn't feel under direct threat. He'd said exactly the same thing to Lev and Kiril when they'd summoned him to the clubhouse. Nikolai Zolotov, the money launderer whose bar Titus had shut down, was ranting at them from way out in Russia. OK, so the man had tracked down their contact details, but that was very different from doing the same thing in person. It was all sound and fury. They should just ignore it, he told them. Block the number and get on with their lives.

Angelica and Amanda listened closely to what Titus had to say. Even before he had finished, however, it was quite clear that he hadn't come close to making them feel comfortable.

'Believe me,' he said, as if to take responsibility for the situation, 'had I known the Crankbait was a front for a criminal's business interests, I would've acted a little differently. The last thing we need in our lives is trouble.'

Titus didn't need to remind them why the family always maintained a low profile, but it was enough to prompt Angelica to press him further about the nature of the threats.

'He was very specific about wanting to eat your family alive,' she pointed out. 'Is he, you know, like us?'

'No,' said Titus quickly, and held up his palms to back it up. 'Far from it!'

'But he claims to devour people,' said Amanda. 'That makes him a cannibal in my book.'

That word. It wasn't something Titus ever liked to hear out loud. In his view, it described the kind of animal under discussion, not the resurrection and refinement of ancient dining habits that his family had come to pursue over the years.

'We celebrate life through feasts,' he told them. 'This man turns on his own to strike fear into his enemies.'

'Well, it's worked,' said Angelica. 'He threatened my babies.'

'And it sounded to me like he meant every word,' Amanda pointed out. 'He's coming for us.'

'We should call the cops.' Angelica tapped the table as she said this. 'Tell them everything we know.'

'Out of the question,' growled Titus. 'Involving the law at any level could cause us all manner of difficulties. We're above that, Angelica. I can handle this.'

In a bid to escape her glare, Titus turned his attention from his wife to the kitchen window. Beyond the lawn and the jetty, which had warped a little in the heat, sunlight turned every ripple on the inlet into glitter. Jupiter was a paradise. Nikolai Zolotov sounded like hell on earth. Even if it was just a madman howling from the wilderness, his calls had cast a shadow of uncertainty and unease over the Savage home.

'You have to do something,' he heard Angelica say. 'We can't just hope he'll go away.'

A rowing boat caught Titus's attention just then, with a single oarsman at the helm. He was moving against the current, making slow but steady progress. Watching the man throw himself into the crossing, Titus considered his position.

'Let's put everything we have into this challenge,' he told them, thinking out loud. 'It was me who shut down the saloon bar, and got us into this. I say we reopen the doors.'

'Really?' Amanda sounded shocked, drawing Titus from the window. 'With the same . . . entertainment as before?'

'I can't believe you took on a job like that,' Angelica muttered at her. 'Not that I condone the way Titus reacted when he discovered what the work involved.'

'I'm proposing a very different business plan,' Titus continued, rising to his feet now. All of a sudden, what he had in mind stirred a feeling in him that he had lost sight of some time ago. It was a drive to succeed, just like that oarsman out on the water. Reaching for his phone, the volume enabled this time, he punched in a number and prepared to update his two friends. Angelica, meanwhile, simply stared at her husband in utter surprise. As he waited for the call to connect, Titus Savage covered the mouthpiece and said: 'Consider the place to be under new management.'

18

As a soldier during the siege of Leningrad, Oleg Savage slept with one eye open. At least, that's what he told his grandchildren, on account of the rumour that some desperate souls were turning on their own kind for sustenance. Yes, Oleg was among that small band that had crossed the line, but still he couldn't afford to drop his guard. After the war, so he said, he made up for such vigilance by sleeping very deeply indeed. As he grew older and his hearing diminished, he found it even easier to slumber through until morning without being disturbed.

It meant Oleg didn't stir that night at the sound of the ambulance siren approaching the nursing home. Nor was he roused by the red and blue lights that flashed across the wall of his room for several minutes.

Waking naturally at nine, as was his habit, Oleg rose feeling refreshed and ready for breakfast with Priscilla on the lawn. While the other residents of the Fallen Pine preferred to eat indoors before gathering dust in the sunroom, Oleg was pleased to find a companion who still had such hunger for life. His first real kiss with her had only happened recently. It had also gone much further than he could've imagined. They'd been out on the porch, enjoying the sunshine, and without word the magnetic attraction between the couple just drew them together. Quite simply, the years fell away for them both. It was a close, fumbling encounter like neither of them had experienced for decades, and proved to be both exhilarating and exhausting.

It also meant that when Oleg left his room he did so whistling contentedly to himself.

With his stick in hand, he made his way to the terrace. Priscilla was an early riser, so it was unusual for him not to see her waiting there. As he shuffled towards his chair, the creak of the conservatory door behind him prompted him to turn. On finding his nurse, Vince, standing with his hands clasped and a pensive, awkward look on his face, Oleg lost his appetite in a heartbeat.

'I'm afraid she won't be joining you this morning,' he said solemnly.

'Has she . . . moved on?' asked Oleg, feeling weak and dizzy all of a sudden. The old man was used to learning that residents had passed away, but this was sounding like news that threatened to overwhelm him. Not only did Oleg fear that their moment of passion on the porch might've killed Priscilla, but he couldn't begin to imagine what the remains of his life without her would be like.

'Easy there.' Vince responded by hurrying to his assistance. He was a broad-shouldered individual and easily supported Oleg with one hand under his arm. 'Priscilla's at the medical

138

centre, under observation. She had a moment, and no doubt there'll be more, but for now she's stable.'

Oleg peered up at the big man, looking like a small boy in the care of his father.

'Will she be home?'

'Oh, you know Priscilla. She's a fighter.' Vince sounded brighter than was natural for the guy. 'And no doubt you'll be spoiling her when she returns, eh?'

Oleg extended his gaze to the empty chairs and the table. He nodded to himself, seemingly transported for a moment.

'A feast,' he said to himself with a note of frustration, as if this was something that couldn't happen soon enough.

'Sounds good,' said Vince, and chuckled at the old man as he blinked back to his senses. 'Want me to order in supplies? Bagels? Donuts? You name it, buddy.'

'I've got it covered,' Oleg told him, and moved to stand without help. 'My family know what I like on my plate.'

Even by his standards, Ivan Savage had endured a miserable morning at school. With football practice that afternoon, he had shown up with his kit bag and every intention of taking part. Bryce, Chad and Ryan had spotted him at his locker, and that's when the trouble began. Now, every time the teacher turned to the whiteboard, someone would flick stuff at him, but Ivan had become immune to that. It was the threats he couldn't ignore, passed to him on strips of paper.

Despite the promise that he would suffer real pain if he dared to show his face on the pitch, Ivan couldn't resist a small smile. Just before lunch break, he even dared to return the messages with the spelling mistakes and grammar corrected in red biro.

'Are you asking to be slaughtered?' growled Bryce, after the bell had sounded. Ivan hadn't even left his chair before the kid came across and pinned him to it. He could smell onion rings on Bryce's breath, which made him wonder what his mother fed him to start the day. 'I swear to God, new girl, if I see you on the field, I will finish you!'

'Unless I get there first.' Ryan slapped the back of Ivan's head as he passed, while Chad chose to kick the chair from underneath him.

'Steer clear, you hear?' Bryce jabbed a finger at the boy on the floor, the creases on his forehead perfectly aligned with the front of his buzz cut. 'Stay out of the way or pay the price!'

Throughout, Ivan remained quite calm. He looked on, as the three boys headed for the corridor, with no sign of distress whatsoever. Alone in the classroom, with everyone else on their way to lunch, he picked himself up along with his chair and sat down again. He only had to consider his plan for payback to feel tranquil. For in the right time and place, the boy would have something to offer them that they could not resist. Food, Ivan had realised, would seal their fate.

Until then, he reminded himself as he fished around in his school bag, he could call upon his first true friend. Crystal was a nice girl, but a little too tactile, and also in a different form to him. Ivan had someone in mind who could be with him every minute of the day, even through the tough times.

'Easy now, Tinky Dinks. Out you come.' At moments such as this, when Ivan felt the need for company, he could console himself with the little gerbil he then lifted onto his lap. He

140

stroked the creature from head to tail a couple of times, sensing the delicate bones just beneath its skin. As he did so, the boy remained oblivious to the chatter and shrieks of the pupils out in the corridor. It felt good, if only briefly, to escape from the school environment in this way. The moment also served to highlight just how alienated he had become at the hands of three individuals. 'Oh, they'll suffer,' he said, as if Tinky Dinks himself had just asked him what he had planned. 'They've picked on the boy who bites back.'

Ivan lifted the gerbil level with his face, observing the creature's tiny nose twitch, and then cupped it with both hands in his lap. Bryce, Ryan and Chad would live to regret the day they singled him out. Even if they welcomed him to training with open arms, it was too late for forgiveness. They would soon know who they had been messing with, he assured himself, feeling tense all of a sudden, and then the tears would fall.

'Ivan . . . *Ivan!*'

It wasn't just the sound of Crystal's voice from the classroom door that stirred him, but the squeak of alarm from Tinky Dinks as the space between the boy's palms constricted.

'You probably shouldn't be seen with me,' he told her, hurriedly returning the gerbil to the bag before it came into her line of sight.

'I know,' said Crystal. 'You're social Kryptonite.'

'Thanks.'

'You're welcome.'

Ivan looked across the classroom at her, just as she broke into a smile. Crystal was wearing an emerald headband. Her hair still sprung out wildly at the back, however. From where the boy was sitting, she could've been illuminated by a ginger halo.

'I like your hair,' he heard himself saying. 'It's like . . . like a stained-glass window.'

Ivan stopped himself as Crystal's expression, hovered somewhere between outright offence and amusement.

'It's gone a little crazy today,' she said next, and dismissed his comment with a shake of her head. 'Anyway, are you coming for lunch?'

'Thanks, but we're good.'

'We?' Crystal looked around, which brought Ivan upright in his chair. 'Is that you and your imaginary friend?'

'Something like that,' he replied, well aware that the folds of his bag were pulsing from time to time.

Crystal caught his eye. It was beginning to dawn on him that she really hadn't been made to show an interest in him as a dare. In a way, this made Ivan feel even more uncomfortable.

'OK, suit yourself,' she said with a shrug, 'but maybe I'll catch up with you when school's out? I promised Grandma I'd help her repaint the porch, but I'm sure she won't mind if I'm a little late. We could walk home together again?'

'It's football practice this afternoon,' said Ivan, a little too abruptly for his liking.

Crystal's smile seemed to freeze at this.

'Is that wise?' she asked. 'I mean, is it safe?'

'Oh, I'll survive.' Ivan pushed the bag under his desk with one foot. 'It's the others who need to watch out for me.'

19

A rib restaurant. That was what Titus Savage had proposed when he called Lev and Kiril about his plan to take over the saloon bar premises. In hindsight, the pair hadn't seemed at all concerned with the nature of the new venture. So long as they could continue feeding Nikolai Zolotov's dollars through the cash register, Titus was free to open the doors on whatever he liked. In return, they had promised, his family would be safe from any threat of vengeance.

'They talked Zolotov round,' Titus assured Angelica, later that week. 'The only condition is that we need to be open for business by the time the next shipment of money arrives. From then on, everyone can sleep easy again.'

Titus was at the wheel of his pickup at the time. He glanced across at Angelica. She saw him, right there, but didn't shift her gaze from the road ahead.

'And this is your way of protecting us from a monster?' she asked. 'By going to work for him?'

'When have I ever let you down?' asked Titus, who had expected this line of questioning. 'In all our years together, I have gone to hell and back to protect our family. If this is what it takes to keep Zolotov at bay, then why not? And if I can level with you for a moment, a rib joint is something I feel I can really sink my teeth into.'

For once, Angelica didn't come back at him with an objection. She just sat there in her sundress and shades, with one hand pressed to her collarbone.

'It all sounds so illegal,' she said quietly, and glanced over her shoulder.

In the cab's rear seats, Katya was strapped into her booster and looking out at the storefronts. Beside her, Ivan sat with his school bag on his lap, clutching it protectively. The red and puffy left eye he'd picked up at football practice was beginning to blacken. It looked suspiciously like he'd been punched, even if he denied it. Across from Ivan sat Amanda, the only one who appeared to be tuned in to the conversation.

'I can't afford to go to jail,' she told them. 'Prisoners don't necessarily have a constitutional right to vegan food.'

'Nobody is going to jail,' Titus assured them. 'Lev and Kiril handle the shady stuff, and we know nothing about that, right? What I'm proposing here is a family-run business selling the best ribs this town has ever tasted.'

'These ribs.' Finally, Angelica turned to face him. 'What kind do you have in mind?'

'The traditional kind,' said Titus, surprised she'd even asked. 'Pure beef.'

'That's a terrible idea,' came a voice from the back. Titus glanced in his rear-view mirror to see his son gesture out of his window. 'Look around you,' he said, as they stopped at the lights. 'There are more rib restaurants in this town than people.'

144

'So, there's a demand,' his father reasoned, lifting his hands off the wheel for a moment.

'Which would be exceeded by supply if we went into ribs.' Amanda folded her arms. 'Besides, there's no way I'd set foot in a restaurant like that. It would be like going to work in an abattoir.'

'Here we go again,' Titus muttered to himself, before addressing Amanda in the mirror. 'So, what do you suggest? The place has a fully fitted kitchen that's just been gathering dust. Food is the future here. Trust me. This could even be the making of us.'

The family were heading out to the former saloon bar at the time. Lev had handed Titus the keys and told him to just do whatever was required. Having dropped by to visit it himself, Titus had returned home to collect everyone else feeling as buoyant as the boats in Jupiter's harbour. Now, as they approached the turn-off in a part of town that looked dusty and a little derelict, he couldn't help feeling disappointed that his proposal had met with such a cool response.

'Do you know what's missing around here?' said Amanda, though nobody replied. 'Something I guarantee will bring customers in their droves.'

'A titty bar?' said Ivan, only for his mother to twist around in her seat and glare at him.

'A vegan café.' Amanda slapped her kneecap as she said this, and then looked around. 'What?' she asked, when nobody replied.

Steering the pickup off the boulevard, Titus followed an uneven road that bordered the inlet. It was late afternoon. With

145

the sun behind the waterside buildings, they drove through broken light.

'Amanda, this isn't a joke,' he said, as the pickup bumped over potholes.

'I'm deadly serious,' she said. 'It isn't easy eating out for me, and there's a growing number who share my tastes. Customers will come flocking.'

'But I don't want to work with carrots all day,' Titus replied dismissively.

'You can leave all that to me,' replied Amanda, as if prepared for such resistance. 'All you'd need to do is help me get the place up and running. After that, you guys could even take a step back and let me prove to you that people are hungry for something like this.'

'But people into this kind of thing are always hungry,' Titus countered, sounding flustered now. 'Nobody ever feels full on a bowl of quinoa.'

He glanced at Angelica, hoping she would back him up. To his surprise, she appeared deep in thought.

'There are a lot of rib restaurants,' she said after a moment.

Titus looked at his wife in disbelief.

'One vegan in the house is bad enough,' he said. 'Now you're proposing that we feed a whole community of herbivores?'

'It would certainly be a challenge – but it would also be the perfect cover,' Angelica reasoned.

'The last place anyone would associate with a family of cannibals,' Amanda added.

Titus was close to giving up asking her to quit with the 'C' word. As the old bar swung into view, however, he decided now was not an appropriate moment to get fractious. Instead, like everyone else, he considered the building before them. In daylight, with no neon to distract attention, there was little to admire. The paintwork was peeling and weeds had sprung up through cracks in the porch. Earlier, Titus had seen only the potential. With his experience as a property landlord, he could renovate the place with his eyes closed and transform it into a handsome establishment for meat connoisseurs. Looking at it now, however, with Amanda's proposal in mind, he began to wonder whether he should've just taken his chances with Zolotov and called his bluff over the threats.

'Whatever your personal tastes,' Angelica said to him, 'we should at least consider Amanda's proposal as a business opportunity. If there's a market for food free from meat and dairy then it does make sense.'

'This is my idea of a dream job.' Amanda unclipped her safety belt and climbed out of the car. 'I'd work so hard to make it a success.'

'A café full of vegans,' said Ivan, and slid across to follow her out. 'Think of the farts.'

Angelica looked set to admonish him, but Titus caught her eye.

'The boy has a point,' he said.

'If that's your only argument against it,' said Angelica, reaching for the door handle on her side, 'I'd say this is a done deal.'

In his short but successful career as a personal trainer, Joaquín was skilled in overcoming injury. He had helped many clients get back on their feet, while muscle strains were a hazard of his job. With ice and rest, the young man knew how to make a quick and full recovery, but this was different. Ever since Angelica Savage spelled out her commitments, which didn't include him, Joaquín had been left with an ache that was proving unbearable.

He'd thought of nothing else since she'd left him at the roadside. Back then, Joaquín had stared in disbelief at the hoarding on the development site that she'd used to illustrate the importance of her family. The young Argentinian had been so sure that she shared his affections. He'd risked everything in making his feelings known to her, and this was how she'd responded.

'You can't just leave me like this,' he'd muttered to himself, glaring at the images of domestic bliss that advertised the proposed new homes. Standing behind a buckled chain-link fence topped with razor wire, Joaquín could easily see himself with Angelica living that sort of lifestyle. Given his tender age, he'd have a close bond with her children, too. 'You need me,' he said, as the cars on the road behind him swished by at speed. 'You just don't realise it yet.'

Like so many young men faced with heartbreak, Joaquín Mendez had thrown himself into his work. That same morning, in fact, he'd run back to the gym and taken several clients to the point of exhaustion in their workouts. Not once, over the days that followed, did Joaquín confide in anyone about what he was going through. His mother called each evening, as she always did, and yet he assured her that everything in his life was just fine.

Had she been able to see her son in the flesh, she would've taken one look at his haunted expression and known that all was not well. Back in Buenos Aires, Joaquín had always been a passionate boy, intense at times when it came to achieving goals in fitness, and though he had little experience of love and relationships, she hoped one day he'd meet someone nice and settle down. Joaquín hadn't intended to fall for a married woman. What's more, Angelica had admitted to pursuing a dream when it came to family life, and so it stung all the more to think that she had rejected him. After several nights of disturbed sleep, the young man found he could no longer just lie there staring at the ceiling fan. He had to get out, despite the ungodly hour, and attempt to escape his torment in the only way he knew how. Slipping on a pair of running shorts and a vest, Joaquín Mendez crept out of his apartment and set off under the street lamps and the stars.

With a water bottle in hand and his head in a mess, Joaquín simply went wherever his bare feet took him. Within half an hour he'd reached the beach, where the sand underfoot was damp but firm at low tide. Dawn was on the cusp of breaking by the time he cut back across the dunes. Unlike the skies, however, his mood was no brighter. He ran at a solid pace with light footfalls, and turned his focus from the way ahead only once. That moment occurred as he wound his way along Riverside Drive, a ribbon of a road that skirted the northern shore of the inlet. For it afforded a generous view of the communities across the water, one of which, he realised, housed the Savage residence. Joaquín had noted Angelica's address in her gym membership details some time ago. Like most things concerning her, it had lodged in his memory with frightening ease. Having made the decision to take a closer look at where she lived, which he did without hesitation, Joaquín set off towards the bridge road. Not once did Joaquín consider that he was torturing himself, or acting on an impulse that bordered on obsession. In fact, when he finally reached the junction to the inlet community, it seemed to him like a small reward for all the miles he had covered. Even Angelica's warning about her husband no longer registered with him. Turning onto the loop road that would take him past Angelica's villa and back out again, the young fitness instructor half hoped she might be up early.

'Angelica! What a nice surprise!' he whispered to himself, playing out how he would respond should she happen to be out. 'Breakfast? I think I've earned it!'

She certainly lived in a nice part of town, he noted on passing all the carefully manicured lawns and water features. He even saw himself living in some of these places, which is when he caught sight of her car. There it was, outside a white stucco villa with a heavy wooden door, snuggled up next to a pickup with a double cab and chrome roll bar.

Without taking his eyes off the vehicles, Joaquín slowed to a halt. Clearly the pickup belonged to Angelica's husband. In his opinion, guys opted to drive these big macho vehicles to make up for their shortcomings.

'You're wasted on him,' the young fitness instructor muttered to himself. He pictured Angelica rushing out to greet some weed of a husband who needed a flash motor to feel big and strong. 'And you're wrong about me.'

Standing there with his hands on his waist and his vest drenched in sweat, he tried to imagine what this loser must be like. At the peak of fitness, and in the prime of his life, the smitten young instructor figured he could handle himself if things ever got rough. A moment later, however, as the front door swung open, Joaquín was forced to drastically revise his opinion.

'You need to slow down,' growled the imposing-looking brute with the shaved dome who appeared at the threshold. He wore a deep frown, almost glowering, and a towel dressing gown that did nothing to soften his presence. 'Otherwise there's going to be an accident.'

Joaquín took a step backwards, still panting but shocked at the sight of the figure who had just emerged from the villa. This wasn't the husband who had taken shape in his imagination. It was the focus of the man's gaze that left him rooted to the spot. There was something so commanding and intense about it that Joaquín felt as though he had just shrunk by several feet. It took a moment for him to realise that the guy wasn't in fact addressing him. This was down to a growing electric hum from behind, which gave him no chance to feel any relief. Joaquín spun around in alarm and promptly jumped sideways to avoid an elderly man on a mobility scooter.

'Watch out!' he snapped, but the old guy seemed to be as deaf as he was blind. Joaquín drew breath to point out that he could've caused him serious injury, only to drop into a thigh stretch instead as the big bear at the door turned his attention on him. Even though he'd barely slept, and had put dozens of miles behind him before dawn, the moment proved quite a wake-up call for the young man. Standing upright again, and with a quick hop from one foot to the other as if to demonstrate that he was just an innocent runner who had paused to loosen up, Joaquín Mendez continued around the loop road without once daring to look over his shoulder. The terrible ache in his heart remained, but now it also carried a note of wariness. For one glimpse into the eyes of Angelica's husband had told Joaquín she had been right to ask him to steer clear. Maybe it was the way the man's focus hardened, there at the front door to his villa, but it told the lovelorn personal trainer of one thing. He had just come face to face with an individual who would not let anyone come between him and his family.

20

Titus Savage watched the early-morning jogger and considered following in his footsteps. There was no way he would get into shape without getting out there and making an effort. One interrupted run to his father's nursing home and back did not amount to a fitness regime, after all. It was more like a cry for help.

'Know what I need?' he said out loud as Oleg parked the scooter beside his pickup. 'A personal trainer.'

'It worked for Angelica.' Oleg climbed off and took a moment to straighten his spine. 'I hear she's going it alone now.'

'The guy clearly motivated her,' said Titus, before breaking off to yawn into the back of his hand. 'She's become all fired up about working with fruit and vegetables in the kitchen at Amanda's crackpot café. I can't say I'm happy, but it seems the need for a fresh challenge is in the air in this household.'

A smile flickered across Oleg's face.

'I heard about the plans for the saloon,' he said. 'My son: the Salad Bar Tsar.'

Titus tightened his dressing-gown sash, the expression on his face in contrast to the bright and sunny start to the morning.

'So, what's with the need to speak to me this early?' he asked his father. 'We haven't had breakfast yet.'

Oleg had left several messages asking to discuss a pressing issue. As Titus had been faced with what felt like a mutiny from his family over his plan to open a rib joint, his time had been taken up pressing them to see reason. With his efforts come to nothing, and another call from his father at suppertime, this was the first opportunity Titus could give him.

'Well, it's delicate,' said Oleg, who had gathered his stick from the clip behind his scooter seat.

'Want to tell me at the table?' Titus jabbed a thumb over his shoulder. 'We're having bacon. The next best thing to a feast,' he added, and rubbed his hands together. 'As I'm sure you'd agree.'

Oleg glanced into the villa. He flexed his nostrils, looking torn for a moment, before asking if they could speak in private. 'You know, between Savages?'

He raised his wiry eyebrows hopefully, supporting himself with both hands on his stick. Titus turned to check that nobody was behind him, before closing the door to the villa and inviting his father to follow him through the yard gate.

Ivan Savage sat at the desk in his room with his eyes locked on the computer screen. The smell of bacon under the grill had reached him some time ago, but first he had some homework to complete. It was a personal project. The class stuff he had got out of the way the night before. As he typed in his search words, Tinky Dinks probed his way across the keyboard, sniffing out crumbs.

'You've just eaten.' Ivan planted the gerbil in front of the little pot of food he'd picked up from the pet store. Turning his attention back to the screen, he frowned at the handful of numbers the creature had added to his search for instructions on how to create a food poison. Not just a strain that caused a sick bug. The boy sought one that killed.

Having deleted the gerbil's digital paw prints, Ivan hit return and waited expectantly for the results. He did so with three boys in mind. A trio of tormentors who would get a taste of his sweet vengeance when the time was right. There would be no proof that he was behind it, but the right people would know. Briefly, he wondered what Crystal would make of his actions. It felt a little bit like she had taken him under her wing, in the same way that he cared for Tinky Dinks. If the gerbil did something unspeakable, Ivan thought, like chewing through the wires behind his videogames console, he would do his level best to forgive him. He couldn't swear by it, of course, but a bond had formed between them that meant the little creature was safe in his care, for now.

'Ivan, it's going cold!'

His mother's voice prompted the boy to shut down the screen, but not before he had added a bookmark to several pages that showed potential. Before leaving his room, Ivan replaced the gerbil in the school bag he had effectively converted into a living space for the creature. Tinky Dinks had come to travel everywhere with Ivan, and grown used to his persistent muttering. He'd also learned to squeak when the cuddles turned into a squeeze, which happened a lot, whenever Ivan had payback on his mind. Even if the boy was a little absentminded sometimes, there was a natural kindness in the way he handled the creature. Carefully, Ivan closed his school bag and prepared to grab some breakfast before school. It felt weird, caring for something so vulnerable. He wondered whether Crystal felt the same way about him.

It couldn't last on both counts, he decided, and headed for the kitchen.

At this hour, the rising sun shone directly across the inlet and through the kitchen window. Titus and his father stood at the foot of the jetty. With their backs turned to the villa, leaning side by side against the rail, they watched sailing boats cross their line of sight in silhouette.

'This lady friend,' said Titus, who had heard his father's plea to allow her to join the table. 'She's really dying?'

Oleg faced into the breeze for a moment, as if to freshen his composure.

'Would I be asking you for any other reason?' he said next. 'Consuming our own kind is the key to life, Titus. We both know that. I'm living proof. Look at me? I'm fit, healthy and 103! My old bones might not be as flexible as they once were, but I'm still here, and with a companion I have come to treasure.' Oleg stopped there, as if to find another way to persuade his son. 'Without Priscilla,' he said finally, 'I would struggle.'

It was quite clear to Titus that Oleg was speaking from the heart. He understood his reasons for this appeal, but just one person had ever joined them around the table for a feast, and that was Amanda. And only then because she had walked in on the family as they dined. Had she reacted with horror, she would've wound up as dessert. Instead, presented with a carnivorous solution to her problem with regular meat eaters, she had helped herself to a plate and never looked back. Of course, it was one more mouth to feed, and Titus felt the weight of responsibility on his shoulders. Inviting yet another individual just increased the risk that their secret would spill out.

'No doubt a feast keeps us in the very best shape,' said Titus, 'but if Priscilla's condition is terminal, there is little we can do.'

'We can *try!*'

Titus was taken aback by the force of Oleg's response. Just then, it was clear that his father wasn't going to return to the nursing home with his hopes crushed.

'Does she know?' he asked. 'About us?'

'Of course not,' said Oleg.

'Could we invite her to join us and just tell her it's a leg of lamb?'

Even as he made this suggestion, Titus knew that his father would never stomach such a thing. As the family had discussed on several occasions, feeding an innocent human flesh without their knowledge could have huge consequences. The experience would bring such elation that it risked condemning them to a hunger they wouldn't know how to feed for the rest of their lives. Chances are they'd exist in a constant state of disappointment, confusion and longing. Besides, it tasted nothing like lamb. People were a cut above pork as well.

'Priscilla trusts me completely,' the old man told him. 'I would never lie to her, and you can rely on me to make sure she never breaks our trust.'

Titus sighed to himself and looked to the lawn between them.

'I accept that she's important to you,' he said.

Slowly, as he processed what this meant, Oleg straightened up and muttered silent words of thanks.

'When can we do it?' he asked. 'This weekend?'

'Out of the question.' Titus looked pained. 'We've only just had a feast. I'm not going to be greedy here. Besides,' he added, and glanced away, 'we have a café to open.'

'Then whenever the time is right,' said Oleg. 'Just, please don't leave it too late.'

Titus nodded, acknowledging that they had an understanding here.

'But if she freaks out at any time,' he finished quietly, 'you do understand what would have to be done.'

Oleg held his son's gaze.

'It won't come to that,' he said in assurance. 'Should Priscilla react badly to the invitation then nature will take her course.'

Titus nodded solemnly.

'She's that close to death, huh?'

'Not if I can help it,' said Oleg, and tightened his grip on his walking stick.

21

Amanda Dias didn't make a habit of skipping breakfast. A healthy eater, she preferred to start the day on a full stomach. On this occasion, however, with the family together in the kitchen, she decided there was no way she could spoon down a bowl of muesli without gagging over the stench of cooked pig flesh. Besides, now that everyone had been persuaded to climb on board with her plans for the café, Amanda was in employment again.

'I'm going to seize the day,' she told them, grabbing the keys for the building, 'and slice it up like a cucumber.'

Things were different for her now. This wasn't some wretched job that earned her no respect and little money. In transforming a run-down strip club into the finest vegan eatery in town, Amanda faced a challenge that could bring her great personal reward. What's more, she would be working with a family who knew how to get a job done with ruthless efficiency.

'What we're planting here are the seeds of a food revolution,' she told Lev and Kiril later that morning. The pair had shown up on request to establish the cost of refurbishing the place. They appeared less than engaged as Amanda took them through the plans, and glanced at one another as she waxed about the wonders of an establishment where everything animal-related was off the menu. 'This is where it all begins, my friends. And you're the ones to make it happen!'

Lev cleared his throat before fishing a wallet from his shirt pocket.

'We appreciate your enthusiasm, sweetheart. Just tell us what you need to get it done.'

'The quicker we're up and running,' added Kiril, 'the sooner we can sleep at night.'

Rather than risk angering Zolotov further, the pair had agreed to advance funds for the refurbishment themselves. Such was their fear of the man that they didn't question the figure, or the terms that the family went on to propose. Calling upon his experience in buying and renovating apartments, Titus presented his costs for the turnaround, fixtures and fittings, while Angelica priced the furnishings. A seasoned homemaker, she insisted on overseeing everything from the painting and decoration to the tables and chairs, and when Ivan showed up after school with his little sister they found that his interest lay with the kitchen and its equipment. It was Amanda who stocked the cupboards, shelves and the walk-in freezer. With religious zeal, she sourced her vegan produce from local markets, smallholders and farmsteads, striking supply deals with a confidence that exceeded her years.

Within days, the old sports bar had been stripped down like a carcass in a cloud of blowflies. A week later, despite his misgivings about the direction this venture had taken, Titus

160

stood outside the building with his family and the lodger, appraising the fruits of their labours. Gone was the neon piping, as had the grilles from the windows. A lick of paint freshened the exterior, and the surrounding weeds had been cut away and replaced by geraniums in planters.

'The Lentil Rebel,' he said, reading from the signage that now graced the front of the porch. Shaking his head, Titus turned to his wife. 'What the hell are we doing here?'

'Going into business,' she said, and then waited for him to look at her. 'Covering ourselves.'

'I'm all in favour of a new challenge,' he said, 'but it sounds about as enticing as a limp lettuce.'

'It sounds honest,' Amanda said to correct him. 'People know exactly what they're getting on their plates, all at affordable prices.'

'Our feasts are free,' muttered Ivan, who stood with his school bag at his feet. 'At least the main ingredient doesn't cost anything.'

At that moment Katya skipped out onto the porch. She was clutching one of the helium balloons that Angelica had commissioned in preparation for the opening. Just seeing his youngest daughter melted away any reservations Titus harboured.

'Well, if it proves to be a success then I'm happy,' he told them. 'I see it as an investment for the family.'

'Kiril and Lev seem relieved,' said Amanda. 'They dropped by earlier with the permits and the first float for the till.'

Angelica glanced at Titus disapprovingly.

'Everything is under control,' he assured her. 'We're doing

161

nothing wrong here. That side of things is for our backers to worry about.'

'Our job is to fill the tables,' said Amanda.

Titus turned his attention to the lodger.

'We're placing a lot of faith in you here,' he told her. 'Bringing in the customers is one thing. Seeing them leave satisfied is another. With no meat in their bellies, I have my reservations.'

'It can't fail,' she declared, grinning in a way that left Titus feeling uneasy. 'On the day we open the doors, all you have to do is be the perfect host!'

Titus heard her clearly, but didn't respond for a moment.

'But my job here is done,' he said eventually, and invited her to look around. 'The kind of people you're hoping to attract? I'm not sure I could look them straight in the eye.'

Amanda glanced at Angelica, who placed a hand on her husband's arm. Immediately, Titus understood that the two women had already discussed the issue.

'When it comes to feasts,' Angelica said, 'you always know how to make it a special occasion. Amanda believes our first customers would feel in good hands with you.'

Oleg Savage was hugely relieved to see Priscilla return from the medical centre to the Fallen Pine Nursing Home. She did so by ambulance, but appeared quite happy and serene as the medics lowered her by wheelchair on the tail lift.

'You scared me,' he told her the next day at breakfast. 'But you don't have to worry, because I've made arrangements for that meal with my family.'

'I hear they've been busy down by the riverside,' said Priscilla, who looked pale from her stay on the ward, but seemed in good spirits nonetheless. 'Will this meal be vegan? I've never eaten vegan. Italian I love, and Mexican, before I stopped eating spicy, but vegan is new to me.'

'It isn't a regional thing,' explained Oleg uncomfortably.

Priscilla grinned at him.

'This family feast,' she asked. 'Is it an aphrodisiac?'

Oleg sensed his cheeks flush beneath his beard. He smiled despite himself.

'Don't you ever stop?'

'In the grave, maybe.' Priscilla reached out to pat his leg. 'But I'm not promising.'

'All I can say is that it'll be the meal of a lifetime,' said Oleg, and pressed his palm over her hand. 'Like nothing you've experienced before.'

'It's never too late to try something new,' she said. 'Even this vegan venture sounds like it might be easy to digest.'

'The café opens at the weekend,' Oleg told her. 'I hope they make a success of it, of course, but the menu is not to my taste.' He stopped to pull some orange juice through the straw in his glass. 'Nothing compares to Angelica's home cooking, which I think you'll find restorative . . . miraculous even,' he added, tapping his nose. 'Priscilla, it could bring us many more happy years together.'

Despite her failing sight, Priscilla held his gaze so intently it felt as if she was looking straight through him.

'Oleg, my condition is terminal. You do understand that, don't you?'

The old man didn't flinch. Not at first. Then he blinked and cleared his throat.

'You know, it often goes unremarked, but some hunting packs will go to great lengths to take care of the sick. African wild dogs, jackals and grey wolves all make sacrifices to save their own. If food is an issue, they'll share it.'

Priscilla tipped her head to one side.

'I thought they killed the weak.'

'Those packs at the top of the food chain have a pecking order,' he agreed. 'But they also possess a strong instinct for protection.'

'That's good to hear.' Priscilla chuckled, enjoying this moment if nothing else. 'Oleg, I will happily join your . . . pack for supper, but in return I want you to face the facts and just help me enjoy what I have left.'

'I'm serious,' he insisted. 'This feast won't just fill your belly. It'll get into your blood, your bones, your *soul*. Priscilla, you'll leave the table feeling born again!'

With some effort, she turned her chair to face him.

'So, level with me,' she said. 'What exactly is your family planning to cook here?'

'Just a meat,' Oleg replied, a little too quickly, but he wasn't planning on revealing any more at this time. The last thing he wanted to do was take Priscilla by surprise. Not in her condition. Aware that she was expecting a better explanation, he reminded himself not to look so tense. 'What we'll be eating is reared responsibly,' he added, 'and cooked to perfection.'

'Well, that certainly sounds promising,' she told him, and her face lit up with her smile. 'I've always loved a roast supper, and clearly you Savages know how to make it memorable.'

'We do indeed.' All of a sudden, Oleg Savage found he couldn't take his eyes away from her.

Priscilla's smile arched to one side and duly transformed into a cheeky grin.

'So, where's my medicine for the day?' she asked.

Oleg frowned, thinking at first that she had confused him for the nurse. Then she puckered her lips, and he knew just what was required.

22

When Joaquín Mendez saw him coming, the young man had been picking his way through a grilled chicken and cornbread salad with low-fat lime dressing. Still struggling to restore his appetite, Joaquín was well aware that the demands of his job required a smart diet. The trouble was that with Angelica still in his thoughts, every mouthful tasted like tissue paper.

This wasn't the reason why he spluttered it across the bench on the gym terrace where he always ate his lunch. It was the sight of her husband, the shaven-headed ape he had spotted at the villa, now striding with a purpose towards him. Joaquín had seen the pickup approach the junction and then pull in, but didn't recognise the driver until he'd stepped out and slammed the vehicle door shut behind him.

'Mary, Mother of *God!*' His chair scraped backwards as he scrambled to his feet. 'There's been a misunderstanding!' he said, as the brute approached. 'Can we discuss this?'

Titus Savage stopped before his table. He looked a little baffled at the greeting, but extended his hand nonetheless.

'You're the man responsible for helping my wife get into shape,' he said, having introduced himself. 'I was hoping you could do the same for me.'

Brushing strands of cress from his vest, Joaquín summoned as much calm into his composure as he could, before inviting the man to take a seat.

'How is Angelica?' he asked, and hid his hands under the table as they had started to tremble.

'I would've thought you'd know that better than me,' said Titus, which caused the young fitness trainer's expression to freeze. 'She trained with you on a daily basis until recently, right?'

'Every day,' said Joaquín, with some confidence in his voice this time. For it struck him that Angelica must have withheld the reason why their working relationship had come to an end. Otherwise her husband wouldn't be sitting pleasantly across from him at the table but reforming his face with his fists. 'She's a dedicated woman,' he added for good measure.

For a moment, Titus appeared not to be listening. Instead, he was studying Joaquín with an unsettling intensity.

'Have we met?' he asked the young gym instructor. 'I swear I've seen you before.'

Joaquín's eyes widened. Even his mouth looked set to do the same thing. He had yet to cast aside the memory of that moment when this man first levelled his gaze at him. Back then, on the loop road outside the Savage villa, it had woken him up to the fact that he'd been flirting with a very dangerous fantasy. Making a play for someone else's wife, as he had quickly come to realise, was forbidden in the Ten Commandments for a very good reason. He only had to look at Titus again, right here in front of him, to see that the guy was capable of striking back with great vengeance and furious anger. It hadn't stopped his feelings for Angelica, but from this moment on staying out of her life had become a basic survival strategy for the terrified young man.

'We may have passed each other on the street,' Joaquín offered eventually. 'When you take out the inlet, Jupiter is not such a big town.'

Titus nodded in agreement, his lower lip pushed up.

'So, what do you say? Can you fit me into your schedule? You've worked wonders with Angelica, after all.'

Just then, Joaquín would've paid Titus Savage to stay away, but he knew that wasn't an option. Instead, with his heart still fluttering from the surprise, he agreed to take on the man whose wife continued to torment his waking hours.

'We can start at the weekend if you like,' he said weakly.

Titus frowned, in an expression of puzzlement that alarmed the Argentinian all the same.

'Has she not told you?' he asked.

Joaquín drew breath to respond, despite not knowing what he was talking about. By now, he had no appetite whatsoever for the remains of his salad. Not when he felt this sick to his stomach.

'Are you busy?' enquired Joaquín, in what was frankly a whisper.

Titus leaned forward, resting on one elbow.

'The café?' he said, as if to jog his memory. 'It wasn't my idea, of course. Our vegan lodger sold it to us, and Angelica agrees that there's a market. You're welcome to join us for the opening,' he went on, gesturing at the young man's chicken

Caesar salad. 'Maybe some of the customers will look at you and realise that what they're missing from their food is the protein, iron and zinc that only meat can offer, but that's another matter. So, what do you say?'

The only thing on Joaquín's mind at that moment was the thought of offering a full confession for stupidly hitting on the man's wife, followed by a profound apology. Sensibly, he opted to keep both of these back and began nodding instead.

'I'll be there,' he said, as if under duress, and was left to stare at the business card that then fell upon the table. With his vision swimming, he barely breathed as Titus clapped him on the shoulder before leaving him alone with his appetite squashed. Only when the pickup gunned into life did Joaquín look up and curse out loud for not skipping lunch altogether and going into hiding instead.

Ivan had no intention of killing Bryce, Chad and Ryan. Not straight away, at least, and only then if he struck lucky with the bait he planned to feed them. Having observed them for some time now, the boy decided that they were at their most ravenous following a football match. The team were locked into an inter-school league title fight, and every player worked up a good appetite on the pitch. Afterwards, there was always a scrum for the snacks laid out in the locker room. If Ivan's targets tucked into the after-match snacks he had planned for them, and the trio dropped down dead, everyone would just blame him and forget all about the torment that had provoked him into taking action. No, there needed to be a window of opportunity for the boy to clear away the plates and remove all trace of the lethal payload that would be slowly multiplying in their guts.

With this in mind, Ivan had chosen the *Trichinella spiralis* worm as his foodborne weapon of choice. Once ingested – in the form of larva cysts in contaminated meat – this microscopic parasite slowly but surely gave rise to a devastating disease that could've been tailor-made to meet the boy's needs. Known as trichinosis, the worm's early incubation symptoms often went unnoticed. It would take up to eight weeks before the victim began to suffer, which made it notoriously difficult to pinpoint the source. Keen to cover his tracks, this appealed greatly to Ivan. When he learned how these pathogenic assassins burrowed out of the intestines and into the circulatory system, ending up lodged in the muscle tissue, the central nervous system and even the brain of their unsuspecting host, he was sold. In good time, when Bryce, Ryan and Chad complained to the coach of joint pains, Ivan could be assured that they would struggle to remain effective team players. When the tremors set in, the boy figured they would have to take his place on the bench. Finally, when the trio experienced the kind of seizures that triggered cardiac arrest and death, he could at least tell himself that he had levelled the playing field.

Naturally, Ivan had to consider safety issues when preparing his food poison. This wasn't something he could just cook up in the kitchen without risk of harm to little Katya and the rest of his family. He needed space, which is why he'd been so keen to contribute some time at the café.

'I'll wash up,' he had volunteered, which was a first. 'That can be my job once we're closed at the end of the day.'

Angelica and Amanda had figured out that between them they could manage the catering and serve customers. Both women were accomplished cooks, and while Angelica had been known to create discomfort with her manner, she could also switch on the charm when it mattered. What's more, should things get busy, Amanda knew that she could call upon a small pool of former lap dancers to work as casual staff. It meant that when Ivan offered his services, Angelica felt they had things covered.

'You're a good boy,' she said, ruffling his hair, 'but the dishwasher can do all the dirty work. Besides, you have school.'

'Then let me clean the equipment at weekends,' he insisted. 'This is a family business. I want to play a role.' Ivan had offered his services on the eve of the grand opening. Titus had been charged with collecting a bulk order of elderflower juice and Amanda was chalking up the specials on the blackboard above the bar. Meanwhile, little Katya had been tasked with laying out natural-fibre napkins, along with the knives and forks, which she undertook while singing happily to herself. A late sun streamed through the windows, which transformed the interior from its earlier shuttered and shadowy incarnation. Standing before his mother, with his school bag at his feet, Ivan lobbied for the job one more time. 'I won't let you down,' he promised, and hesitated for a second before adding, 'not this time.'

Angelica folded her arms.

'Promise me you're not planning any pranks.'

Ivan knew that she was mindful of those moments in his past when a bid to amuse had ended in bloodshed, but he was fifteen years old now. His sense of humour had matured to the point where it didn't end in injury or the occasional death demanding a cover-up from his father.

Besides, what Ivan had planned here wasn't a prank. It was payback, pure and simple. Not that he told his mother that just then.

'There won't be a single germ on the surfaces by the time I've finished,' he assured her, and meant every word. For the nasty stuff would be sealed away inside a container, once he'd finished preparing his creation, and then carefully stashed until the time was right to strike. Totally unaware of his true intention, however, Angelica beamed at her son and told him where to find the cleaning equipment.

'Look at us,' she said admiringly, as he headed for the kitchen. 'We Savages know how to get things done properly.'

23

The next day at noon, Titus Savage drew back the bolt from inside The Lentil Rebel and opened the door. With some reverence, he stepped out onto the porch, looked one way and then the other, and then let his shoulders sag.

'They'll come,' said Amanda, who was standing anxiously behind him. She glanced at the rest of her adoptive family. 'My people won't let us down.'

'Your people,' muttered Titus, with his back still turned. 'I feel like we're catering for the weak and feeble.'

As a man who had reinvented himself on several occasions in order to avoid the full force of the law, Titus Savage had come to accept his new role as the proprietor of a vegan café. It was a business venture, pure and simple. He didn't need to share his customers' values in order to cater for them. Hosting this opening day was hardly the fruit of a lifetime's ambition, but he considered it a duty to his family. Nevertheless, the calm and quiet troubled him. According to Amanda, vegans were on the rise. As far as Titus was concerned, they were a dying breed, and only had themselves to blame if they became extinct.

'All that leafleting for nothing,' grumbled Ivan, who had taken Tinky Dinks on a tour of the neighbourhood mailboxes over previous evenings. Such was his trust in the gerbil that he had even walked with his bag unzipped. What's more, the creature seemed to enjoy peeping out to feel the breeze on his whiskers. 'Damn those sausage dodgers.'

'Ivan!' Angelica glared at her son. 'Let's not write off this business straight away.'

'You should listen to your mother.'

The voice came from over by the counter, where two men dressed in tropical shirts sat on high stools. Nursing glasses of wheatgrass juice, both Lev and Kiril looked distinctly tense.

'If the café flops,' added Kiril, 'we'll all pay the price, and not just financially.'

'He'll find us,' Lev went on. 'Zolotov will hunt us down.'

'Will you relax?' Titus pinned the door open and strode between the tables towards the pair. 'For one thing,' he added, gesturing at Ivan and little Kat, 'there are children present. Secondly, I won't allow any harm to come to my family. If Zolotov has a problem with the way this business is run, the man can talk to me.'

'Titus will take care of things,' Angelica told them. 'He's never let us down yet.'

'And here comes our first customer.' It was Amanda who was first to spot a figure heading their way. She had remained by the door to scout the waterside road. Immediately, all eyes turned in that direction. Angelica was first to recognise the flame-haired girl as she crossed towards the steps.

'That's no customer,' she said, sounding disappointed.

'Crystal,' said Ivan under his breath, bristling at his mother's tone.

Titus turned to his son with his expression brightening.

'A girlfriend?'

Angelica shot her husband a look, as if to suggest that his optimism was misplaced.

'She keeps wanting to spend time with me,' said Ivan, whose pale face was beginning to flush.

'Well, that's a start.' Titus beamed briefly, before concern came into his expression. 'It also means you need to treat her with kindness, OK?'

'But it doesn't qualify her for freebies,' Angelica warned, before summoning a smile as the girl stepped into the café.

Crystal was wearing an emerald-coloured summer dress that exposed her freckled shoulders and arms slick with sunscreen.

'Hey there,' she said hesitantly, looking around as everyone stared at her. 'Am I early?'

In response, all eyes turned to the boy whose cheeks had now turned scarlet. With his head bowed, Ivan looked up at the girl who had come to offer her support.

'Do you want a drink or something?' he asked.

Titus switched his attention from his son to Crystal and back again.

'Of course she'd like a drink!' he declared, extending his hand to welcome her in.

'I can pay,' she said, much to the relief of the two men in floral shirts at the bar. 'Actually, Ivan, I was wondering if you'd like to have lunch with me?'

By now, the boy appeared set to burst into flames of

embarrassment. He stared at the school bag at his feet for a moment, looking as if he wished he could tuck himself away inside it, and then nodded solemnly. A young couple climbed the steps to the porch just then, though it was the baby strapped to the man's chest that commanded everyone's attention, given that it was facing outwards and crying lustily.

'Someone's hungry,' observed Amanda, which came as no surprise to Titus if the poor kid was restricted to soya products.

'Do you serve children?' asked the man, sounding apologetic and harassed, just as another family squeezed in around him.

Titus considered the man's request, his spirits lifting as the tables started to fill, and wished he could reply that sadly kids were off the menu. This was a meat-free establishment, after all.

'Everyone is welcome,' he told him instead, and realised that he meant it. Nothing compared to a feast, of course, but here was something that could bond his brood, even if the food they served only looked fit for squirrels. 'Just be sure to spread the word,' Titus said to finish, noting Ivan hurrying into the kitchen to deposit his school bag. Smiling for the customer still, he steered Angelica away before addressing her under his breath. 'If Amanda is right about the broccoli-botherers around here,' he said, and beamed at the next party to walk through the door, 'The Lentil Rebel could soon be the café that everyone is talking about.'

Three hours later, Joaquín Mendez approached the café at a slow jog and then drew to a halt. The place was doing good business, he noted at a glance, with the sound of chatter and laughter matched by the clink of cutlery. It certainly looked welcoming, but that did nothing to take away from the fact that this was the last thing he wanted to do. It was all too much to bear, knowing that Angelica would be present, and yet the invitation from her husband had sounded non-negotiable.

'You go in, say hi, you leave,' he told himself, and then paused to catch his breath.

Joaquín had opted to run all the way from his apartment to burn off the adrenaline. All morning, as soon as he pictured himself faced with the woman who had asked him to step out of her life, the nape of his neck began to blister with sweat. It wasn't just the force of his feelings for Angelica that quickened his pulse. The thought of facing Titus in her company was proving almost unbearable. Joaquín gathered the front of his vest and mopped his face with it, exposing a trim and contoured abdomen.

'OK,' he said, shaking his limbs down. 'Let's do this.'

Such was the extent of his nerves that Joaquín found himself challenged by an unusual lack of coordination as he made his way towards the porch. Having finally sorted it out, so his left arm didn't swing forward with his left foot, followed by the same action on his right, he dropped his head and mounted the steps. Midway up, with a jackhammer for a heart, he spun around on the ball of one foot and walked back down again.

It was pure instinct that persuaded Joaquín to turn. Faced with fight or flight, he'd been struck in an instant by the sense that only bad things would befall him if he walked through the door. No way, he decided, was he going to face Angelica in the presence of her protector. It would be like entering a lion's den, and just felt all wrong to the young man. The decision served to ease his heart rate as he strode away from the building, only for it to spike once more when a voice called out from behind him.

'What's the matter, my friend? You don't need footwear to join us. No doubt the people here are used to that kind of thing.'

Slowly, Joaquín turned on his bare soles to find himself under a penetrating gaze. The man on the porch was smiling, but that did nothing to soften the intensity in his eyes.

'Good to see you, Mr Savage,' he said, before clearing the catch in his throat. 'I thought you were closed.'

Puzzled, Titus glanced back at the café. With almost every table taken, this opening day appeared to have turned into quite a party. He faced Joaquín again and waved away his observation.

'I hope you're hungry,' he said, beckoning to Joaquín. 'Although between us, I doubt the food on offer meets the dietary needs of a man of your profession.'

'Oh, there are many health benefits to be had from veganism,' said Joaquín, who felt briefly relieved to be on a topic he knew something about. As a fitness trainer, many of his clients came to him with questions about their diet. 'For one thing, it's low in cholesterol and saturated fat.'

Having reached the top step, Joaquín found Titus with that bemused look on his face again. It was as if the answer he'd just provided did not compute with the man.

'Well, let's just say what we have to offer won't spoil your supper,' said Titus, placing a guiding hand between Joaquín's shoulder blades. 'I see you as a lean meat kind of guy.'

Struggling not to spin out completely, Joaquín nodded

politely and succumbed to the slight pressure he felt from his host's guiding hand. He didn't register the chatter of the customers inside. Nor did he glance at the blackboard to pick something to eat. Instead, his eyes fell upon the figure behind the counter, who froze on seeing him.

'Angelica!' With Titus looming behind him, Joaquín adopted an expression much like a hostage being forced to face a camera. Angelica glanced at her husband, and then stepped out from the counter. 'What a surprise to see you here.'

'Mr Savage invited me,' he told her, and cleared his throat in case his voice wavered again.

'It didn't seem right to let Joaquín go to waste.' Titus clapped him on the back. 'I've hired him to help me rediscover my form.'

If Angelica was shocked to hear that her husband had signed up with the young man she had recently cut from her life, the terrified fitness instructor failed to detect even a flicker in her composure. The way she stared at him just then, it was a surprise he hadn't turned to stone.

'If there's one thing I'll say about Joaquín,' she remarked finally, 'he doesn't give up.'

'Well, he's got his work cut out with me.' Titus chuckled and patted his belly. 'Let's hope he doesn't live to regret it.'

24

Amanda had never been happier. If she couldn't promote the virtues of a diet derived from human flesh, then a vegan café was the next best thing. Both forms of eating spared blameless animals, after all, and so she felt comfortable in each camp. With the backing of her adoptive family, who seemed increasingly at ease with setting aside their personal food preference during opening hours, this spirited young woman threw herself into the role of running a meat-free establishment.

Within a week, Amanda could count on regular customers. Ten days after opening, she had got over the allergy that came from dealing with so many people whose clothing was covered in cat hair. A fortnight later, there were times when those who showed up without a booking had to wait for a table to become clear. By the end of the first month, The Lentil Rebel was running at full capacity.

'Nikolai Zolotov sends his congratulations,' Lev announced, on dropping in after the doors had closed one evening. 'The café is turning over more money than the saloon bar, so you're doing good here.'

As had become routine, Lev brought a bulging Manila

envelope with him, which Kiril took to the till. Amanda noted how the man always counted up the takings from the day by mouthing the digits on each intake of breath. She figured it was a habit he had developed from years of laundering hot money.

'Just don't sit back on your laurels.' Kiril swatted the till shut, having filled it with the next float of cash that needed cleaning. 'An aggressive strategy is what you need.'

Amanda had been wiping down the counter when they showed up. It annoyed her to see Kiril reach for one of the remaining cookie-dough truffles, carefully made with gluten-free flour and xanthan gum, because inevitably it crumbled as he swept it to his mouth and he never used a plate.

'We're happy as we are,' she told them, balling the cloth in her hands.

'But you could be happier.' Lev used a tone that sounded like a warning. 'Think about it. Talk to Titus. Sound him out.'

'He'll be here soon to lock up,' said Amanda. 'Why not stick around and ask him yourself?'

'Sweetheart, it's nearly suppertime,' said Kiril. With the envelope filled with the day's takings, he rejoined his business partner, who looked set to leave.

'There's a good rib restaurant further up the boulevard,' Lev told her. 'We got a table booked in half an hour.'

'You can join us if you like,' Kiril added, only to wince when Lev jabbed an elbow into his arm.

'Amanda isn't like us, dumbass. If the food on her plate had a mother or a face then it's off the menu.'

Unless it's food that's had a birth certificate, passport or a driving licence, she thought, but opted to bite her tongue. Since the café opened, Amanda hadn't been on a single dinner date, nor did she have any desire to do so. Waiting the tables here, she'd met plenty of nice guys who shared her views, but somehow that wasn't a challenge. In time, she knew that someone would walk into her life in desperate need of seeing the error of their eating ways. For now, however, The Lentil Rebel took up all her energies.

'They do salad where we're going,' said Kiril hopefully.

'Thanks, but no.' Amanda smiled sweetly and gestured at the door as if to remind them it was there. Outside, the sun had settled under blankets of orange, peach and turquoise. A stiff breeze caused the palm trees to shiver and sway, while lights from the villas across the inlet were beginning to twinkle. '*Bon appétit*, fellas. Hope it chokes you.'

Lev shared her grin before turning to leave, while Kiril hung back for a moment, his tall frame and narrow shoulders in silhouette to her.

'Well, when you come to your senses,' he said, 'supper is on me.'

'Good night, Kiril.' Amanda crossed the floor to hold the door open for him.

The two men had arrived in Lev's sports car, which chirruped as he disabled the alarm. Amanda watched him squeeze into the driver's seat, while Kiril had to practically fold himself up to fit in beside him.

'*I always think those two would taste a little too sour for my liking.*'

Amanda turned on hearing the voice behind her. Ivan was standing at the kitchen door with his school bag slung over

182

one shoulder, watching them leave.

'You should've come out to say hi,' she told him. 'It's only polite.'

Ivan turned his attention to her for a moment, but it was clear by the look on his face that he hadn't registered the advice.

'I was busy working,' he told her.

Amanda returned to the counter to clear up the crumbs.

'I admire your dedication to the job,' she told him. 'It's good to know that someone's on top of the kitchen hygiene.'

This time, Ivan heard her clearly. He looked quietly surprised, as if she'd just reminded him of something.

'I'll be right back,' he said, and disappeared through the door.

He left Amanda looking puzzled. Just what was the kid up to in there if he wasn't disinfecting the equipment? She set down the cloth to follow him, only for headlights to sweep across the opposite wall of the café.

'You'll have to hurry!' she called out to Ivan. 'Your parents are here.'

As agreed, now that the building was refurbished, Titus had stepped back from day-to-day involvement with The Lentil Rebel. He offered advice and guidance to Amanda, and had done a great job fixing the extractor fan, but seemed content to keep a low profile.

'How was business today?' he asked on stepping inside.

'The best ever,' said Amanda. 'You just missed Lev and Kiril. I think they'd like us to expand.'

With a guffaw, Titus slapped his sides.

'I'm already fighting one expansion,' he told her.

Angelica joined them just then. She had spent the day at

183

home baking biscuits and cakes for the counter. Katya clasped her hand. The little girl was wearing a pair of mesh fairy wings that hung at an angle from her shoulders. Angelica let her go to run around, before looking up and around in admiration.

'This is such a welcoming place,' she said, noting the recent addition of a community corkboard. It already featured a cluster of business cards and flyers that added a note of green against the cream walls. 'You should be proud of your achievements, Amanda.'

'It's a team effort,' she insisted, as Ivan returned from what was evidently a hasty clean-up operation.

'It seems everyone has made a contribution.' Angelica smiled proudly at her son.

Ivan stopped by a table, resting his bag on the floor.

'Do you know what this calls for?' he said, looking hopefully at his father. 'A feast.'

All eyes turned to Titus. Given the success of the café, Amanda expected him to agree straight away. Instead, it seemed as if some invisible weight that had been hanging over him just settled on his shoulders.

'I've been meaning to discuss this with you,' he said, and gestured for them to join him at a table. Amanda took a seat across from Titus, who waited for Angelica to deal with Katya's request to straighten her wings. Ivan remained standing, however, right beside his school bag.

'Is this about the ginger and garlic marinade again?' asked Angelica. 'I like the flavour it brings as much as everyone else, but it takes hours to soak into the meat and we don't have that kind of room in the fridge.'

'It's Grandpa,' he said, leaning in. 'Oleg has asked to bring a guest.'

'To eat?' asked Ivan. 'If it's his friend from the home, she looks too old for the table. There's no meat on her bones.'

'To eat *with* us,' said Titus, to clarify. 'He believes it could save her.'

Angelica closed her eyes, sighing at the same time.

'We Savages have always stuck together. Amanda is the only exception.'

'And she didn't let us down,' Titus pointed out. 'Under any other circumstances, I would've refused, but this means everything to my father.'

'I bet it does,' Ivan muttered under his breath. 'The old fox.'

'Then it comes down to trust,' said Amanda.

'He knows that.' Titus sat with his hands clasped. 'Oleg is aware of the consequences should Priscilla break that trust.'

'It also means a lot of mouths to feed,' complained Angelica. 'I know people tend to be a little more fleshy around here, but that's still less of the best bits for each of us.'

'I know someone suitable,' Ivan piped up. 'Actually, I know three. They're all in my class!'

Amanda tutted and shook her head.

'Then they're only fifteen years old,' she pointed out. 'That makes them minors, which is sick, Ivan. No way *that's* going to happen.'

'Amanda is right,' said Angelica. 'We have principles.'

'Then who?' asked Titus. 'I have some lovely tenants at the moment. None cause me any trouble. I'd hate to lose them in a hurry.'

It was Angelica who rose first from the table.

'I have someone in mind.' She began to button her coat once more, deliberately keeping her gaze from her husband.

'Who?' asked Titus, as she waited for him to join her at the door.

'We can discuss this over dinner,' she told him, and fluttered her hands to summon Ivan and Katya.

Amanda fetched her coat, well aware that if Angelica had made up her mind about what meat they would be eating, Titus would simply be required to bring it home.

25

Water aerobics was always popular among the more mobile residents of the Fallen Pine Nursing Home. It was gentle on the joints and offered a chance to exercise communally. The session took place in the home's outdoor pool, which had been purpose built without a deep end. The participants faced the instructor at the side – an overweight lady in unflattering Lycra called Dionne – and performed star jumps with differing degrees of success.

'This is killing me,' muttered Oleg, waist-deep in water, as his fellow residents splashed about around him.

'Well, I think it would be a fine way to go.' Priscilla was positioned beside him in her bathing suit and cap with the plastic flower detail. She had made a good recovery since her hospital visit. Even so, the staff had frowned upon her insistence on joining Oleg in the pool. With her arms spread crookedly, she looked as if she hoped to flap into the air. 'Might as well bow out having a good time!'

Just then, the cell phone in Dionne's fanny pack began to bleat. She sighed wearily, as if she knew the call would be from her divorce lawyer, and then waved at her class to stop.

'Well done, everybody,' she called out. 'You've earned yourselves a rest.'

Slowly, the elderly folk in the pool began to gravitate towards the steps. Oleg waited for Priscilla to move alongside him, holding her hand to keep her steady.

'You're not leaving this world,' he told her. 'Not yet.'

'Oleg, how many times?' Priscilla smiled and rolled her eyes. 'You're very sweet, but there's nothing anybody can do. It's OK, though.' Oleg felt her squeeze his hand. 'These are happy days for me.'

By now, a line had formed as two nurses helped each resident up the steps. Oleg and Priscilla joined the queue, the sun drying their shoulders.

'The meal I mentioned . . . ' Oleg addressed her quietly, keeping his eyes on the nurses. 'I've spoken to Titus, and my family would love you to join us.'

'Well, that's sweet of them,' Priscilla replied. 'So, when are you going to tell me what's on the menu? I'm partial to a bit of pork.'

Oleg gasped on feeling her pinch his bottom. He wheeled around in the water and found her grinning at him. Through his eyes, the moment was both startling and sad. He hadn't felt like this since his teenage years before the war. He also knew that without a feast he wouldn't be feeling this way for much longer. Now Titus had confirmed that Priscilla would be welcome at the table, under strict conditions, the old man knew she had to be told. It was a gamble, of course. What Oleg had to share went against nature, after all. He also knew that she wasn't the sort of lady who liked to make a scene. And so, to be on the safe side, he decided there and then to strike in public with what she could expect on her plate.

'A human.' Calmly, Oleg clasped her hands under the water. 'Listen to me, Priscilla. We're not fiends. I swear it. This is dining undertaken in the best possible taste, and with health benefits that mean you and I can spend a lot longer together than your doctors believe. Think of this meat as a medicine,' he told her, keeping it as casual as he could. 'I guarantee you'll finish your final mouthful in a state of rapture, as if you could live forever. Now, can I trust you to process what I've just shared without screaming?' Oleg held her gaze, waiting for her to close her mouth. 'Whatever you're thinking right now, just give yourself some time to digest it.'

A moment passed before Priscilla appeared to pull focus on him. Then, with a blink, her mouth eased into a smile, followed by a chuckle.

'You're such a kidder!' she said. 'Some time to digest it, indeed! You almost had me there, you wicked man!'

'Priscilla –' Oleg drew breath to stress that he was being deadly serious, only to falter as her amusement gathered ground. Aware that a number of residents at the poolside were turning to see what the old lady in the water found so funny, he forced a little smile for her benefit. 'Well, I tried,' he said, mostly to himself.

Cackling now, Priscilla took her turn on the steps, where the two nurses helped her up and into her towel.

'Oleg, you make me laugh, but you really shouldn't joke like that. What if someone took you seriously?'

Oleg glanced nervously at the nurses, but they were used

189

to the residents' babble and generally tuned out. It was only when they had finished with Priscilla that the two men paid him any attention.

'I can manage this myself,' Oleg grumbled, thinking that he now had a serious challenge on his hands. Not just with leaving the pool, but with persuading an elderly lady to explore an extreme form of eating for the sake of their future together.

On several occasions, usually when things got too much at school, Ivan Savage headed for the sand dunes overlooking the boardwalk and the ice-cream stall. The boy always chose to sit amid the long grass where he couldn't be seen, cross-legged with the gerbil in his lap. There, he watched the vendor serving up treats that nobody questioned or even knew they wanted until it was too late to resist.

It was with this in mind that Ivan had volunteered to help some of the moms provide post-match refreshments whenever the football team played an inter-high-school league match. Given that Ivan only ever spent his time on the bench, as he had explained to the coach, serving snacks would allow him to make a contribution in the closing minutes.

'That's a wise move, buddy,' the coach had told him, as the rest of the squad goofed about during warm-up by performing body slams on one another. 'A safe option.'

And so, with nothing more sinister in mind than watching how the team filed into the changing rooms to devour the drinks and snacks laid out for them, Ivan had made himself useful by buttering the bread.

By his third game in the role, he had worked out exactly

what sandwiches Bryce, Ryan and Chad favoured. All three ate the ham and gherkin, deriding anyone who took the tuna or the egg as 'snack faggots'.

'Leave those for new girl, although he'll probably want to cut off the crusts first!'

Ryan was the ringleader on this occasion. He was sweating profusely, having just come off the pitch from another physically intense game. Ivan watched him drain a cup of orange squash before crushing it in his fist.

'Can I get you a refill?' he asked.

Ryan dropped the cup at his feet, his eyes narrowing.

'Sure,' he said cautiously.

Ivan filled another cup without word, just as Ryan swapped glances with Bryce and Chad.

'It's important to keep your fluids up,' said Ivan, and handed him the drink.

Ryan took the cup and gulped it back. Then, with his cheeks bulging and his two friends grinning, he blasted it back at the boy.

'Whoops!' he crowed, as Ivan took the full force in the face. 'Careless!'

'You're all wet,' said Bryce.

'Same goes for his panties,' added Ryan, and burst out laughing.

Ivan didn't respond. Even when the trio peeled away from the refreshment table, he just stood there with his eyes closed and juice dripping from his lashes like amber tears. Despite the indignity, however, Ivan held onto the fact that he knew just what to prepare in time for the next fixture.

Having thrown themselves into the match, Ryan, Bryce and Chad would come to him in a state of exhaustion, hunger and dehydration. That meant their immune system would be less effective than normal, which was ideal for what Ivan had in mind. No doubt he would face more ridicule and torment in serving them refreshments, and all three would walk away as they had done just then. The only difference would be what they had unwittingly taken with them in the pit of their guts.

It would be just like the kiddiewinks buying ice cream on the boardwalk, Ivan thought. He might've been wrong about the seller's intentions – no doubt the tarpaulin in the back of his car was for the stall, not an incumbent body in the boot – but just supposing he was there to incapacitate his victims? If so, it was the perfect set-up. So long as the treat was presented to them as just what they needed, nobody would question what was in it. That was the thing about food, he decided. It could seduce the senses with devastating efficiency.

'Next time,' he muttered to himself, and wondered what it might be like to be a pathogen working slowly through the bloodstream from the stomach to the brain stem.

Ivan reached for a paper towel to dry his face. His mother wouldn't be happy that the juice had stained his school shirt. He just hoped she'd be distracted by the planning currently underway for the family's next feast.

26

Since he had begun working out under Joaquín's guidance, Titus found that he could now tighten his belt strap by an extra notch. He felt fit and looked trimmer, which was down to a ruthless running regime alternated with weight-training sessions. He knew he still had a long way to go, of course, but the recent improvements meant by rights he should've arrived outside the gym in good spirits. Instead, on seeing his trainer stretching in the sunshine outside the entrance, Titus just felt his heart grow heavy.

'All set?' asked Joaquín Mendez, who stopped reaching for his ankles and began skipping on the spot.

'As ready as I'll ever be,' said Titus. 'How about the forest road circuit?'

Joaquín seemed surprised, but not in a bad way. The route Titus had just suggested would take them several miles further than he had run before, including an isolated track through the pines where it was easy to twist an ankle.

'You're feeling brave,' he said, falling still for a moment. 'Reckon you're up for it?'

'I'm ready for anything,' said Titus, well aware that only

one of them would be coming back again.

'Well, that's good to hear.' Joaquín began jabbing his arms back and forth at the elbows. 'It sounds like my work is almost done with you.'

Titus was dressed in his shorts and, unusually, a long-sleeved sweatshirt. The sleeves served to hide the garrotte, which he had carefully wound around his left wrist for safekeeping. While the pine trail carried some risk of turning a foot, it also presented the perfect opportunity for Titus to dispatch Joaquín in private. With the job done, Titus planned to remove the cell phone from the pouch strapped around the young man's forearm, access his diary for the day and delete his digital footprints. With the body hidden in the undergrowth, he'd jog back to collect the pickup, which was parked as a precaution several blocks from the gym, and then bring the body home. Technically, it was a straightforward operation. Where Titus struggled, for the first time, was with his feelings about it all.

'Let's not push too hard,' he asked, and gestured at the sky. 'On a beautiful day like this, it's important to enjoy the moment.'

Joaquín eyed him warily, which wasn't unusual, thought Titus. Ever since he'd signed up with his wife's ex-trainer, the guy had related to him as if he might bite. Even so, Titus was keen to make sure the young man made the most of what would be his final run. He even consoled himself with the fact that his victim was about to die doing something he loved.

'You're welcome to lead the way,' suggested Joaquín, only for Titus to decline the offer.

'After you,' he said, and gestured for him to set off. 'I insist.'

When Angelica nominated Joaquín as a suitable candidate for her to cook, Titus had reacted with surprise. She had often spoken fondly of him, he pointed out, which was an observation backed up by Amanda. As an unwritten rule, the family always opted to feast on the troublemakers and the irritants. Surely Joaquín was one of the good guys? In response, Angelica had argued that the young Argentinian would offer them something that Titus had been longing for: lean meat with the minimum of fat.

'He's in peak condition,' she argued. 'And there's no point in working out unless you're going to eat healthily, too. You need to take a holistic approach to fitness, Titus. Joaquín is just what we need to make this a feast that hits the spot but won't leave us feeling bloated for days afterwards.'

When Angelica spoke with this intensity, Titus knew not to stand up to her. They had plenty of respect for one another, but his wife called all the shots in the kitchen. Amanda often poured scorn on this arrangement, accusing Titus of being a dinosaur who needed to man up and wear a pinny with pride, but the fact was it worked for them as a family. When it came to the feasts, Angelica's cooking was peerless. With no recipe books to draw upon for inspiration, she had forged a culinary pathway for herself, which her family hungrily followed. As the provider, it was down to Titus to take care of the hunting. He was keenly aware that Ivan had reached an age where he really needed all the experience he could get. On this occasion, however, it wasn't football practice that got in the way. It would just be weird, Titus figured, to show up for a training session with his son in tow, and he didn't wish to unsettle Joaquín in any way. Ultimately, he wanted the young man's final run to be something he enjoyed without distraction.

'Let's do this thing,' said Joaquín on breaking into a stride. 'No pain, no gain.'

After less than twenty minutes of jogging under the glare of the sun, it became clear to Titus that his personal trainer was completely free to soak in his surroundings. Even when he called out to the young man to ease up the pace, he was so far back his voice just failed to reach him.

'Slow down, dammit,' Titus muttered to himself, and made an effort to quicken his footfalls.

Of course, he knew that this was Joaquín's way of pushing him. It just meant he had burned up every last ounce of energy by the time he reached the trail through the pines. This was where the kill was supposed to happen, were Titus not fit to drop. As he struggled to catch up with the young man, twice turning his ankle on the uneven surface, Titus sensed the muscles in his chest and legs scream out for him to stop. If his body was trying to tell him something, his mind made every effort to do likewise. Not only was Joaquín currently well out of his reach, he couldn't ignore the fact that he was pursuing a nice guy with a good heart. It simply didn't justify his selection for the table in any way. By the time Titus found Joaquín waiting for him at the trail exit, he was in no fit state to speak to the man, let alone strangle him.

'How are you feeling?' asked Joaquín, jogging from one foot to the other as if he'd merely been warming up all this time.

Titus dropped his hands to his knees, panting so acutely he

made a rasping noise with every inhalation. Metaphorically speaking, he wanted to murder the guy, but only for testing him to the very limit of his physical ability.

'I'll survive,' he said eventually, and looked up. With the sun in his eyes, Titus saw only an upright figure with his whole life ahead of him. 'But I'll pay for this when I get home.'

'Dinner has been delayed,' Angelica Savage told Oleg several days later. 'We'll have to wait a little longer for the next feast.'

The pair were browsing the chilled-meat aisle in the grocery store at the time. Angelica often took Oleg to assist her in the weekly shop. She didn't really need his help, but he appreciated the company and the change of scene.

'We can't wait,' he said quickly and with a note of panic at what he'd just been told. 'Priscilla doesn't have much time left.'

Angelica was pushing the cart while Oleg rode alongside her on the store-issue scooter, though he had braked on hearing the news.

'Then our guest will have to learn to be patient.' Angelica turned to face him. On seeing his troubled expression, she tipped her head to one side. 'Unless you mean she literally can't wait because she's, well . . . dying?'

Over the public-address system, a store worker broadcast details of the daily deal for sliced white bread as if he might burst into tears of boredom. Oleg looked to the basket of his scooter for a moment, waiting for the announcement to finish.

'A feast is all I can offer her.'

'It's certainly one to tick off the bucket list,' agreed Angelica, thinking that at least the old lady wouldn't have long before she took the secret to the grave. She didn't like the idea of anyone joining them. It had taken her a while to feel comfortable with Amanda. On this occasion, it was Titus who had persuaded her that it would make an old man happy. Angelica didn't share Oleg's belief that somehow human flesh would save Priscilla. Even so, she didn't want to crush what hopes for the future he might have left.

'I'm sorry, Oleg, but your lady friend will have to hold on for a little while,' said Angelica gently, and swapped her attention between the shelves as if each one was as disappointing as the other.

'Oh.' The old man looked crestfallen. 'What happened to the personal trainer?' He drew level with her once more. 'From your description, he sounded like the meat would just fall off the bone.'

Together, they moved towards the mince.

'You'll have to ask Titus . . . He came back with the promise that he'd find someone more deserving for the table.'

Oleg sighed and rolled his eyes.

'My boy is getting a little long in the tooth, perhaps,' he said. 'Given the opportunity, I imagine Ivan wouldn't let us down in that way.'

Angelica paused to pick up a beef fillet. She examined the sell-by date, her mouth tightening, and then set it back down on the shelf.

'Letting Ivan loose wouldn't be wise just yet,' she told him. 'For his own reasons Titus hasn't delivered this time, but he's meticulous. Ivan will follow in his father's footsteps one day, but he isn't ready. He needs to learn not to get too caught up in the kill and to think about the bigger picture.'

'A hunter's eye.' Oleg nodded as he spoke. 'It'll come with practice.'

'So, what shall we have instead of a feast?' she asked, as they moved along the aisle. 'Lamb is good.'

'It isn't in season,' grumbled Oleg. 'Not that it stops the stores from flying it in from halfway across the world. It's so excessive when we have all the meat we can eat right here on our doorstep.'

'Oleg, local produce is off the menu this weekend.' Angelica caught his eye and held it until she felt sure that he understood. 'We're not going to rush into serving up anyone. That's how mistakes are made. So, what'll it be? The lamb or a shin of beef?'

'Either meat will have to tide us over.' Oleg shrugged, grasping the handlebars of his scooter in readiness to move on. 'Let's just hope Priscilla lasts until we dine upon the *finest!*'

'So, you've told her?'

'In a sense.' Oleg broke from her gaze. 'Actually, she thinks I'm joking, but I will find a way to make her realise that joining us could *transform* the time she has left. I just need to be assured that we'll have something to eat.'

'It's important that you relax. It's not good for you to be this stressed.' Angelica prepared to cut through the refrigerated ready-meals aisle, which was badly congested with shoppers and their trolleys. 'You shouldn't worry yourself about where the next feast is coming from.'

'But I can't afford to have faith in others at my time of life,' Oleg shot back. 'If Titus doesn't put food on the family table soon then perhaps it's time he let his son take over!'

27

The ham contained the fate of the three jocks from the school squad. Once Ivan was ready to strike, it would assume the filling for a Last Supper in sandwich form. The boy had invested a great deal of time and effort in researching the project. The trichinosis parasite, his chosen means of food poisoning, was most commonly associated with pork. Unfortunately for Ivan, public health measures across the state's pig-farming industry meant any cut from the supermarket shelf was unlikely to be contaminated. And so, having trawled online through recent court records, Ivan located a farm shop that had twice been prosecuted for poor hygiene standards. It was a bus ride out of town, sported fly strips from the ceiling that really needed changing and staffed by a dull-witted man in a duckbill cap whom Ivan had marked down as inbred.

'Everything you see has been raised and slaughtered by Papa himself,' he had said, as Ivan inspected the pork for sale behind the smeared glass counter. The boy had wondered if the man might be referring to his uncle or some such, but reminded himself to stay focused on the task at hand. The man had leaned over his chopping board just then, seeking Ivan's ear. 'You'll find our prices are real appealing,' he had promised. 'It's what comes from cutting out the pen-pushers.'

Having read up on the subject extensively, Ivan figured the man was referring to Agricultural Law Enforcement officers. Without a doubt, unless the farm tightened up its act before the next inspection, the place would be shut down or even condemned at a stroke. Ivan had passed the pig shed on the walk up the track to get here. The place stank of slurry, was clearly overstocked and the ground showed evidence of rat runs. The produce on offer here had to be *riddled* with the trichinosis parasite.

'I'll take three slices,' he had told the man, holding up the same number of fingers for good measure.

Next came the preparation stage. There was no way Ivan could fool his victims into eating raw pork, after all. Basic cooking presented a problem, too. According to Ivan's internet research, trichinosis could be killed off at a high temperature, As an oven-roasted ham would present Ryan, Bryce and Chad with no health risks at all, the boy had to consider other forms of processing the meat to make it look like a tasty treat while still preserving the parasites.

Curing was an age-old process and met Ivan's needs perfectly. By entombing the ham in a salt mixture, all the moisture in the meat would be drawn out that otherwise allowed bacteria to thrive. What it didn't kill, however, was his now favourite form of roundworm. Ivan had discovered that advanced preservative techniques in the commercial food industry had eliminated that risk, which ruled out just purchasing a pack off the shelf. So, to be on the safe side, in order to serve up a ham sandwich from hell, the boy had decided to cure his own slices from scratch.

The evening after his visit to the farm shop, while Amanda mopped the café floor, Ivan had set about putting his research into practice in the kitchen. His first task was the creation of a dry-curing mixture. This involved blending table salt with sodium nitrite, which he had lifted from the school lab. Ivan was precise in his measurements, anxious to get it right, before pouring the mix over his slices. With his plastic container filled to the brim, the boy was set to let time take over. By leaving it for three days in a cool environment, he could look forward to a ham that looked and tasted delicious, while still delivering a deadly charge.

The problem, he had discovered, centred on where to stash an open container of meat intended to maim and kill.

Ivan recognised the risk involved in hiding it anywhere in the kitchen. This was a vegan café, for one thing, and both Amanda and Angelica would easily sniff it out. He knew that nobody would find it out in the yard, but then the torpid Florida heat, coupled with the flies, would turn his hard work into something frankly stomach-churning. It was only when Ivan read about the effectiveness of using a water bath that he fell upon a solution. It was a method that provided a constant, cool temperature, which suited the curing process. What's more, as Ivan stood upon the rim of the toilet in the café restroom, having carefully floated the container in the cistern above and then replaced the ceramic lid, he could be assured that it was a safe hiding place for the long countdown that followed.

Now, at the end of the process, alone in the kitchen after the café had closed, Ivan stood before the worktop and studied the fruit of his labours. Wearing a pair of disposable latex gloves, he shook away the salt mix and found that the meat slices had changed in texture and colouring. They were no longer so moist, springy or fleshy pink, but had acquired a darker, more leathery look.

'Do you want to be the taster?' he asked, addressing Tinky Dinks, who had just peeped out from his school bag on the floor. Ivan removed a slice from the container for a closer inspection. Holding the ham to his nostrils, he found it didn't smell off at all. For a lethal time bomb in food form, this was just the appearance and aroma he had been hoping to achieve. What's more, having effectively preserved the meat, it would keep until the time was right for him to strike. Ivan glanced back at the gerbil and grinned. 'Only joking,' he said, returning the slice to the container. 'But if you're hungry, I can find you something to eat. Let's face it, this place is stocked with food that's only fit for woodland creatures.' He looked up and around as he spoke, scanning the shelves for something suitable. It was only when he reached for a jar of porridge oats that he stopped and tutted to himself. 'Now that would be careless,' he said, and stripped off his gloves.

'*What would?*'

The voice from behind him caused Ivan to gasp. Hurriedly, he tossed the gloves into the bin and turned around. Crystal stood at the door. She smiled wryly at him.

'Hey there!' Ivan leaned against the kitchen counter as casually as he could. 'You startled me.'

'Amanda let me in. I was curious to see how this place was working out.' Crystal wore her hair in bunches, which made her look like an overgrown five-year-old. Just then, however, Ivan felt in no position to question her appearance. 'So,' she said, and closed the door behind her. 'What are you hiding?'

A spike of dread passed through Ivan. Having attempted to shield the plastic container from her view, he suddenly felt completely exposed. Crystal was looking at him intently. Lost for words, the boy just stood there without blinking. At that moment, all his efforts threatened to come to nothing. He couldn't simply tell her he'd been curing meat. She'd want to know what it was doing in a vegan kitchen, and no doubt an interrogation would follow. Just thinking ahead like this left him close to crumbling.

'Crystal . . .' He considered offering to make her a cured-ham sandwich. It would be a pity, he thought, having got to know her lately. Here he was facing the only person at school who showed an interest in his life, and now he'd have to dispose of her. Ivan took a breath to ask if she liked mustard or mayo, only to see her eyes drop to his school bag.

'Don't move,' she said suddenly, and took a step back. 'Ivan, this place has a vermin problem.'

It took a moment for Ivan to realise that Crystal was talking about the gerbil. He glanced down to see the creature padding over the top of his bag, and seized his opportunity to shove the plastic container behind a bag of flour.

'That's no vermin,' he said, sounding markedly relieved. 'I saved Tinky Dinks from a life of being prodded half to death by pre-schoolers. He goes everywhere with me now.'

Ivan crouched to pet his little charge. When he returned his attention to Crystal, she looked like she had slipped into a trance.

'You are weird,' she said eventually, nodding as if confirming something to herself. 'But also kind of wonderful!'

For the second time since Crystal walked in on him, Ivan sensed some heat in his cheeks. The boy felt funny all of a sudden. A little lightness in the head and heart. He didn't like it one bit.

Amanda had just put the mop and bucket away when the two figures appeared at the café door. She had locked up after letting Crystal in, which forced Lev and Kiril to knock on the glass for her attention.

'Are you trying to tell us we're not welcome?' asked Lev when Amanda opened the door for them.

'Just keeping the carnivores at bay,' she said, as Kiril followed him in. 'Business is good and word is getting around. The last thing I need is some meat-eating punk robbing us of our takings.'

Kiril nodded, while Lev looked at her quizzically.

'So, what are you saying?' he asked with a hint of amusement in his voice. 'Vegans never commit a crime?'

Amanda consulted her thoughts for a moment and then shook her head.

'We're the ones with the ethics,' she told him. 'You can almost smell it in here.'

Kiril lifted his nostrils.

'All I can smell is bleach,' he told her, and then gestured at the till. 'Bleach and nice, clean dollars.'

She watched him cross the café floor, well aware that his bag contained the next delivery of notes to be laundered.

Amanda wasn't at all comfortable about this aspect of the new venture. Lev and Kiril were harmless enough, however. She could've grown to like them, in fact, if they weren't just here to feed the till with dirty money. At the same time, she was well aware that without this financial backing, she'd still be fending off men in cheap bars who thought it acceptable to hit on her just because she served them drinks.

'Everyone is happy with how this has turned out,' Lev told her. 'Zolotov is so pleased he's willing to finance a whole chain.'

Judging by the way both men appeared to hold their breath for her to respond, Amanda realised that a plan was underway here. The pair had hinted at it on their last visit. Now, Lev had spelled it out.

'I don't do big business,' she told him. 'This is a local enterprise. We serve the local community and hope to enlighten others. That's as far as it goes.'

Lev listened to her reasoning with his eyes crinkled at the corners. A moment later, he beamed and nodded like a father hearing out a small child's outlook on life. Then Amanda finished, and tightened her gaze. Slowly, as he realised that she wasn't going to let up, Lev's expression faded.

'It wasn't meant as a suggestion,' he mumbled, and turned anxiously to his associate. Amanda found Kiril was already looking directly at her.

'We're just the messengers here,' he told her. 'It's in all our interests if we go back with positive news. You should at least talk it over with Titus. No doubt he'll see sense.'

Amanda didn't respond for a moment. First, she consulted the floor. Then she began to chuckle to herself.

'Do you want to know what I think?' she asked finally, facing up to them both once more. 'I think your boss man doesn't exist. You've cooked up this guy with the teeth to scare us into doing your dirty work.'

'Nikolai Zolotov is very real,' said Kiril darkly. 'And very powerful.'

'Well, he can eat my falafels,' Amanda declared, sounding increasingly defiant. She gestured towards the door. 'Now, if you'll excuse me, gentlemen, I have a café to close for the evening.'

28

Sitting on the beach, watching his youngest daughter build a castle with a bucket, Titus was in a reflective mood. He had come here to give Angelica some space. Ever since he'd returned empty-handed from his workout with Joaquín, she had been uncomfortably brittle with him.

'That's beautiful,' he told Katya, as she patted the turrets flat on her castle. 'Who lives there?'

The little girl turned to face him, pushing back her floppy-brimmed sunhat that her mother insisted she put on.

'Vegetarians,' she told him, before turning without warning and smashing the structure with a single sideswipe. 'And the vegans!' she added with a kick.

Titus tried hard not to look taken aback. He understood the sentiment, naturally, despite his involvement with a meat-free café, but that was business and this was his precious little angel. While Ivan appeared to be coping much better with the difference between right and wrong since their arrival in Florida, he was reluctant to go through it all again with little Kat.

'Honey pie,' he said, climbing to his feet, 'it's important that we show respect for everyone. Look at Amanda. She feasts with us but still has her own beliefs.'

Katya frowned, clutching her plastic spade like a pitchfork now.

'Why can't we all just eat the same thing?' she asked.

Titus smiled to himself. Little Kat really was pure sunshine. The last thing he wanted to do was see shadows creep into her innocent mind.

'How about an ice cream?' he suggested, changing the subject. He offered to hold her hand. 'Everyone likes ice cream.'

Titus knew she wouldn't be able to resist. Sure enough, Katya reached out for her father, trampling over the remains of her sandcastle as she went. They had come to a popular stretch of the coastline just off the Ocean Trail Way. A stiff offshore breeze kept the heat at bay, though Titus could feel his bald dome beginning to burn. So long as his daughter was protected, however, nothing else really mattered. Heading for a small parade of beachfront stores and kiosks, he found himself reflecting on all the efforts he had made through the years to support his family and keep them united. In many ways, he had simply taken the baton from his old father and run all the way here with it. Only now – ever since the thing with Joaquín – things felt different. For the first time ever, he had set out to bring back meat for a feast, only to return home with an excuse.

'Does cookies and cream taste nice?' asked Katya, as they left the sand for the boardwalk and crossed towards the kiosk.

'It tastes great!' Titus stopped before the serving hatch and cupped his brow against the sun to scour the flavours. 'Do you know what I like on a hot day?'

'Vanilla?'

'Lemon sorbet. It's my favourite.'

Katya pulled a face, which made Titus laugh.

'OK,' she said, peering at the board again. 'Let me see.'

'You can have anything you like,' said Titus, still clasping her hand. When she didn't answer, he looked down at her. 'Which one is it, honey pie?'

'Maybe we need to ask.' Katya switched her attention from the list to the man in the striped apron and hat awaiting their order. 'Sir, do you have human flavour? I'd like two scoops, please.'

Immediately Titus steered his daughter back a step and took her place.

'She's joking,' he said, and forced a chuckle. 'We'll take two cookies and cream.'

Katya looked mystified when Titus turned his back on the man and glared at her. Even so, he took responsibility for the situation. Waiting for his order, Titus resolved that there would be no more disappointment in his family. Everyone was clearly hungry for a feast, from his elderly father to his youngest daughter, and that was down to him alone to deliver. With this in mind, he decided that his son really should lead the way. Now that Titus had to fight to keep in shape, it was only right to pass that baton on to Ivan. He was a decent kid, Titus reflected. In fact, lately the boy had displayed a real sense of commitment and enthusiasm towards his cleaning work in the café. By all accounts, he got the job done in good time, calmly and without error or complaint.

It was qualities like these, thought Titus, as he passed one ice cream to Katya and took a lick of the other, that would serve his son well as a hunter.

Astride his mobility scooter, with the hems of his boot-cut jeans flapping wildly, Oleg Savage hurtled along the sidewalk at such a rate that his eyes were watering.

'Coming through!' he yelled at the pedestrians, who turned and flung themselves from his path. '*Emergency!*'

Wearing the faux-leather jacket that Amanda had given him one Christmas, with the Confederate flag emblazoned on the back, the old man could've been mistaken for a retired dare devil. He certainly showed no sign of caring for his own safety as he clattered across a red light at the junction and caused several cars to brake.

Oleg had been enjoying lunch when he heard the news. Priscilla had been taken ill once more. This time, his nurse's reluctance to go into detail had told him it was serious. Vince had sat down across from him with that uncomfortable look on his face. Just the mention of her name had been enough to make the old man ball his napkin into his bowl of liquidised chicken, rice and peas, before shuffling to his scooter as fast as his walking cane would allow. Wrenching the battery charger cable from the vehicle's socket, and ignoring the marker, Oleg had twisted the speed dial full circle and torn off for the medical centre. It was only as he approached the building, when the scooter began to lose power rapidly before purring to a halt, that he realised why Vince had pleaded to drive him there.

'What is this? Some kind of test?' he asked out loud, and

shook his fist at the sky. Grabbing his cane from the clip behind his seat, Oleg eased himself onto his legs, which appeared to bow as he righted himself, and then continued on his way at a hobble.

Priscilla had no family. He knew that. Her only son had died in a climbing accident thirty years ago. Following the passing of her husband, she had lived alone with the company of friends. Now that they had all moved on, Oleg considered himself to be her only companion in this world. If the time had come and she was dying – and he desperately hoped that wasn't the case – then Oleg wanted to be at her side. It took him several minutes to make the last block to the main entrance. Inside the lobby, people turned on hearing the automatic doors slide open for the wheezing, breathless geriatric. Before he could ask for directions, two porters had rushed to support him.

'OK, sir. You're in good hands now,' said one, before yelling for a medic.

'Let's make you more comfortable,' the other one added, helping his colleague to scoop the old man onto a gurney. 'What is it? Your heart?'

'Damn right it's my heart,' protested Oleg, struggling uselessly to be free of their attentions. 'I'm a visitor, not a patient, and it's going to break clean in two unless I get to see my Priscilla!'

Ten minutes later, as a compromise with the doctor who really wasn't happy with his blood pressure, Oleg was taken to a private room by wheelchair. The patient under the covers looked as if she was hovering between two worlds. This wasn't the Priscilla he had come to adore. Her face, at rest, lacked spirit and expression. She wore an oxygen mask that fogged and cleared and then fogged again, while her eyes remained closed as if she had retreated deep inside herself. At her bedside, a machine on a trolley beeped rhythmically.

'Sleeping through the snooze alarm, eh?' Oleg glanced up at the porter, who told him he'd be waiting outside. 'That's all she's doing,' he called after him. 'Having a rest!'

The porter placed a finger to his lips, backing out into the corridor at the same time.

'Take it easy, sir,' he said as the door began to close behind him. 'Doctor's orders, remember?'

Alone with Priscilla at last, Oleg positioned himself at her bedside, applied the brake to his wheelchair and sat for a moment with his hands in his lap. The window blinds were turned against the sun and framed by the glare. He could hear kids laughing and shrieking in a playground below. It felt as if he had found himself in some kind of waiting room here; cocooned from a world that one of them had outlived. Oleg smiled weakly to himself, and then wiped his cheek with the heel of his hand.

'I'm sorry,' he told her. 'I promised you something and I've let you down. But I meant what I told you, Priscilla. It was no joke.' Oleg paused there to compose himself. Outside, in the fresh air, the children continued to play. 'We're cannibals, Priscilla. *Cannibals*. There. I said it. And no bolt of lightning has struck me down. The word is loaded with fear and misunderstanding, of course, but there's so much more to it than the simple consumption of human flesh. The experience is life-changing in so many ways. Believe me when I say that eating your own kind is the purest form of sustenance there is. As a family, we are bound together by what we eat. It's cleansing and restorative, turning sickness into health, and that's why I wanted you to share in it. By dining with us, you – *we* – could've had so much more time. Now I know you'd have been shocked to the core, Priscilla, had I held my nerve back in the pool when I tried to tell you about our little secret. I just wish I'd had the courage to believe that, despite it all, you would've placed your faith in me.'

Oleg stopped there, aware that he was talking to himself, and gazed at the back of his hands for a minute. Over the years, they had become more defined by the bones underneath. It was as if death was in there somewhere, slowly revealing itself but held at bay for now. He found it upsetting to return his attention to Priscilla. Lying there, she looked like a woman without the resources he possessed to continue the battle. Oleg glanced at the door, confirmed that it was shut, and then leaned in to find her ear. 'I wish that you could taste a slow-roasted shoulder with garlic and sea salt,' he said. 'Just a mouthful, Priscilla. Nothing more. Believe me, I know how hard it is to swallow the first time, but the rewards make it all worthwhile.'

The old man sat back again, as if awaiting her answer. Beside him, the heart monitor continued to punctuate the silence. 'My family are different, of course. They were brought up to relish the sheer sense of *being* that comes from eating our own kind, and I respect them for it. But you and me, Priscilla, *we're* different. Way back, during the siege, I was faced with dying long before my time. What I had to do to survive was desperate in the extreme, but only by taking that step did I discover what it means to feel *super*human, and that's what I was hoping to offer you. So, I'm sorry, my love. I wish I had been stronger for you and just spoken from the heart. I had been so looking forward to enjoying each other's company for far longer. I guess with a feast off the menu now, I'll have to wait until I see you on the other side.' Oleg paused for several beeps and then chuckled to himself. 'Although after the life I've led, there's a good chance we won't be heading to the same place.'

It was a knock at the door that turned his attention. Oleg looked around to see a doctor enter the room. His first thought was that she looked far younger than the juniors who followed behind her, even if she did hold herself with more authority.

'Just checking up on the patient,' she told him, and then asked the porter to draw Oleg's wheelchair away from the bedside.

'How long does she have left?' asked Oleg, before falling quiet as the team checked her pulse and heart rate.

The doctor glanced over at the old man, and then at some of the juniors who had begun to titter.

'Well, let's ask Priscilla,' she said, and clasped her hand. 'What do you think, my dear?' she asked, her voice raised by a notch. 'You gave us cause for concern earlier, but your stats are back where they should be.'

On seeing this, Oleg leaned forward for a clearer view. When he saw Priscilla with her eyes open, blinking as if to communicate her awareness, he felt an overwhelming sense of both relief and sheer dread. It meant, as she turned her head to face him, he could only respond with a rictus grin.

'Seems like she's come round for you,' observed one of the juniors.

'So it does,' said Oleg, who felt pinned to the back of his wheelchair by the sharpness of Priscilla's gaze.

29

Finishing a weekend lunch of clam chowder, Ivan Savage was first to ask if he could leave the table.

'Manners,' said Angelica. 'It won't kill you to wait until everyone finishes.'

She had summoned the boy from his room just as he was researching notorious food poisoning outbreaks in recent history. Since coming up with his plan of action, the subject had become a source of keen interest to him. Ivan could barely wait to see his three victims complain of neck stiffness or involuntary twitches as the trichinosis worm wriggled towards their brains. He didn't want to miss a thing.

'Your mother is right,' Titus added, with a napkin tucked into the neck of his shirt and his mouth full. He gestured at the salad bowl, which had gone largely untouched. 'How about some greens?'

Ivan shared a grimace with Katya. Even Angelica, who had prepared the side dish, pretended not to hear.

'Where is Amanda?' asked the boy, prompted by the sight of all the untouched lettuce leaves.

'At the café,' said Angelica. 'I'm sure she'll finish it for us later.'

'That young lady is doing a fine job,' said Titus, and waited for Angelica to meet his gaze across the table. 'I think it's fair to say she's earned herself a feast.'

Angelica's eyebrows lifted by a fraction. She set her spoon down and dabbed at her mouth with a napkin.

'Should we get our hopes up?'

Titus slowed his chewing, aware that everyone was looking at him.

'Let me take care of that,' he told her, before switching his attention to Ivan. 'Hey, buddy, what do you say to helping your old man down at the condo this afternoon?'

'Do you mean, like, chores? I'm kind of busy right now.'

'Your apprenticeship,' said Angelica directly.

'We feel the time is right,' Titus added, with a glance at the boy's mother.

'Whatever you had planned,' she continued, 'nothing is more important than learning how to provide for the table.'

Immediately, Ivan's thoughts returned to his research. The ice-cream seller didn't just show up looking dodgy and simply hope for the best. He took time to dress the part, and was forever wiping down the counter so that nothing could distract from the treat he had to offer. OK, so the guy wasn't slipping poison into the passion-fruit flavour – at least, Ivan didn't think so – but the principle still stood. Preparation was essential, and he could not afford to skip it. With the next football fixture just days away, it was vital that he felt completely in control of the situation. He needed to know every fact about the parasite his three targets were set to ingest in order to feel calm and collected on the day. Then again, Ivan didn't want to disappoint his dad. Ever since he'd failed to bring the fitness trainer home for the table, the boy's mother just hadn't let him forget it. Everyone in the family knew that nothing could ever seriously come between his parents, of course. How could it when they lived this kind of life? Still, in Ivan's view she really seemed to be questioning his ability to deliver the goods on learning that the barefoot guy had outrun him. What was the big deal anyway, the boy thought? Yes, it was disappointing that they didn't get to dine on some prime Argentinian man steak, but, you know, nobody had *died*. Still, judging by the way his parents awaited a response, Ivan figured that his poisoning plans would just have to wait.

'I'll help,' he told his father, who closed his eyes in apparent relief. 'Just let me shut down my computer first.'

The tenant who had called Titus to report a cracked shower tile sported an impressive body mass index. Ivan could only estimate the man's fat content based on his height and weight, but he had a good eye. He owed this to his father, who shook hands with the guy when he answered the door and then introduced his son.

'Call me Lou,' the man said to Ivan, smiling warmly, before apologising profusely for bringing them out at the weekend. 'I'm just worried that water is leaking into the apartment below. I'd hate to think I was causing a problem.'

'You're not a problem,' said Titus, who had brought his toolkit with him. 'To be honest, most tenants in your situation wouldn't care less.'

This didn't stop Lou from expressing his gratitude as he led them into the apartment. Ivan knew damn well why they were here. He had been on hunting trips with his dad a couple of times before. Mostly back in England when he was younger and prone to making mistakes. It felt good to know that finally he was being considered mature enough to give it another shot. If his mind wasn't weighed down by revenge plans, the boy might even have relished this moment. Just then, Ivan was tempted to tell his dad all about Chad, Bryce and Ryan. Preparing a fatal food poison took planning and precision, after all. Then again, it was all theory so far, which persuaded him to keep it to himself for now. Once he'd quietly laid waste to his tormentors, without leaving a single crumb of proof that he was behind it, Ivan had no doubt that his dad would be very proud of him indeed.

'Here's the tile,' said Lou, crouching in the bathroom with one hand on the floor of the shower. Ivan and Titus stood over him. It was the perfect moment to reach for the garrotte stashed in his toolkit. Instead, the boy's father observed the cracked tile with one hand on his chin.

'We could just seal it up, but it's better to put in a new one,' he told his tenant. 'I always like to do a thorough job.'

Offering to make them a coffee, Lou left the pair alone in the bathroom, apologising for the inconvenience one more time. Ivan waited until the man could be heard at work in the kitchen before rounding on his father.

'You missed your moment,' he hissed. 'We could've had it done by now.'

Titus looked pained, as if his son had just yelled in his ear.

'Let's not rush things,' he said, and proceeded to rummage through his toolkit. When Titus produced a chisel and a grout remover, it became clear to Ivan that his father's primary goal here was to waterproof the shower.

'What's going on, Dad?' Ivan glanced into the hall. 'He's good to go, right?'

Titus looked wearily at his son. He drew breath to reply, only to be stopped by the sound of footsteps in the hallway.

'Here you are, gents,' said Lou, and handed them two steaming mugs. 'Now, I should get out of your way, but if there's anything you need, just ask.'

'Thanks,' said Titus, who seemed well aware that Ivan was looking at him incredulously.

'Do you want me to do it?' asked the boy, and reached for the hammer.

'Not now!' Titus grabbed his arm. 'Not him,' he added quietly.

'*What?*'

'I like my meat to be mouthy,' said Titus. 'The ones who bitch and complain. The disrespectful and the rude. Those that come too close to our lives for comfort. They are fit for consumption, Ivan. Not people like Lou. He's polite. He's kind. He's considerate. The world needs guys like this, Ivan. Eating him would be a waste.'

Ivan listened to his father as if he had no understanding of the words. From the kitchen, Lou could be heard humming to himself as he did the washing-up.

'Is that why you spared the trainer, too?'

'The stamina was mostly the issue there,' said Titus, nodding

221

as if to himself. 'That young man was quick on his feet.'

Ivan stared at his father for a moment before shaking his head.

'You're past your prime,' he said.

'It's important to be selective,' countered Titus.

'Look, just let me take care of things!' Ivan snatched the hammer. 'Someone's got to feed the family!'

'Are you crazy?' Titus grabbed his son and wheeled him around to face him once more. He did so with such force that Ivan dropped the tool, which clattered to the floor. 'I am *not* going to let you pick off a good man,' he hissed, struggling to contain the force of his feeling. 'If Lou had behaved any differently, then believe me he'd be dangling by his shoelaces from the shower rail by now, but that didn't happen and it saved his skin. Now, maybe the time has arrived for you to step up as the provider, but first there's an apprenticeship to be served, and that begins by doing as I say!'

Ivan considered his father for a moment.

'We can't go home empty-handed. Mum will slay you.'

From the kitchen, the jaunty whistling sounded completely at odds with the darkening atmosphere in the bathroom. Ivan had no intention of being the first to break his father's gaze.

'We'll pick up something on the way home,' he told the boy. 'Let's just focus on what we came here to do.'

Ivan watched his father get to work on chipping out the tile. His old man wasn't getting any younger, he thought, and dropped to his knees beside him.

'Let me do this for you,' he said, and gently took the chisel from his hands.

'But you've never taken out a tile before.'

'I can learn,' said Ivan, and he continued to tap around the edge where Titus had left off. 'It's why I'm here, isn't it?'

Amanda Dias was at the cash register when the cop entered The Lentil Rebel.

She froze on seeing him, before summoning the presence of mind to blink and close the drawer.

'Don't panic,' she muttered under her breath, on sensing her heartbeat quicken. 'Be cool.'

It was approaching lunchtime, which was a busy time for Amanda and the former lap dancer she had just hired to waitress at weekends. The girl was busy dealing with a customer in a suit who had just taken a seat in the corner by the window. She hadn't noticed the lawman come through the door, but he had seen Amanda. The guy wore his uniform like a second skin, as if he'd been in the job for decades. On finding his gaze levelled on her, Amanda's only option was to step out from behind the counter and greet him as brightly as possible.

'Ma'am,' he said, and removed his hat to reveal a crop of salt-and-pepper hair. 'Can I speak to you for a moment?'

'Of course.' Amanda cleared her throat. 'I'd offer you a seat, but as you can see every table is taken.'

As the officer looked around, Amanda did her level best to control her breathing. For a moment it felt as if the café itself had started spinning. A cop had paid a visit and Titus was an emergency call away. She had him on speed dial, but even that was too late to help her now.

'It's an impressive operation you got here.' The officer was still peering around as he said this, which made Amanda all the more nervous. 'Must be making you guys some serious bucks, huh?'

By now, Amanda could feel her ribcage strain to contain her hammering heart.

'We felt confident about the demand,' she said, as coolly as possible. 'Vegans are no longer a minority. People are beginning to wake up to what they're eating.'

The cop nodded, meeting her eyes once more.

'Can't say I could live without a good T-bone,' he told her, 'but I admire what you've done for the community. It's good to see young people like you make a commitment.'

Sensing that her worst fears weren't about to happen for real, Amanda felt an urge to breathe out long and hard. With the cop still scrutinising her, however, she thanked him for the support.

'Can I get you anything? A coffee?'

'Is it drinkable?' The cop held up his hands, grinning now. 'I'm kidding. The guys at the precinct were joking about it recently. Said you served up liquid cardboard. I volunteered to come in and take a sample back. If it's good, you can count on our custom.'

Maintaining her smile, Amanda Dias wondered whether it was possible to pass some cardboard and hot water through the blender in the kitchen. Anything to prevent The Lentil Rebel from becoming a police magnet.

'Our coffee tastes great,' she told him all the same, and held her chin up proudly. 'Even better when you know it's ethically sourced.'

As she offered to fix the cop a cup on the house, Amanda noticed the new waitress making her way towards them. She seemed a little harried, which was unsurprising for someone on their first lunchtime shift. Then Amanda caught her eye. In a blink, she knew the girl had something to say.

'The man in the corner would like a moment of your time,' she whispered, and seemed relieved when Amanda asked her to fix the officer his drink to go.

'Will you excuse me?' she asked.

'The customer is king,' the cop said. 'Especially when they're paying.'

Amanda shared his smile but felt only relief to be moving on. Whatever the guy in the corner wanted, it couldn't test her any more than this.

30

Joaquín Mendez was a haunted young man. Ever since the Savages came into his life, he had found it impossible to escape from them.

Recently, during a jogging session with Titus through the pine trail, it had actually felt as if the man was *pursuing* him. Joaquín had kept glancing over his shoulder and there he was; struggling to keep up but with his eyes narrowed in a way that made the trainer involuntarily pick up his pace. It had all been in his imagination, of course. He knew that. Nevertheless, Joaquín couldn't help but feel deeply intimidated by the guy. It was inevitable, he supposed, having fallen for his wife.

Angelica may have spelled out her commitment to her family, and yet still he couldn't move on. In fact, almost every time Joaquín attempted to clear his head with a training run, he would catch sight of her. He had seen her so many times over recent weeks that it felt as if Jupiter must be full of her clones. From a distance, Angelica had appeared emerging from the superstore, exiting the hair salon and visiting her father-in-law at the retirement home. It was uncanny, Joaquín reflected, as he pounded barefoot across the lighthouse park. He couldn't fail to notice her, because she practically lit up through his eyes. Just then, for example, as he followed the path around the tennis courts, he pulled up on seeing her pass through the main gates. Her youngest daughter was with her. She sported a pair of those toy fairy wings and was riding around her mother in wide circles on a pink bicycle. Angelica, dressed in a lilac summer dress and oversized shades, practically floated into the park. Panting lightly, Joaquín stared at this siren in his life and felt a knot pull tight in his digestive tract.

'Why?' he asked himself, his voice cracked in anguish. 'Why me?'

Watching Angelica, who was too far away to notice him, Joaquín crossed to a nearby bench and sat down. He shook his head, barely able to believe how this could happen. At least that's what he kept telling himself. Deep down, the young trainer knew he couldn't exactly put such frequent encounters down to destiny. Even if he left his apartment with the best of intentions, somehow he would find himself running through locations across town where he knew she was likely to be. Only recently, Joaquín had forced himself to stop heading for the loop road around the inlet community in case a neighbour called 911. He'd done it so many times he was on nodding terms with a pool maintenance guy working at a nearby address.

As he pondered his actions, Angelica appeared to drift along the path towards the little museum they had there. Her daughter followed behind, her wings wobbling as she trundled along. It tormented him to see the woman, it really did, and yet Joaquín continued to seek her out. In a way, she had become the sustenance he needed, because since coming face to face with her at the vegan café, his appetite for food had completely dwindled. Every time he sat down to eat, he found himself picking at his pasta and even pushing away the bowl. It wasn't good for someone who burned through the calories, and it had begun to show in his face.

If this was love, Joaquín had reflected that morning in front of the bathroom mirror, it was consuming him.

The last time his mother had reached him by webcam, all she could talk about was how haunted he looked. Joaquín had insisted it was down to the poor connection, unwilling to admit that he had fallen for a married woman. Back home, she'd never taken to any girl who'd shown an interest in him. There was no way she would welcome this relationship, even if it only existed in his dreams right now. It was just something he would have to tackle on his own, despite having no previous experience of managing feelings this intense. Joaquín found himself grasping the crucifix around his neck as he watched Angelica inspect the park's flowerbeds. Coveting another man's wife was one of the Good Book's alarm-bell Commandments. Having to face that man on a regular basis and help him get into shape just made things so much worse. Joaquín was committing a sin here, and as he couldn't stop himself then he deserved to be punished. Looking up at the sky, feeling utterly torn, the young Argentinian wondered out loud what his maker might have in store for him.

Just make it soon,' he muttered. 'She's in my bones.'

Ivan Savage sat alongside his father in the pickup and wondered if they were here to eat. Titus Savage had just pulled up in the parking lot outside the burger bar. After reversing carefully into the vacant bay, he'd killed the engine and then just sat there. Ivan glanced across at him. Clutching the ignition key, which he turned in his hands like a rosary, his father was focused on the pastel-painted building in front of them.

'Dad,' said Ivan, a little hesitantly. 'Are you hungry?'

'Hungry?' Titus appeared to stir from some inner contemplation. 'Sure I'm hungry. Aren't we all?'

Ivan knew what his father meant by this, but for once he wasn't talking about that deep-seated longing to fill his belly with a feast. It had been a while since lunch. That was all. A cheeseburger and a shake would bridge the gap, which is what Ivan had assumed they had pulled in to purchase.

'This joint is a real low-budget number,' he pointed out all the same. 'People come here because the burgers are dirt cheap. That's if you can call them burgers at all. We'd be better off at the chicken wing joint two blocks up. At least with a wing you know what meat is on the bone.'

Titus responded by sitting up in his seat, his focus fixed on the main doors to the restaurant.

'How about that one?' he asked.

Ivan followed his line of sight to see a man waddle out in a pair of wraparound shades and flips-flops. With every step, his shirt buttons over his belly strained at the seams. He was munching on a takeout as he headed for his car, having simply scrunched open the wrapper to get to it.

'Really?' The boy faced his father side-on. 'Do you want fries with that as well?'

'Or her?'

When Ivan turned to see another overweight customer squeeze out of the restaurant, he realised what was going on here.

'Dad, this isn't hunting. It's convenience food.'

Titus shrugged.

'I promised your mother.'

Ivan looked back at the man, who by now was struggling into his car with the burger clenched between his teeth.

'But this stuff is supersized!' the boy complained. 'Even you've admitted that the cholesterol and fat content in the meat we've been eating lately can't be good for us. Imagine the junk these guys contain! You're looking at a heart attack waiting to happen here. Besides, after all the effort you've put into working out lately, a blowout like this would only put you right back at square one.'

As the silence between them thickened and stewed, a kid hauled himself out from the restaurant to catch up with the woman. Through Ivan's eyes, any exercise was better than nothing for a junior carrying more pounds than most. It still didn't whet his appetite, though.

'I won't take out a tenant,' Titus told him abruptly. 'Unless they're trouble, it just wouldn't be right.'

'Whereas the obese are fair game when all else fails? Especially the impoverished with nothing to lose, right?'

When his father sighed to himself, Ivan knew that he'd called him out.

'I just didn't want to make it difficult.' Titus tipped his head back against the seat rest and then turned to face his son directly. 'With nothing on offer at the condo, this seemed like a good place for you to start.'

'Me?' Ivan touched his chest with one hand. For a second, he considered confessing to the sophisticated strategy he'd put in place to punish his school tormentors. Then he figured there was a chance his dad would want to know details, and he couldn't risk the interference when everything was going to plan. 'It's cool that you're ready to let me do the honours,' the boy said instead, 'but I can do better than this. I'm not a kid any more. I'm fifteen years old. Even Katya could round up one of these human doughnuts.'

Titus tried hard not to smile.

'I feel bad for bringing you here now,' he said, and then gestured towards his suggested targets. 'At least these guys can live to eat another day.'

Ivan looked hard into his father's eyes. He shared the same intensity of focus and Arctic-blue colouring, and yet what he had to say would mark them out to be very different in outlook at that moment.

'When I was little, Dad, you didn't spare a thought for someone's feelings in selecting them for a feast. Something's changed with you. It's as if you've gone soft, and not just in the belly. Ever since you got sweet-talked into opening that vegan café . . . it's awakened something weird in you. What do they call it?'

'A conscience?' Titus turned to face the restaurant doors again. 'Maybe it comes to us all eventually.'

Ivan didn't answer. His father began to fiddle with his keys again.

'So, what are we going to tell Mum?' Ivan asked quietly.

Finally, and somewhat decisively, Titus slotted the key back into the ignition.

'We're going to tell her to prepare for one of the finest feasts ever to grace the table,' he said, and brought the engine to life with a roar. 'The meat is going to be truly special. I promise you, it'll be worth the wait.'

31

'Excuse me?' Amanda Dias stood before the customer who had summoned her to the corner table. The man held a menu in his hands. He was reading it so closely that all she could see of him was a sweep of hair, pushed back over the crown of his head and trimmed neatly at the sides. The primitive black tattoos on his knuckles also caught her attention, which looked scratched in by a pin. 'Could you repeat that order, please?'

'I said,' the man replied, slowly and deliberately in a voice that bordered on a growl, 'do you cater for real meat eaters?' He lowered his menu on delivering the question and flashed a smile at her.

Amanda had heard him correctly the first time. It was the sight of the grater-like grills encasing his upper and lower teeth that told her exactly who she was facing here.

'This is a vegan establishment,' she said, struggling to keep the shock out of her voice and suppress any hint that she recognised the man. 'You'll find plenty of rib restaurants in town.'

Nikolai Zolotov continued to peer up at Amanda. His face was creased and weathered, as if it had been exposed to harsh winds, and his skin appeared closely moulded to his skull.

'I'm joking with you,' he said, in what she recognised now to be a Russian accent. 'But I am interested in learning more about the business.' He stopped there and extended his hand.

'I know who you are,' said Amanda, dropping the pretence in his surprisingly gentle grip. 'When someone threatens me and the family I live with, Mr Zolotov, I don't forget in a hurry.'

Another smile stretched across Zolotov's face. He ran a hand through his hair, exposing sharply receded temples.

'I apologise for any distress that may have caused,' he told her, 'but as a business incentive, it worked.' Nikolai gestured at their surroundings. 'This is far more rewarding than some crappy bar, don't you think? It brings in a much bigger cash turnover, too.'

By now, Amanda had regained a grip on her composure. Seeing the man in the flesh had come as a shock, but now that he was talking he came across as someone who was all bark and no bite. Glancing over her shoulder to see the cop leaving with his free coffee, she took a seat across from him and rested her elbows on the table.

'Something tells me you didn't travel halfway round the world just to toast our success.'

'Of course not.' Zolotov leaned back in his chair and admired the view through the window for a moment. He was wearing a smart suit, open at the throat, which again revealed a hint of black tattoo work. Amanda figured it could only have been etched in a prison cell. When she realised she was staring, she looked up with a start to find him waiting for her full attention. 'I came to visit my nephew,' he continued. 'Rolan had offered to show me the sights, but since he lost his job when the bar shut down, he's busy seeking new employment. No doubt Lev and Kiril will act as my tour guides, but I'd like to do something to help out my boy, which is where you come in.' Zolotov leaned in closer. Raising his eyebrows, shot through with grey, like his hair, he pulled back his lips to reveal just a hint of metal. 'What do you say, Miss Dias?'

Amanda only had to picture Rolan's face to be sure she never wanted to see him again.

'We're fully staffed,' she told him.

'Oh, not in this fine establishment.' Zolotov held her gaze for a moment, as if what he had to say next was evident. 'I'm talking about the first of the new places. Fully funded by me, managed by you, and with someone running the show we both trust. I think you know who I'm talking about, right?'

The café door opened just then. Amanda glanced across at it, before returning her attention to Zolotov.

'When Lev and Kiril first passed on your request,' she said, 'we made it quite clear that we weren't interested in building a food empire. The bigger we grow, the more compromises we have to make with the food on offer here. You can leave that to the fast food chains and the supermarket giants. Perhaps our response was lost in translation.'

'Maybe.' Zolotov shrugged. 'So, why don't I ask you again nicely, right here, so there's no room for misunderstanding?'

'Oh, it's not for me to say.' Amanda smiled, matching his expression, and then gestured at the bald-domed man who had just walked into the café with his son in tow. 'You'd have to ask the boss.'

Ivan slipped into the café restroom with a purpose. Having spent the afternoon on a hunting trip that had revealed a great deal about his dad, he was determined not to let any kind of compassion get in the way of his own personal project. Bryce, Chad and Ryan didn't deserve his forgiveness. What Ivan planned to give them instead was a post-match sandwich that would slowly eat them up from the inside out. It was his father who had wanted to drop in here on the way home, just to check that Amanda was coping with the late-afternoon crowd. He was losing it, the boy reflected, as he climbed up onto the rim of the toilet and lifted the cistern lid. Finding the container with one hand, he smiled to himself before putting everything back in place. It wouldn't be long before it was time for him to assemble the sandwiches. By then, he guessed, those little larva cysts would be itching to get into his victims' guts so they could start their fantastic fatal voyage.

'We're good to go,' he muttered under his breath, as he unlocked the restroom door. Finding Amanda preparing to knock caused him to start and take a step back. 'Hey, can't a boy get some privacy?'

'He's here,' she hissed. 'I thought you'd seen him and were hoping to escape through the restroom window.'

'What?' Ivan felt stung at the suggestion that he'd act like a coward in any situation. Just then, however, he wasn't sure what he was supposed to be running away from. 'Who's here?'

'Do you see him?' Amanda gestured with her eyes to encourage him to look over her shoulder. 'That man in the corner with the metalwork in his mouth. It's him!'

'Zolotov?'

Still holding the restroom door handle when he said this, Ivan had to resist the urge to lock himself away.

'He's for real, Ivan. The cannibal criminal. Titus is talking to him right now, but I don't think he's going to be leaving unless he gets what he wants.'

Ivan considered this for a moment, wondering whether he would be expected to lend his support. Given how his father had become a little flabby around the edges lately, the boy felt a sudden sense of duty conflicting with his instinct to hide. He glanced at the figure in the corner one more time, no doubt listening to his dad drone on about how wonderful it was to be kind and charitable. When he turned back at Amanda, he found her looking a little tense and freaked.

'Let me speak to him,' he said, and gestured for her to step aside. 'Someone needs to tell this guy to back off.'

'That's not a good idea,' Amanda cautioned, but the boy was on a roll. Stepping out across the floor, he even found a hint of a swagger return to his stride. 'Ivan, you really should leave them to talk!'

The café was still bustling, but only one table commanded his attention. Ivan could just see the back of Zolotov's head from where he was standing. For all the stories about this guy eating hands and ears ripped from his victims, he just looked like someone who had come to discuss a business loan. Well, as his old man was clearly floundering, he would just have to take over. It was time to step up, he told himself, as he weaved between the tables. There came a time in every son's life when he had to take over from the father, and that moment had arrived. He sensed a power within him, drawn from his dad's failure to put food on the table and what he knew he would be feeding his three tormentors at school. Nikolai Zolotov might have earned a reputation for devouring his fellow prisoners during a spell in jail, but Ivan had been raised on human flesh since his first teeth had come through. Now *that* was hard core. The boy curled his hands into fists, wishing that the place was empty and the garrotte nested in his pocket. As it was, all he planned to do was ask nicely for Zolotov to leave the premises. If he refused, Ivan was ready to face him off. What was the guy going to do? Eat him alive in front of the customers?

'Sir,' he said, and tapped the man on the shoulder. 'Can I have a moment of your time?'

Ivan glanced at his father, who fell into shadow as the man rose to his feet

'Hello, Ivan.'

The boy was shocked to hear his own name, and rattled, too, as this lean-faced figure turned and loomed over him. Then Nikolai Zolotov broke into a grin and all the courage that had steered Ivan there evaporated. In that moment, it felt as if he had come face to face with a shark in human form, one whose jagged molars had been embellished with miniature plates of grating blades.

'Sorry to interrupt.' Ivan swallowed uncomfortably. 'I was wondering if I can get you a drink on the house. All our coffee is gluten free.'

32

Oleg Savage purposely steered clear of Priscilla after her return to the nursing home. He was deeply relieved to learn that she had made a good recovery from the scare that saw her rushed to the emergency room. According to Vince, she was still a very poorly lady, but that wasn't why he left her in peace.

She knew.

Lying in her hospital bed, with Oleg at her side, Priscilla had heard every word he'd said. When she'd opened her eyes, it was brutally apparent that she now believed his admission that cannibalism was the elixir he could offer her. It was a change in the way she looked at him. Something he had never seen in her gaze before. What he didn't know was what it meant.

Three days after she had been discharged from hospital, Oleg braved knocking on her door. If Priscilla had shared his secret with anyone else, he decided, the cops would've been all over the home by now and his family in custody. Oleg felt that at the very least it would be safe to speak to her.

'May I come in?' he asked, having heard no response. Oleg knew Priscilla was in her room. He had seen the nurse leave just moments earlier. 'You're quite safe,' he said to reassure her, before a quiet smile crossed his face. 'I've already eaten.'

'*Then by all means step inside.*'

Taking a breath, Oleg clicked open the door. Priscilla was propped up on pillows, strikingly pale behind a bed tray that supported her lunch. She held a teaspoon in one hand, which was poised over a bowl of soup.

'Smells good,' said Oleg, sniffing the air. 'Carrot and coriander?'

Priscilla nodded and set the spoon on the tray. 'Oxtail is usually my favourite,' she told him, looking directly into his eyes, 'but I'm off meat for now.'

Oleg felt his heart kick.

'May I sit down?' He gestured at the armchair beside her window.

'Go ahead. You look a little unwell yourself.'

'I'll be fine.' Oleg felt his bones creak as he eased himself into the chair. 'I've just been worried about you.'

Priscilla said nothing for a moment.

'Worried about my health,' she asked eventually, 'or what I might say?'

It was another fine day outside, but inside the heat was oppressive. Even though the residential home was fitted with a sophisticated air-con system, Oleg felt his shirt begin to stick to his back.

'I'm concerned about you,' he told her, 'just as I care very much for my family.'

'Everything you say right now feels like a threat.'

Oleg looked to the floor for a moment.

'Please don't think of me as a monster,' he asked. 'I would

never do anything to hurt you.'

Priscilla observed him warily, as if he were a dog and she wasn't yet sure if he'd bite.

'I let you into my life,' she told him. 'Into my *heart*.'

'It's all for love, Priscilla. Whatever happens, I want you to know that.'

Priscilla looked hard into his eyes, though she didn't look convinced.

'People do some terrible things in the name of love,' she said next. 'What you've admitted to is an atrocity, Oleg, and yet you speak of it as some kind of miracle food.'

'That's what it is,' he said with a shrug. 'I can't lie to you.'

'But these poor souls that you're . . . eating, they surely don't deserve –'

'Every feast is carefully sourced,' Oleg cut in. 'We don't just carve up anyone.'

'But they're still *people*,' Priscilla insisted. 'And eating people isn't right.'

Oleg rested his head against the back of the chair, preparing to explain.

'You know, what we do has a long history. It's a ceremonial custom among many ancient tribes. Take the Wari' from the rainforests of Brazil. Way back in time, when a loved one died, their body would be roasted and consumed by the family, friends and relatives as a way of mourning. They believed that it allowed the soul of the deceased to live on within them. Many might think that's gruesome. If you can just see beyond what are simply cultural values, however, you'll recognise that it's the *ultimate* act of love.'

241

For the first time since he'd sat down, Oleg saw her smile.

'What's wrong with your basic cremation?'

Oleg grinned despite himself. 'I like my meat cooked medium rare, not cindered.'

Priscilla chuckled, sounding like a hen before a scattering of seeds.

'Well, that's another thing we got in common,' she told him.

Oleg's expression brightened considerably.

'So you'll dine with us? It'll bring you a fresh lease of life. I guarantee it!'

In response, to his surprise, Priscilla dipped her spoon into her soup and took a mouthful. She closed her eyes, seemingly savouring the taste. Oleg looked on, perplexed.

'This is surprisingly good. You should try some. You really should.'

'Priscilla, I need to know. It's important for my family so they can be prepared.'

Priscilla looked as if she was about to scoop her spoon into the soup once more. She studied the bowl for a moment and then looked back across at Oleg.

'What you told me,' she said, 'about how those ancient people grieved.'

'The Wari'?'

Priscilla smiled, some colour in her cheeks at last.

'I liked that story.'

'This isn't going to end well for him,' was the first thing Angelica said when she learned about the café encounter with Nikolai Zolotov. She faced Titus directly, who was seated at the far

242

end of the kitchen table, and let her expression do the talking before she put it into words. 'I think it's safe to say we have a candidate for cooking. The man has caused us enough trouble, and no doubt you'd appreciate a taste of the old country.'

She watched her husband consider this for a moment. He often came home with treats from the Russian deli, such as cold meats and candies. Judging by the way he seemed to be turning things over in his mind, Angelica figured she'd soon have to think about how best to prepare a feast featuring cabbage, beetroot and cranberries.

'It's a nice idea,' said Titus eventually, 'but the man has a ruthless reputation as a killer. Lev and Kiril speak fearfully of him and his past in prison. As for his taste for human flesh, Angelica, let's not forget that Zolotov skips the cooking stage. I dare say I could take him on, but if I meet my match then it may not be Nikolai who ends up as a meal. It could be me. In the raw.'

With every reservation Titus gave, Angelica's sensed her sympathy for his position thinning. Ivan and Amanda sat on either side of the table, listening intently as they curled their forks into the spaghetti she had prepared for them: one with a bolognaise sauce, the other with organic garlic and chilli. Katya occupied the chair beside Angelica, close enough to be corrected every time she favoured using her fingers to feed herself.

'It's OK,' said Ivan. He waited until he had everyone's full attention. 'I'll do it.'

Amanda was the first to chuckle.

'I don't mean to be unkind,' she said, 'but you couldn't kill

243

a conversation.'

'Don't push me!' he snapped hotly. 'You'd be surprised at what I can do.'

'The only thing that really surprised me was how quickly you fixed Zolotov his latte.' Amanda laughed at the memory, before pausing to compose herself. 'Leave him to me,' she offered. 'I've been sharing your feasts for long enough. It's time I brought something to the table.'

'That's sweet of you,' said Angelica, 'but you're doing a fine job at the café. If there's a problem here,' she added, with a long look at her husband, 'I'll deal with it.'

'OK, stop right there.' Titus raised both palms over his bowl in surrender. 'I know what you're trying to tell me. I get it. But you're wrong. I can still provide for the family. I just think we'd be taking a big risk in attempting to serve up Zolotov.'

'It would be a challenge,' muttered Ivan, who was clearing his plate.

Angelica watched Titus hesitate, distracted by their son's comment, before clearing his throat.

'We should at least reason with him first,' he suggested.

'That didn't get you far in the café,' Amanda pointed out. 'I hardly think he's going to sit down at the table again and negotiate this with you. Either you kill him, or cave in to his demands.'

'There has to be another way,' insisted Titus. 'None of us wants to build a vegan empire or have anything more to do with his money. As the café is perfect cover for our lifestyle, I propose that we buy him out.'

Angelica blinked and sat back in her chair.

'Oh, Titus.'

'Give me a chance. Let me soften him up.'

Ivan glanced at Amanda.

'Isn't that what the meat tenderiser is for?' he whispered, only to shrink back into his chair when Titus glared at him.

'OK, so I could bring him back for the table, but do you honestly think a man like Zolotov is going to taste good? He's spent decades in a Russian gulag, surviving on uncooked body parts, gruel and turnips. You only have to look at him to see that he's carrying a lot of gristle, and that's not something I look forward to in a feast.' Titus paused for a moment, as if to calm himself down. 'There's one thing we don't do in this family, and that's kill and let the corpse go to waste.' Again, he stopped himself, but only because Ivan had shifted uncomfortably and scraped his chair in the process. 'We slaughter for food,' he said to finish, 'and that's where it ends.'

'Sounds like another excuse,' Amanda muttered while pulling the air between her teeth.

Angelica opened her mouth to reprimand their lodger, but she couldn't disagree. In her eyes, despite his reasoning, her husband really did appear to have lost his killer instinct. In the past, a man like Zolotov would've sealed his place on the menu by causing such upheaval. She had been married to Titus for long enough to know that he would never let the family down, but he was certainly testing her patience right now. Still, Angelica was well aware that Titus always looked to her for support.

'If you need to work on Zolotov then perhaps you should arrange to spend some time with him,' she suggested, and reached for her napkin. 'But if he still refuses to back off then promise me you'll do the right thing. Even if there isn't much meat on his bones, we could always use him for a broth.'

Titus collected his fork from the side of his plate. He glanced up at Angelica, this guiding force throughout his life, and then targeted his last meatball.

'These are good,' he said, and waved it in the air. 'Your best yet.'

As Titus popped the meatball into his mouth, Angelica noted a drop of tomato sauce fall upon his shirt. It was only a slight mark, well hidden by the garish colours of his tropical shirt. Even so, she knew it was there. No doubt it would be a stubborn stain to remove, but he could rely on her to deal with it.

Angelica just hoped that Titus would take care of the other matter with the same conviction.

33

Joaquín Mendez blamed Angelica for the fact that his eating habits had gone haywire. Essentially, she had now killed his appetite. As passion swelled in his heart, so his belly had just shut down. Every time he found himself feeling just a little hungry, he'd run into her once more and supper would be written off. It had reached the point where his colleagues at the gym were beginning to ask if everything was OK. Joaquín insisted that he was fine.

He also hated himself for it.

This was no state for a young man like him to be in. He hadn't come to this country to be eaten up by a woman who was completely out of bounds to him. In his role as a personal trainer, it was vital that he took on board enough carbohydrates and protein to power him through each day. Joaquín understood this. Love was no substitute for food, and yet it had become his driving force.

In a bid to keep starvation at bay, once or twice a week, when sleep evaded him, the young man took to calling up Round Da Clock Pizzas on the waterfront and ordered the eighteen-inch deep crust Feastzilla with extra anchovies. He never had any intention of eating such a giant delivery, and yet, somehow, as the hours ticked away in front of the cable talk-show repeats, Joaquín would wind up with an empty box. It never left him feeling good. Sometimes, the bloating and indigestion was worse than the guilt and self-loathing, neither of which helped when tasked with taking his clients through their paces.

When that client was Titus Savage, Joaquín considered it to be close to torture.

'You look as if you've lost a few pounds,' Titus told the troubled Argentinian later that week. 'If there's an alternative to working out, I'll do whatever it takes. Go on. Tell me your secret, Joaquín.'

Titus was lying on a bench press at the time. It was the final machine on the circuit, where he was preparing to pump weights the size of dinner plates. Joaquín avoided his eye, desperate not to give away the fact that his client's wife was responsible for him looking so hunted.

'You're shaping up nicely,' he said instead, and tentatively patted Titus on the belly. 'That looks like the beginning of a six-pack.'

Titus looked down the length of his torso, quietly pleased with himself.

'I haven't seen that for some time,' he said. 'Feels good.'

Relieved to have moved on from the subject of his own appearance, Joaquín circled the bench press and encouraged Titus to grip the bar above him.

'Nice and easy,' he told him. 'If it feels too much, just let it drop back on the support stand. You don't want to bite off

248

more than you can chew.'

Titus glanced at the young trainer.

'Tell that to my wife,' he muttered, which caused a chill to wash through Joaquín's veins. Every time Titus arrived for a workout he felt tense in his company. It wasn't quite so bad when they were jogging. Joaquín could stretch ahead to avoid eye contact and conversation. Here in the gym, it just felt suffocating, especially when Angelica came into the conversation.

'Problems at home?' he dared to venture.

'The café.' Titus grasped the bar. 'Our backer is in town. He's a little determined with his plans for the business. Angelica and I disagree about how to deal with him. She feels a meeting would be fruitless, but I'll figure something out.'

Joaquín watched carefully as Titus took a deep breath and tightened his grip on the bar. Then, as his face turned red and began to quiver, he inched the weights upwards.

'You could take him for a trip on your boat,' the young trainer suggested. 'That nice one with the cover down by your jetty.'

Joaquín hadn't intended to distract his client. Nor had he expected to see him practically drop the weights back onto the rack.

'What was that?'

'Oh, nothing.' Immediately, Joaquín realised that the only way he could know that Titus had a small vessel under tarpaulin was if he'd been scoping out the family villa from the other side of the inlet. He drew breath to make some excuses, but by then Titus was sitting upright on the bench.

'Joaquín,' he said finally, seemingly unaware that the young man now stood before him like an infant bunny in the headlights of a big rig truck. 'That's a *terrific* idea!'

'Really?'

'What better way to bond with someone here than by taking to the water?' Titus focused on some imaginary spot just above the young trainer. 'I could head upriver with him for some creek fishing,' he continued, and began nodding to himself. 'That would give us plenty of time to talk and nobody would even know we were there.'

Joaquín couldn't be sure what Titus had in mind at that moment. He just knew that he was crumbling under the pressure of being this close to someone whose wife had come to possess him.

'Do you want to try a couple less kilos?' he asked his client, desperate to move on.

Joaquín Mendez took a step back when Titus rose from the bench, and then another when his client faced him looking ponderous and brooding.

'I don't think I ever mentioned that I owned an outboard, did I?'

This time, Joaquín retreated by a further step and banged his head on a power rack. The blow caused him to gasp and wince. Titus didn't even blink. If his question was one asked out of curiosity, Joaquín's response now summoned an air of suspicion from the man.

'Just a guess,' he offered weakly. 'Jupiter is a popular place for boat owners.'

As his voice trailed away, the thumping beats playing over the sound system also seemed to fade, along with the rhythmic slide and creak of the gym equipment surrounding them. Even the floor seemed to tip to one side as Titus intensified his gaze. For a moment, Joaquín thought he might cry. He was still reeling from the blow to the back of his skull, but this was all too much.

'Well, you guessed right,' said Titus eventually, who blinked and shrugged. 'And it would be good to get the outboard engine running. I just never find the time.'

Joaquín should've felt only relief that this moment had passed. Instead, he found he just couldn't hold out any longer. Half-starved and overwhelmed by the force of his conflicting feelings, he placed one hand on the crown of his head and stumbled into a confession.

'I've seen your boat many times,' he said, his resolve all but crushed. 'From the opposite shore, when I stop to look across at your villa in the hope of seeing . . . *her*.'

Titus tipped his head to one side. He looked perplexed, as if this was the last thing he had expected to hear, and yet also the most likely. Joaquín swallowed uncomfortably. Opening up like that hadn't come as a release, he acknowledged to himself with a start. If anything, it just invited the possibility that his emotional pain was about to become physical.

'Well, frankly I'm not surprised,' growled Titus after a moment. 'Amanda is a good-looking young woman.'

It took a second for Joaquín to process the name, and another to realise that this was his one chance to slide out of the most stupid thing he had ever done.

'She is,' he said, and tried hard not to sound relieved. 'She really is.'

'Want me to make an introduction?' asked Titus. 'Miss Dias can be a little intense, but if you take all the preaching with a pinch of salt, you'll find a soft centre on the inside.'

'Sure,' said Joaquín, who didn't mean to sound so hesitant. If he had to spend an evening out with the man's lodger, it was better than being flayed alive for confessing he was in love with his wife. 'That would be good, Titus. Thank you.'

'No, thank *you!*' he countered, and reached for the towel he had slung over the machine to mop his brow. 'Now, if you'll excuse me, I have plans to make for a little boat trip.'

Ivan had come a long way in recent years. That was his view on the eve of the football match. He had left the practical jokes behind, grudgingly conceding that people didn't find them funny if it meant a trip to the emergency ward. Instead, the boy had turned his attention to the fine art of food poisoning, specialising in fatal strains, and soon his tormentors would know how it felt to taste payback. What's more, it seemed Ivan's father had finally acknowledged that he was ready to provide for the table. It was just a shame, he thought, that his offer to deal with Nikolai Zolotov hadn't been welcomed. OK, so the man's metal molars had taken Ivan aback when he first faced him, but now he'd had a chance to recover his composure, it was time to step up to the plate. Maybe not the dinner plate, if his dad was right about Zolotov carrying a little too much cartilage, but he'd make sure the man was no longer a problem. Well aware that his family would fear the worst outcome for Ivan, the boy shared his intentions with just one individual. A kindred spirit he considered to be his listening ear.

252

'If only they knew what I could do,' he muttered at Tinky Dinks on the walk home from the café. 'Soon they'll see that I can be trusted to get the job done.'

Ivan was clutching his school bag to his chest. With the zipper open, his adopted gerbil was able to pop its head out from time to time to take in their surroundings. It had been a breezy day, but the turn of the tide saw the palms stop swaying. Now, as the sun settled over Jupiter, Ivan's thoughts turned to his plan for the weekend. He glanced down at the bag, not to check on the gerbil, but to be sure the package in silver foil was still safe in the side pocket. Earlier, on completing his cleaning duties in the kitchen, Ivan had set about assembling his sandwiches. It was to be the final part of the preparation process, and he had carried it out with great reverence.

First, he'd carved the bread slices from a loaf baked freshly that day. Next, he applied a coat of mayonnaise. He'd had to pick up a pot from the grocery store, because the vegan variety in the fridge was egg free and he couldn't afford for Bryce, Ryan or Chad to grimace with their first mouthful. The boy had also considered chopping up some lettuce, but figured that kind of food was too feminine for his targets. Instead, he'd opted for gherkins. The next step had required him to don disposable gloves. Using a pair of tongs and a knife, Ivan had carefully lifted a slice of his precious ham into each sandwich. Having undertaken a deliberately amateur curing process on meat sourced with malice, and with no modern-day methods to make it fit for human consumption, he had every confidence in his product. It had to be riddled with larval cysts, the boy assured himself; each one primed to go off like

253

a foodborne grenade. Finally, having snapped off the gloves, he closed the sandwiches and stood back to admire his hard work. They looked good, in his opinion. Generously filled for hungry young men after a match. The three jocks would not be able to resist. Despite the fact that it would condemn them to a progressively horrible death, Ivan wanted them to think of it as a post-game snack they would never forget.

It was only disappointing, Ivan thought as he crossed the bridge, that he couldn't ask them what they'd like to go with it. Some deep-fried chicken nuggets, perhaps? A giant strawberry shake, peach pie and thirty-seven chocolate bars? Wasn't that the kind of thing prisoners on Death Row requested for their final meals? What the trio faced was pretty much the same thing, the boy decided. Then again, after the misery they had caused him, he didn't think they deserved the privilege.

Ivan was so lost in thought that at first he didn't pay any attention to the sound of the car slowing behind him. With the late sun on his back, flaring against the windows of the riverside villas that lined the other side of the water, he continued to ponder the fate of his tormentors. Then the vehicle's horn sounded, causing him to spin around.

'Want a ride home?'

Nikolai Zolotov drew up alongside the boy in an emerald-green Chevy Spark. The little two-door hatchback was a surprising choice of rental for a man with his reputation. He would've placed him in a muscle car, not a run-around. In fact, Ivan might not have recognised him at all, given the dark glasses he was wearing. It was only the smile he flashed him that left the boy in no doubt as to who had just pulled up here.

'I'm good,' he said, clutching his bag protectively.

'Jump in,' insisted Zolotov, gesturing at the passenger seat. 'What's the worst that could happen?'

Facing the man once again, Ivan felt his stomach shrink in fear. He had to be joking, judging by the grin on his face, but something told the boy to stay on the sidewalk. Yes, he'd had it drummed into him from an early age that there were strangers out there who might want to interfere with him. In this case, he just didn't want to get eaten.

'I'd really rather walk,' he said quietly.

'Get in the car, Ivan.'

'Yes, sir.'

34

Sometimes Angelica Savage felt as if she spent more time at the supermarket than she did at home. Despite carefully planning the weekly shop, there was always something else to pick up each day. That afternoon, having discovered an empty bread bin, she bundled Katya into the car and set out to pick up a loaf.

'Mommy,' little Katya piped up on the way there, 'are we getting ready for a feast?'

Angelica glanced in the rear-view mirror, her lips pressed together disapprovingly.

'Not yet, I'm afraid,' she said. 'Your father's had some issues sourcing the ingredients, but it won't be long now. Are you hungry, honey?'

Katya nodded at her in the mirror. She was wearing red bows in her hair that matched her dress, along with white tights and shoes with silver buckles. Despite her rosy cheeks, Angelica couldn't help thinking she looked in need of some nourishment.

'Mom?'

Angelica reminded herself not to snap. Continually criticising the child for her accent couldn't be good for her self-esteem. She just hoped that eventually the influence of her family would win out.

'What is it?' she asked her daughter.

'When can we just buy someone to eat from the store?'

Smiling to herself, Angelica made a note to share the observation with Titus.

'Not in our lifetime,' she told her daughter. 'Once the human race wakes up to the benefits of eating its own kind, you can be sure to find the shelves filled with bodies on polystyrene trays, shrink-wrapped and stamped with a best-before date.'

'Yum.'

'Oh, I'm not so sure,' said Angelica, and slowed for a scooter. 'When food becomes big business it can leave a bad taste in the mouth. I dare say the meat would be cheap, but also somewhat tasteless. Plus we'd have no idea where that person came from. I'm not sure I want to eat someone if there's a risk of horse content or contamination by veterinary drugs. In fact, when you think about it like that, Katya, let's hope society *doesn't* develop an appetite for itself any time soon.'

'Daddy says that good things come to those who wait.'

Angelica glanced in the mirror. She hadn't expected her daughter to comprehend something so central to the family's values at her age, and so Katya's response earned her a smile.

'Let's hope so,' Angelica told her. She slowed a little on seeing a cop car coming the other way. 'Though if Daddy makes us hold out for much longer then your brother might do something about it.'

It was the change in tone that persuaded Ivan Savage to hurry around to the passenger door of the Chevy Spark. Zolotov hadn't sounded threatening, just insistent, but it was entirely reinforced by a glint of sunlight on all that metalwork in his mouth.

'You can dump your bag on the back seat,' he told the boy, before easing the vehicle away.

Pretending not to hear, Ivan reached for his seat belt instead. He was too frightened to insist that the bag should remain on his lap. Even with the car's air con set to maximum, he suddenly felt hot and claustrophobic.

'So, how was your day?' the boy asked while looking straight ahead.

'It can only get better,' replied the Russian. 'Lev and Kiril took me for a round of golf. Man alive, that game is dull! No wonder it hasn't taken off back home. Those pussies had to get home for their suppers, so I figured I'd take a drive. Hired a car that won't attract me any attention and took to the road. Now, where is good to eat around here, my friend? I'm famished.'

Ivan clutched his school bag tightly. To find himself hitching a ride with Nikolai Zolotov had come as a complete surprise. The fact that the man was being so nice just made it all the more unsettling.

'It depends what you like.'

Zolotov smiled to himself.

'What do you know about me?' he asked.

Ivan glanced sideways at the man. Just then, he was equally worried about what Zolotov knew about him and his family.

'I heard you like your meat raw,' he said delicately.

'You heard right,' said Zolotov, and thumped his chest once. 'You're looking at the cannibal criminal.'

The boy couldn't actually remember when he'd first tasted human flesh. A third birthday, perhaps. Something like that. What was imprinted on his memory was his father's repeated warning never to mention it outside the family. Ivan had also been encouraged to steer well clear of using the 'C' word. Hearing it now didn't leave him feeling any kind of connection with Zolotov. His mother was good at serving up a couple of ribbon cuts as sushi, but wolfing down uncooked body parts just sounded gross and nothing to boast about. Still, Ivan was aware that Zolotov was simply looking for a reaction here.

'Wow,' he said after a moment, though all he could think was: *big deal*.

Zolotov glanced across at him.

'Are you not worried about your safety?'

'Yes, but you're driving right now.'

Zolotov chuckled and then nodded, as if he couldn't argue with that.

'Relax, kid. I've no plans to eat you. I was locked up in a labour camp the last time, way out in Siberia. Discovered my cellmate had been paid to murder me, so I took action first.' Zolotov shot a look at the boy, as if to check he had his full attention. 'I hacked off his ear and ate it in front of him.'

Ivan responded by telling Zolotov that they needed to go straight across at the next junction. Just then he couldn't wait to get back to the protective bosom of his family. Whether the guy was trying to show off here or scare him, Ivan didn't feel at all comfortable. Even Tinky Dinks had vanished from sight inside his bag. Then, as he felt the gerbil wriggling inside, an idea came to the boy's mind that promised to solve a lot of problems. He glanced across at Zolotov, noting the tattoo ink just visible behind his shirt collar.

'If you're hungry, I have some ham sandwiches.' Ivan cleared his throat. 'They're freshly made.'

'At the café?'

'Don't tell Amanda.'

Zolotov laughed, throwing his head back in a way that alarmed the boy. Not least because he took his eyes right off the road.

'I like you, kid. You must have some big *yaytsas*, no?'

With his heart rate rising, Ivan opened the side pocket of his bag and removed the foil-clad package. With each baited sandwich cut in two, and until that moment just three victims in mind, he felt sure that he could afford to sacrifice a segment.

'I'm helping to serve refreshments at a football match tomorrow, but you're welcome to take one.'

Nikolai Zolotov looked across at him, back at the road, and then returned to meet his eyes.

'I'll last until supper,' he said, 'but thanks anyway.'

'Consider it a snack.' Ivan peeled back the foil at the corner. 'It would be rude to let a guest in this town go hungry.'

Zolotov chuckled to himself.

'You're quite the host, huh? Just like your father.'

'Go ahead. Take one.'

Zolotov pulled up as the lights turned red at the next block and then casually reached into the package. Ivan watched him take half a sandwich, sliced diagonally and with the crusts intact. Without taking his eyes off the lights, the Russian opened his mouth and took a bite right out of the middle. It left a jagged crescent through the layers of bread, meat, gherkins and mayo. Zolotov chewed for a moment, seemingly switching the mouthful from one side of his jaw to the other, and then his face contorted.

'Oh, man, what's in this?'

Ivan flinched at the sight of shredded ham and bread snagged in among the man's grills. Nikolai Zolotov was facing him, awaiting an answer with the remains of his sandwich in one hand. It was only the sound of a car horn behind that prompted him to notice that the lights had turned green. As the Spark moved off, after Zolotov had leaned out of the window and threatened to make mincemeat out of the other driver, Ivan realised he had missed his chance to throw open the door and bail.

'It is good?' he asked helplessly.

'Good?' Zolotov shifted up a gear. 'It's *incredible!*'

'Really?'

Ivan tried hard not to sound as flabbergasted as he felt. The man had actually taken a sandwich, loaded with a killer pathogen, and actually enjoyed his first mouthful. It boded well for his intended victims, but this was still a bonus he hadn't foreseen.

'It's so rich and salty, set off nicely by the creamy mayo.' Zolotov stuffed the rest of the sandwich into his mouth, followed a gesture from Ivan to hang left and then asked for another.

'We're nearly there.' Unwilling to sacrifice any more, Ivan scrunched up the package, stowed it in the bag and pointed out the turning for the inlet road. 'This is me.'

Zolotov switched on the indicator and sighed. Ivan dared to glance across at him. The man was picking at his teeth with one hand.

'Well, I guess you've kept the wolves at bay,' he said, pinching a strand of meat from the metalwork inside his mouth. 'I wouldn't want to deprive your players of a snack like that.'

'Oh, they've earned it,' said Ivan, who figured it didn't matter if the man knew where the sandwiches were heading. He could expect to feel a little off colour in the next day or so, as the larvae migrated into his system, but it wouldn't floor him. The serious business, like the tremors and the fits, came later. With at least thirty days ahead before he showed any signs that a deadly worm had invaded his nervous system, there was no way it could be traced back to him. Ivan calculated that Zolotov would consume something like another ninety meals before he'd feel the need to seek medical attention, and by then he'd be home in Russia. Effectively, this eradicated any culinary footprints back to the boy. As Zolotov followed the gentle curve of the road, passing mailboxes and close-clipped lawns, Ivan spotted his mother in the drive. She was unloading the groceries from her car with little Kat. His first instinct was to ask Zolotov to keep driving, but by then it was too late.

'Someone's been to the supermarket,' he said. 'It must be good to come back to home cooking.'

Ivan knew full well what the man was hinting at here. Having just fatally poisoned him, the boy felt a strange duty of care.

'I'm sure there'll be enough food for one more,' he said, as Angelica noticed the car slowing down. 'You'd be welcome to join us for supper.'

'I can't think of anything better.' Zolotov cranked up the handbrake, grinning broadly at the woman who had twisted around and was now glaring directly into the car. 'Once your mother gets to know me,' he said, 'I'll have her eating out of my hand.'

35

When Oleg arrived at the villa and found the hire car parked outside, his first thought was that Titus had finally delivered. Since they'd moved here, it was a rare thing for the family to have a guest at the table. Usually, they ended up on it.

'Good boy,' he muttered to himself. 'I knew you wouldn't let us down.'

For a moment, he considered performing a half-circle on his scooter and zipping back to the home to fetch Priscilla. She would be ready, he told himself. He had prepared her for the best and worst of what a feast involved. Just as he turned the handlebars, however, the front door opened and his granddaughter skipped out to greet him.

'Guess what's for supper,' said Kat, reaching up on her tiptoes for a kiss. Oleg's beard always tickled her, which meant he never actually planted his lips on her cheek. 'Steak!'

Oleg had just placed his scooter into park mode. Hearing this, he grasped the ignition key once more, with Priscilla in mind, only for the lodger to appear at the door.

'*Beef* steak,' she said, to clarify. 'The alternative is eggplant and polenta casserole, which I made this morning.'

Oleg knew that Amanda always made provisions for herself at mealtimes. The only exception was in preparation for a feast, when she helped Angelica with passion and gusto.

'I'll pass on the polenta.' Easing himself from the scooter, the old man gestured at the hire car. 'I got my hopes up there for a moment.'

'Same for me when I got back from work.' Amanda glanced over her shoulder, and then stepped out into the late sunshine. 'Then I found out who was joining us for supper and lost my appetite a little.'

Oleg responded with a puzzled expression, before following the two girls inside.

Titus had told him all about Nikolai Zolotov. He recognised the man just as soon as he rose from the table to shake his hand.

'Is this business or pleasure?' asked Oleg, who took note of their guest's teeth but offered no hint of surprise or shock.

'Both,' said Zolotov. 'Doing something you love for a living means never having to work again. Isn't that right, Amanda?'

Amanda took her seat beside Ivan, who was watching their guest closely.

'If you mean the vegan café,' she said, inspecting the food on her plate, 'then yes, it's a pleasure to be there.'

'So double the pleasure and open another one. Hell, open three! I can fund them.'

Titus crossed the kitchen with the first of the plates just then. Angelica had prepared the meal Mexican-style. It was a dish that involved marinating the meat in lime and pepper, before flash frying it to seal the flavours and serving it up with a freshly chopped salsa. As ever, Oleg's would arrive in liquidised form. The old man watched Angelica fire up the food processor. Even with her back turned away from the table, he could tell that she was listening closely.

'The simple fact is that expanding the business goes against Amanda's principles,' said Titus, serving their guest first. 'Now, I propose that we let everyone enjoy their meal and we'll discuss the matter later.'

'Agreed.' Zolotov sat with his hands in his lap and watched as Titus served Oleg and then little Katya. He caught her eye across the table and smiled. 'Such a cutie,' he observed. 'Good enough to eat.'

Oleg only had to see Titus falter as he collected the next plates to know the comment carried a message. That Angelica seemed to freeze just confirmed it. Even Amanda tensed in the neck. Only Ivan looked relaxed, and continued to stare with interest at the visitor. Aware of the thickening silence, Oleg reached for his glass and raised it over his plate.

'*Za vashe zdorovie*,' he said, addressing Zolotov. 'Your good health, and may your visit to Florida be pleasant . . . and peaceful.'

Zolotov lifted his own glass with a small smile.

'Then let's hope everyone does the right thing.'

By now, Titus and Angelica had taken their seats at opposite ends of the table. Oleg noted them exchange a look as they gathered their knives and forks. It was certainly conspiratorial, but there was a problem with this guy if they planned to slaughter him for his flesh. As soon as the old man set eyes on Zolotov, his taste buds failed to trigger. Plainly, the guy was tough-looking, and not the first choice for the table. Even so, judging by the atmosphere he had brought with him, on top of his unwanted proposition for the café, Oleg figured the family might just have to make an exception here. Back in the day, living under siege, he had grown used to eating whatever flesh he could find. Nobody was entirely inedible in his view. It was just a question of being creative with the cooking. With this in mind, the old man began to slurp through his straw in the belief that their guest would be history by the time dessert was served.

'So, what do you make of Jupiter?' asked Titus, as he sliced into the steak.

'Lot of rib restaurants and a lack of lap-dancing clubs.' Zolotov spoke with his mouth full. 'Apart from that, I believe I like it for the same reason as you guys.'

'Why is that?' asked Angelica, who sounded to Oleg as if she was forcing herself to join the conversation.

Zolotov sat back in his seat and swallowed noisily. 'It's quiet. Tucked away from the hustle and bustle of the big city. The kind of place', he said to finish, and looked around the table, 'where people could get away with murder.'

'Well, it's home to us,' said Titus calmly. 'But unless you've explored the town by her waterways then you've hardly scratched the surface.'

'There sure is a lot of water.' Nikolai Zolotov reached for his glass.

'Which is why we own a boat,' said Titus.

Once again, Oleg noticed him share a look with Angelica. It was just a glance, a lifting of the brow, but enough to cause the old man to choke as he drew his supper through a straw.

'Excuse me,' he said, having spluttered into his napkin. 'Something just went down the wrong way.'

Angelica was loading the dishwasher with Amanda when Ivan returned from the Fallen Pine. He had accompanied his grandfather home, and came back looking unusually upbeat.

'What's wrong?' she asked her son, a note of worry in her voice. Whenever Ivan was anything other than sullen or quiet, she immediately concluded that something bad was about to happen.

'Everything is cool.' Ivan picked at what was left of the cheesecake on the side.

Angelica glanced across at Amanda.

'Did you see Grandpa back to his room?' she asked. 'He's not stuck in traffic with a flat battery or anything?'

Ivan looked hurt at the very suggestion.

'He's fine,' he said, 'although I was tempted to turn around when he started going on about Priscilla all over again. Mum, if she does come to eat with us can we slip him something to calm him down?'

'They're sweet together,' Amanda cut in. 'Like little kids.'

Ivan shivered to himself and appealed to his mother once more.

'At least make sure they sit apart from one another.'

Angelica looked a little mystified for a moment, only for her attention to return to the dishwasher as Amanda went back to slotting plates into the rack.

'Priscilla will dine with us in due course,' she told her son, 'but don't bother your father about that now. He's out on the jetty preparing the boat for tomorrow.'

Earlier, at the table, the family had slowed their eating when Titus invited their supper guest to join him on a trip upriver. He had sold it to the man as the best way to get a flavour of the town and its surroundings, as well as an opportunity to discuss the business matter at hand. When Nikolai Zolotov took up the offer, claiming it would beat another round of golf, Angelica was the first to go back to her plate with a smile on her face. At the same time, she noticed Ivan silently but urgently attempting to interrupt his father as he outlined the wildlife they could expect to see. Whatever he wanted could wait, she had told him crossly, and reminded him of his table manners. Now, at the very mention of the trip once more, Ivan stood before his mother and Amanda with his chest puffed out proudly.

'There's no need for a boat trip,' he told them. 'I've already dealt with the guy.'

Angelica succeeded in covering her amusement by tightening her lips. Unlike Amanda, who chuckled and rolled her eyes.

'Ivan,' she said, 'you can't kill someone by creeping them out.'

'I'm not joking,' he protested.

'Your time will come,' Angelica told him. 'Until then, leave this to your father. We can't afford to make mistakes with a man like Zolotov.'

'But I –'

'If you want to make yourself useful,' Angelica cut in, knowing that he'd only be a nuisance down at the jetty, 'go and make sure that Katya is in her pyjamas and not parading around in her angel wings.'

When Ivan dared to glare at his mother, all she had to do was return the gesture to persuade him to leave the kitchen.

'I'm telling you, he'll soon be worm food,' the boy muttered, but by then Angelica and Amanda were focused on finishing the dishes.

'He's just frustrated,' said Angelica, as Ivan slammed the door behind him. 'A feast would lift everyone's spirits.'

'So, when is Titus going to deliver?' Amanda found a cloth to wipe down the table.

Angelica plugged a tab into the dishwasher.

'Have faith,' she told him. 'His sole aim in life is to take care of the family.'

'You can say that again.' Amanda crossed to the table. 'He's set me up on a date with that personal trainer you guys have been using.'

'Joaquín?' Angelica froze for a second, and then considered what this meant. 'Well, I think that's a wonderful idea,' she said, before nodding to herself. 'He's a passionate individual, just as you are. It could be the perfect match.'

'He is kind of hot for a carnivore.' Amanda blushed and balled the cloth in her hand. 'Let's hope he sees the light.'

THIRD COURSE

36

As the sun climbed over Jupiter the next morning, and egrets fed on shrimp in the shallows, Titus Savage hauled anchor on a boat he had barely used. He'd unfurled the pilot's canopy the evening before, dusted down his fishing rods, filled the bait box and finally made room for the picnic basket that Angelica had just handed over to him. It should have felt good stepping on board for a day on the water. A chance to relax at last. That had been his intention when he'd purchased the vessel, only for the demands of family life to keep him away from it. On this occasion, however, the trip was wholly business, not pleasure.

'She's a good woman, your wife,' observed Zolotov, as Titus waved goodbye to Angelica and little Katya on the jetty. He was seated at the boat's aft with his arms spread wide. 'Traditional.'

Unlike Titus, who was wearing a colourful Hawaiian shirt, cargo shorts and deck shoes, his passenger looked as if he was being ferried to a funeral. The only thing missing was a black tie and a mournful expression. Instead, the man kept grinning at him.

'We have our values.' Titus was perched on the cockpit seat

in the centre of the hull. He tightened his grip on the wheel and steered the boat parallel with the shoreline. 'We also treat each other with respect.'

'That's good to hear.' Zolotov was wearing tinted shades that glinted like his teeth. He ran a hand through his hair, pushing it back at the temples. 'It would be a shame if something were to happen to them.'

Titus didn't answer. He understood the threat, which was why they were heading upriver. If Zolotov refused to back down with his plans for the café expansion then the stretch was secluded enough to dispose of him without witnesses.

At least, that was the plan until two unexpected passengers had joined them.

'Everything will work out just fine.' Lev was sitting upon the gunwale to his starboard. Like Titus, he wore a tropical shirt, only his was unbuttoned to the belly. He had already worked up quite a sweat under the sun, which left his face glistening.

'Titus will see sense. Isn't that right, skipper?'

Kiril sat opposite, also dressed colourfully, and was in the process of applying sunscreen to his long, bony arms. He looked to Titus, who simply flared his nostrils in response. The pair had claimed they didn't want to miss out on the fun. As soon as they had let themselves through the villa's side gate, however, it was plain to Titus that they wanted to come aboard to be sure he would bow to Zolotov's demands. He only had to see them glance nervously at the man to confirm that they were terrified of him.

'I always do the right thing,' he assured them, and looked over his shoulder. Zolotov had dipped one hand into the water, watching the disturbance it created. With a sigh, Titus steered the boat towards deeper channels.

The Loxahatchee River was a branching ribbon of water flanked by cypress trees and thick, tropical vegetation. It was also home to a lot of alligators, as Titus warned Zolotov one mile into their journey.

'You really should stop trailing your hand back there,' he told him. 'That's if you want to keep it. They can get big and bad upstream, and I dare say their blood is colder.'

'Nothing scares me.' Zolotov flashed a grin at him. 'I bite back, remember?'

They had left the last villa behind some time ago. As the waterway began to narrow, Titus slowed the boat. Having taken the northwest fork, the river here was punctured by knuckles of tree roots and dotted with lily pads. Storks watched them pass from their outposts in the mangroves, an eagle circled in the thermals overhead and from time to time a sudden splash would remind Titus that there were predators in the water as well as in the boat.

'Is it safe to fish here?' asked Lev, as Titus coasted to a halt beside a small island in the waterway. He looked warily at his partner, who was busy applying anti-mosquito spray to his neck.

'What's the worst that could happen?' Kiril observed, before holding out the spray to Titus and then Zolotov. Both men declined the offer.

'There's no going back now.' Having removed his jacket and rolled up his sleeves to reveal a display of crude prison tattoos, Zolotov crossed the gunwale with a fishing rod in hand. 'This is going to separate the men from the boys.'

Stepping out from under the canopy, Titus donned the fisherman's cap that Angelica had insisted he bring with him to protect his dome. Next, he slipped the little anchor overboard.

'Here is good for snapper and snook,' he said, with one eye on Lev. 'Also the bottom feeders.'

'Are we cut out for that?' It was Kiril who understood what this meant. 'Those feeders can be big mothers, man. We don't want to get out of our depth here.'

In response, Titus collected his rod and stood alongside Nikolai Zolotov, who had already cast his line into the water.

After so much careful planning and preparation, Ivan Savage arrived outside the changing room feeling calm and relaxed. He could hear members of the football team horsing around inside, and braced himself for the usual reception when he opened the door. On this occasion, it took the form of a warm jockstrap in the face.

'How do you like that, new girl?' crowed Bryce, as he locked his shoulder pads across his chest.

'I'm guessing he likes it a lot.' It was Ryan who had been responsible for throwing the undergarment.

'Just don't go using it as a comfort blanket,' warned Chad. 'That's mine for the match.'

Solemnly, with his bag in one hand, Ivan picked up the jockstrap and deposited it on the bench beside Chad. He glanced around, looking to check that the long foldaway table had been delivered by the janitor. Later, after half-time, he would join the small band of moms who had volunteered to prepare the refreshments and lay out a spread for the team's return.

'I just wanted to wish you guys good luck,' he said, having laid eyes on the table, and then backed away towards the door. 'I'll be watching the game from the bleachers. Most of it, at any rate.'

Chad glanced at his two friends. They seemed bemused by Ivan's warm wishes.

'We don't need luck,' he told the boy. 'We're invincible!'

Ivan Savage smiled quietly and opened the door. As he did so, the jockstrap connected with the back of his head, which he continued to hold high as he made his way along the corridor. In a way, the boy could allow them this one last bid to humiliate him. It only served to strengthen his convictions.

'The countdown has begun,' he said, glancing down at his bag. As ever, he'd left a gap so that Tinky Dinks could peep out. Just then, the gerbil felt like his partner in crime. 'Those boys are going to suffer, buddy. Mark my words!'

'Talking to yourself is the first sign of madness, but talking to a gerbil is kind of cute.'

With a sigh, Ivan drew to a halt.

'Crystal.'

He turned to find the girl hurrying to catch up with him. When he met her eyes, she beamed at him. Ivan struggled to look pleased to see her. He had grown to quite like her company over recent weeks, but now was not the time to practise social skills.

'Have you brought Tinky to watch the match?' A little breathless from the run, Crystal covered the gap that had risen up between her T-shirt and jeans by clasping one arm by the wrist.

'Something like that.'

'Room for one more?' she asked hopefully. 'You can explain the rules.'

'You're asking me?' Ivan laughed despite himself. 'My understanding of the rules is part of the reason why those guys give me such grief. You'd be better off quizzing the gerbil.'

With a giggle, Crystal reached out to take the bag from the boy. Ivan reacted as if she had just attempted to stab him.

'Whoa!' She pulled back with her arms raised as he snatched the bag away from her. 'I'm not going to hurt him.'

'Just . . . *don't!*' Ivan clutched the bag protectively, struggling to regain his composure.

Crystal watched him take a step away.

'What else you got in there?'

'Nothing!'

'Well, something's about to fall out.' She gestured at the bag. 'Careful.'

Ivan dropped his gaze to see the crinkled silver foil package peeping from the side pocket. Hurriedly, he stuffed it back in.

'Team sandwiches,' he said, regretting it immediately. 'Not for now.'

'What kind?'

'Never mind what kind!'

'Hey, go easy! What's eating you today?'

All of a sudden, Ivan felt under interrogation. The girl might have only been making friendly conversation, but he really needed it to stop. Outside, beyond the doors at the far end of the corridor, the cheerleaders could be heard going through their routine.

'We'd better find a place to sit,' he said quietly. 'Are you coming?'

37

In the corridor outside Priscilla's room, Oleg Savage sat upon a plastic chair with his hands on his knees and his gaze fixed upon the wall opposite. When the door beside him opened, he took a moment to raise himself with his stick and then faced the doctor who had been called to the nursing home in such a hurry.

'Will she be OK?' he asked. 'What's happening to her?'

Judging by the identity badge around her neck, the doctor was at the tail end of her call-out shift from the hospital. The woman looked considerably less tired in her photo, and yet she had come promptly when the staff found Oleg's companion struggling for breath in her bed.

'Priscilla is comfortable,' she told him, resting a hand on his shoulder. 'And it's important for her not to be worrying about you.'

'I'm fine,' said Oleg hotly before reaching for the door.

The doctor moved her hand from his shoulder to his wrist, which she held firmly this time.

'That means rest,' she said. 'No drama.'

'Is she awake?' Oleg glanced at the door, which was ajar.

Inside the room, one of the nurses from the home was straightening out the foot of the bedspread. 'I need to see her.'

The doctor considered his request for a moment.

'Sir, you do understand what's happening here?' Oleg found she held his gaze now with the same purpose that she gripped his wrist. 'Priscilla is dying. We need to make sure she does so comfortably and in peace.'

The old man heard her clearly, but didn't register a change in expression.

'We're all dying,' he muttered eventually. 'Every single one of us, from the moment we're born. What's important is that we make the most of our time. No matter how little is left.'

'I understand that –'

'*Nobody* understands that better than me.' Oleg kept his voice down, but cut in with such passion that the doctor blinked in surprise and released his wrist. 'Life is here to be devoured, ma'am, until there's nothing left on the plate. Not a scrap. Not a crumb. Not a morsel!'

Within half an hour of dropping anchor, it became clear to Titus that Lev and Kiril were hopeless fishermen. Lev had let a beautiful snook get away by reeling in his line too forcefully, while Kiril had succeeded only in snagging the riverbank. He'd wrestled to free the hook for a couple of minutes, and then abandoned his rod in favour of a beer from the cooler. Titus didn't consider himself to be a seasoned angler. He knew how to fish, of course. Oleg had taught him as a little boy, along with the hunting and trapping skills that he deployed to this day. Still, like the boat, it was something that he just never found the time to pursue.

'Well, this is the life,' said Zolotov. 'It's a far cry from a Russian winter.'

Lev and Kiril mumbled in agreement. Titus focused on his float. It had jabbed under the water a couple of times in the last minute. Something, he figured, was nibbling at the bait.

'Jupiter has been good to us,' said Titus. 'I wouldn't do anything to change that.'

Nikolai Zolotov glanced across at him.

'What I want you to do for me can only improve your life here,' he said. 'You'll still be running a vegan enterprise.'

'But not just one little place by the waterside,' said Titus. 'A chain.'

Zolotov shrugged, like it was no big deal.

'Doesn't every business want to expand?'

'Maybe,' said Titus, who had noticed Zolotov's float was also stirring. 'But this isn't a business. The Lentil Rebel is a front for money laundering, and I have to think of my family. I am not prepared for us to take further risks by expanding your criminal enterprise. So let me make *you* an offer,' he finished, sounding increasingly determined. 'We've served you well since the café opened. No doubt we've washed more cash than your previous venture, and now I'd like to buy you out.'

Zolotov seemed surprised at first. Then he faced Lev and Kiril and burst out laughing.

'You have to admire this guy. He has some guts! Does he really think I came all this way to make a few dollars?' Zolotov turned to face Titus once again, and the smile vanished from his face. 'No deal, my friend. I was upset when you closed down the lap-dancing bar. You put my nephew out of work, and though I see him make no effort to find another job, you saved your skin with this vegan venture. I had no idea there was such a demand. Now it's time to stop playing pocket money games and build an *empire*!'

'The public are hungry for it,' said Lev.

'It's the golden goose,' added Kiril with a shrug, and then frowned at the boat deck. 'OK, not a goose, that would be wrong. Maybe a grape. That's what you've created here, Titus. The golden grape.'

As the pair spoke, Zolotov placed a hand on his belly, as if in a little discomfort, only to be distracted when Titus's float bobbed and twitched in the water.

'Let's just enjoy this moment,' suggested Lev, and looked pleadingly at Titus.

'You'll make the right choice.' Kiril nodded, as if to prompt some kind of confirmation.

'Gentlemen, we didn't come here to discuss choices,' said Zolotov. 'I'm here with an *instruction*. Titus, if you value your family as much as you claim then we'd be using this opportunity to consider likely locations for the next cafés.'

Titus caught a glimpse of the man's teeth once more. The metalwork was menacing, without a doubt, but for once Zolotov didn't seem to be carrying himself with the same air. If anything, thought Titus, his waxy pallor and the fact that he had to steady himself against the boat's wheel suggested he was a little unwell. Above all, it revealed a hint of vulnerability.

'Everything OK?' asked Lev, who had also noticed.

'Just finding my sea legs, I guess.' Zolotov stood upright

once more, rolling his shoulders as if to demonstrate that the moment had passed. Then he lowered his head and glared at Titus. 'No doubt we'll all feel a lot better when you stop playing with the lives of your loved ones.'

Titus drew breath to stand his ground, only for his attention to be drawn by a disturbance in the water.

'Hey, Nikolai, you got a catch!' Lev stood and pointed at the ripples where his float had disappeared.

Zolotov grabbed his rod and began to reel in the line.

'Nice and easy.' Kiril rose to his feet, glancing at Titus as if they both knew just what he was up against here. 'We can't have another one get away.'

Ivan Savage sat upon the bleachers with his bag between his feet. The two teams had reached the final quarter, which is when the boy had begun to jog his knee up and down.

'Nervous?' asked Crystal. 'It's a close game. Hard to call.'

Ivan glanced across at her, still processing what she'd just said. 'What's the score?'

'You don't know?' Crystal looked at him side-on. 'Thirty five, thirty eight.'

'Oh, right. So, who's winning?'

When Crystal didn't respond, Ivan stopped focusing on the three players he had been watching intently since the match began and gave her his full attention.

'Well, right now, we're losing,' she told him. 'You really have no idea how to play this game, do you?'

On the pitch, Ryan had just attempted to smash his way through the opposition, only to drop the ball as they dragged him down. The pair watched him rise to his feet again, spitting insults at the little cornerback bitch who had been in the right place to catch it.

'All I know is that sometimes it isn't just about brute force,' said Ivan. 'Cunning can also bring results.'

Crystal nodded, still watching as Bryce backed up his buddy by shoving the cornerback into Chad, who responded with a helmet headbutt.

'That's true,' she said, as the referee intervened. 'But we really need to push the big boys forward if we're going to snatch a victory here. I know those three have been hard on you, but they're our best chance in the time we have left.'

'Which is running out fast.' Ivan glanced at his watch. 'Anyway, I should go help out with the refreshments,' he said, before collecting his bag. 'These sandwiches won't serve themselves.'

'Aren't you going to stick around to see who wins?' asked Crystal.

Ivan picked up on her surprise as he rose to his feet, but didn't glance back in case she saw the purpose in his eyes.

'I already know,' he muttered to himself on making his way towards the steps.

With his feet planted squarely on the deck of the boat, Nikolai Zolotov began to reel his fish in.

'This is too easy,' he said. 'There's no resistance, but that's just how I like it. Saves on the time and sweat.' Preparing to flick the rod, he faced Titus and grinned at him. 'The sooner I get my own way, the better.'

The moment the snook sailed out of the water and onto the

deck, it was clear that Zolotov had massively overestimated the size of his quarry. One jerk of the line had been enough to land what was clearly an infant. Now, the tiddler flapped desperately by his shoe.

'Better luck next time,' observed Titus. 'Just release it and toss it back in.'

Zolotov appeared uncomfortable at the sudden landing.

'Release how?' he asked, before peering up at Titus helplessly.

'By taking the hook out of its mouth.' Titus frowned. He hadn't expected this from a man with such a ruthless reputation. 'You can do that, can't you?'

Nikolai Zolotov looked aghast. He reached down and then promptly recoiled when the snook flipped over. When Titus took care of the task, gently returning the fish to the water, an expression of sheer relief crossed Zolotov's face.

'What was the problem?' asked Lev.

He looked at his partner, who appeared equally bemused. 'Are you . . . squeamish?'

Titus didn't need to hear another word from Zolotov, who now seemed as rattled as he did feverish. For in that brief moment with his catch – a tiny creature that he couldn't even bring himself to touch – the man had revealed a great deal about himself. Titus rose to his full height, ready to square up to him, only for his attention to return to the water when his own float snapped sharply to the right.

'Fish on!' cried Zolotov, seizing upon the distraction.

For a second, Titus considered ignoring it while he attended to the matter at hand. When Lev and Kiril crossed the deck to see what was dragging the float, which caused the boat to rock, he sighed to himself and grasped the reel handle. This time, the curve of the rod told them all that the catch was considerable. Titus was forced to brace himself as a fight took shape, which he did both capably and without a word, while his two expat friends offered their encouragement. Only Zolotov hung back from the edge.

'Is this wise?' he asked at one point, and then promptly swatted at a mosquito.

With every turn of the reel, Titus considered the situation he had just uncovered. No doubt Nikolai was an underworld player. That was apparent in the packets of money they'd been forced to put through the cash register. Certainly the crude tattoos marked him out as a man who had served time in the Russian penal system. What didn't stand up any longer, however, were the stories that preceded his arrival. On several occasions the man himself had called upon such infamous episodes from his past in order to deliver his threats. Still wrestling with his quarry, Titus glanced across at him. This figure, who claimed to have gorged on severed body parts, just flinched from a teensy fish. Could he really have a taste for human meat? From his experience, crossing that line left nothing to fear in the world but the safety of your own flesh and blood. Ultimately, Titus concluded, Nikolai Zolotov was no cannibal. Just a con artist.

'Here it comes,' said Lev, leaning over the side.

'It's a big one,' Kiril added, who was ready with the landing net.

'What is *that*?' asked Zolotov, peering warily from behind them as something very large took shape from the depths.

'Catfish,' said Titus, who saw his chance to land it.

'King of the bottom feeders,' said Lev, nodding sagely. 'There are monsters around here.'

With one final heave, Titus drew his quarry to the surface. He then grabbed the net from Kiril, who was just looking on in horror like the other two. It was way too small to cope with the great fish. All Titus could do was use it to support the body of his catch as he swung it on board. The beast had to be at least forty pounds, with a huge mouth, alien-like whiskers and sharp quills fanning from behind its fins. Unlike the little nipper, which had flipped about helplessly, this one thrashed from one side of the hull to the other, causing all three passengers to scramble back smartly. It was Kiril who was first to hop off the boat and onto the island, followed quickly by Lev, whose desertion caused the boat to push away.

'Hey, wait a minute!' This was Zolotov, who had been preparing to follow them. The boat drifted to a halt when the anchor pulled tight, but by then the gap was too far for him to jump.

'Will you give me a hand here?' yelled Titus, who was struggling to remove the hook from the mouth of his giant catch. The catfish – a flathead – continued to thrash wildly. Zolotov simply looked on, frozen to the spot, it seemed. With the hook free at last, Titus grabbed the beast in a bear hug and wrestled it back overboard. The fish hit the water with a heavy splash, but Titus only heard it. By then, he was hurriedly hauling anchor, a plan of action rising with it, before throwing himself into the pilot's seat.

'Don't go anywhere!' he called across to Lev and Kiril, and promptly fired up the engine. 'Zolotov and I have a matter to discuss in private.'

38

Ivan found that the football moms had already set to work in the changing room. The long table, covered with Stars and Stripes crêpe paper, was in the process of being laid out with plates of home-prepared treats for the team.

'How kind of you to help out,' said Felicia, whom Ivan regarded as the mom-in-charge. Felicia was dressed casually but carefully in yoga pants and a pink zip-up sweat top. Despite the welcome, her tight smile told Ivan that she didn't relish his presence. The other moms just ignored him completely. Ivan was well aware that they regarded him as a threat to their system. He wanted to tell them that they had nothing to fear. This was just a one-off, after all. Instead, he offered what he hoped looked like a smile and fished out the wrapped sandwiches.

'I've had to guard these carefully,' he told her. 'I've already lost one.'

'Well, they're in safe hands now.'

Felicia reached for the package, only for Ivan to withdraw it from her reach.

'It's no problem,' he said, and headed for the table. 'I'll take care of this.'

Collecting a plastic plate from the stack on the table, Ivan made a space at the far end. With his bag placed against the wall, he began to lay out his sandwiches. Bryce, Ryan and Chad always strong-armed their way to the table, so there was a good chance that nobody else would fall upon the plate first. Even so, there was no guarantee. It would be a shame, Ivan thought, if another couple of players got in before. Then again, as his father always said, collateral damage was sometimes unavoidable.

'There,' he said to himself, and stood back to consider the surrounding plates.

At a glance, there was no sign that his offering contained killer meat. Only Ivan could be aware that these sandwiches contained a fatal filling. If everything went to plan, those boys would leave the changing room like ticking time bombs. Ivan knew that he could see it through. He had already taken care of the guy who dared to threaten his family. It was annoying that he hadn't got out of bed in time to catch his dad that morning and put him in the picture. Still, at least it didn't matter now if it turned out that his old man really was past his prime. Nikolai Zolotov was a dead man walking. As far as Ivan was concerned, it meant he was ready to take over as the family's hunter-in-chief.

Just then, the sound of whooping and high-fives from the corridor drew Ivan from his thoughts. The team were on their way back to the changing room.

The boy glanced back at his bag. Tinky Dinks was watching him from the gloom behind the half-open zipper. In Ivan's mind, it was clear he was waiting for his master to strike.

Titus Savage had set out with a master plan for dealing with Nikolai Zolotov. The moment Lev and Kiril showed up, however, that plan had been laid to waste. All he had wanted to do was talk to the man at length and reason with him. Titus figured that their shared Russian heritage would help them bond. He had hoped that by the end of a peaceful trip upriver, Zolotov would've agreed to his proposal for the café. If Angelica and the rest of his family assumed he had brought him out here simply to kill him off then they were mistaken. They'd already ruled that the guy was inedible, and you didn't just murder someone because they stood in your way.

It was only if Zolotov failed to be reasonable that Titus had intended to resort to measures such as that.

Now, with Lev and Kiril yelling at him from the little island in the waterway where he had just abandoned them, Titus Savage seized the chance to get his day back on track.

'What are you doing?' growled Zolotov, and promptly staggered backwards as Titus hit the boat's accelerator. 'Turn around, man!'

It wasn't easy, negotiating the river here. Titus slammed the wheel one way and then the other in a bid to avoid mops of weed and overhanging branches. He glanced over his shoulder, saw Zolotov struggling to stand and a boiling wash of water in the boat's wake.

'Just hold on!' he called back. 'All I want is some space to talk.'

'It's too late for that!' Zolotov spat at him. 'Now stop this tub or I plant a bullet in the back of your skull.'

This time, when Titus looked around, he found that Zolotov had grasped a canopy strut for balance. He'd also produced a pistol. Holding the grip horizontally, he levelled the weapon at Titus and repeated his demand. By now, the island they had left behind was obscured by a bend in the river and banks thick with mangroves. Titus shut down the engine, letting the boat drift to a halt. Turning to Zolotov directly, he then raised his hands in surrender.

'I'm surprised to find you're armed,' he said. 'A man with your reputation.'

Nikolai Zolotov broke from his gaze at this, looking a little gassy. The colour had drained from his face, while the neck of his shirt was beginning to take on sweat.

'Give me a moment,' he said, and rested his brow against the support. 'I feel like I might heave.'

'Just take it easy.' Slowly, Titus extended one hand towards him. 'Put down the gun and have a seat. We can talk business back on dry land.'

'How many times?' Zolotov forced himself to stand upright, reasserting his grip on the gun. 'It's too late to talk. If you're not prepared to expand the business, Titus, then only one of us will be going home.'

With a frown, Titus considered the gun. He'd never faced a weapon before and it rattled him. In a situation such as this, he usually enjoyed the element of surprise. Bugs flitted all around them in the sunlight, which was dappled by the canopy of leaves and branches. Something stirred in the water towards the opposite bank, but nothing that could help him here. It left him with no choice, Titus decided. Unarmed, his only weapon was the truth.

'You know, I'm not so sure that being on water is your problem right now. All that perspiration tells me you have a fever, not motion sickness, Nikolai. And cramps, judging by the way you're wincing. Could it be something you've eaten?'

Zolotov didn't answer for a moment, gripped as he was by another abdominal cramp.

'I ate with your family last night,' he said eventually, and looked up into his eyes once more. 'I don't see you suffering.'

'How about lunch?'

'I skipped it. Got by on a sandwich your boy gave me.'

Titus looked away for a moment, focusing on a point midway between the boat and the opposite bank. His boy would never be so generous. There had to be a reason why he would freely hand over something like that. Without doubt, he realised, Zolotov had been poisoned.

'Well, maybe it is just the rocking of the boat,' he said, to cover his thinking.

'Food has never turned against me,' agreed Zolotov, clearly in some discomfort. 'Some of the things I've digested would turn most people's stomachs.'

'So I've heard.' Despite the gun, Titus sensed his control over the moment begin to return. 'Can I ask you something?' he continued. 'I'm curious about your experience of eating human flesh.'

'What about it?' asked Zolotov, who briefly dropped his gun hand to clutch his abdomen.

'What does it taste like? In your experience.'

Zolotov met his eyes again, this time looking for some kind

of reasoning behind the question.

'Hard to say,' he offered uncertainly. 'Like beef?'

'Oh, really?'

Titus raised one eyebrow.

'OK, more like pork.' Zolotov mopped his brow. 'I meant pork.'

'Are you sure?' he asked, pretending to sound even more surprised.

'Chicken?'

This time, a note of desperation came into Zolotov's voice. Titus offered him a knowing smile.

'Nikolai, those are the kind of answers people give when they've never tasted such a thing. If you'd said venison, which is a common guess, then I would've come to the same conclusion. You see, if human meat is in good shape, it should *transport* you. Quite simply, there is no comparison. It goes beyond the taste. Isn't that the draw? The thing that keeps you coming back for more?'

With his mouth dropping a little as his listened, Zolotov appeared to remind himself to nod.

'Sure it is,' he said after a moment, and laughed nervously. 'Who doesn't get totally out of it gnawing on a severed limb?'

'That's not what I mean.' Titus grimaced. 'When my family and I sit down for a feast, we make sure the person we're eating has been considerately sourced and cooked to perfection. If we went about gnawing on just anyone raw, we'd be no better than jackals, right? What you and I are talking about is *evolved* eating. In my opinion, fine dining on our own kind places us right at the top of the food chain.'

Now Zolotov simply stared, his eyes widening.

'Are you serious?' he asked quietly.

Titus lowered his hands, not taking his eyes off the man for a moment.

'Nikolai,' he said plainly, 'you're not a cannibal, are you? It takes one to know one, after all. But that doesn't make me any more of a fiend than you. No doubt as a meat eater you're happy to tuck into a steak, sausage or burger with little thought for the miserable existence some poor creature suffered in order to end up on your plate. Me? I make every effort to ensure that the people we eat deserve what's coming to them. They might've lived a happy, free-range life, but ultimately their conduct means they won't be missed. Now that, my friend, is ethical consumption. I've become a goddamn *humani*tarian!'

'You're sick,' whispered Zolotov.

'Take a look at yourself,' Titus said with a chuckle. 'When we heard all about the incident in the prison cell, everyone marked you down as some kind of twisted psychopath. I'm guessing you invented such a story to command fear and respect, and reinforced it with that demonic dentistry. It persuaded people to do things your way, right?'

'This isn't about me.' Grimacing once again, with his insides clearly in uproar, Zolotov tightened his grip on the gun. 'You got one last chance, Titus! Do I have your word that you'll build that chain, in which case your secret is safe with me, or should I kill you for the confession you just made?'

'Nikolai, you're a man who has relied upon a terrible lie to build your business. It's one thing to pull a weapon on me, but now I'm having difficulty believing that you'd actually shoot.'

With a glint of the metalwork wrapped around his molars, Nikolai Zolotov squeezed the trigger. Titus reacted with a jolt, unlike Nikolai, who took a moment to realise that the gun had jammed. With a roar of dismay, he threw his hands in the air, cursing Lev and Kiril.

'I ask them to source me a firearm, here in America, and what do they bring me? Some crappy Russian ex-army model!'

As he moved to free the weapon's hammer, Zolotov doubled up in pain. Titus considered kicking the gun from his grip, but the moment escaped him when the man's cheeks bulged and he rushed for the back of the boat. At the sound of retching that followed, Titus pulled a face and raced to consider his next move. There was no way that he would agree to Zolotov's demands, and the man was clearly willing to kill him if he could make the gun work. In no mood to reach for the garrotte he had packed in the pocket of his shorts, he took to the captain's chair. Strangling a man while he was being sick would be messy, and there was a strong chance that Ivan had slipped something into his sandwich that was set to kill him anyway. Whether or not his son had intended to cause such a severe reaction, there was only one course of action available now. Under the circumstances, it came down to what was kindest. As the Russian criminal behind him continued to be violently unwell into the water, Titus twisted the ignition key. He then pushed the boat into a turning circle with such momentum that the nose of the vessel rose up like a stallion.

As a cry of surprise broke out in his wake, followed by a heavy splash, Titus turned his thoughts to Lev and Kiril. He'd only been gone a few minutes, but no doubt he'd find the pair thoroughly shaken from the experience. The alligators were rife around here, after all, he noted, on passing one such beast as it slipped into the river and headed at speed towards the boat's point of departure. There was nothing more terrifying than thinking you might end up as supper, as Titus knew from experience.

Which is why he always aimed to make sure it was over quickly for his victims.

39

Ivan Savage was pleased to discover that the team had clawed to victory in the closing minutes. It meant the players were particularly boisterous and upbeat when they bundled into the changing room.

'Well done, boys!' declared Felicia, who had been standing in front of the table but then stepped smartly out of their way. 'Just form a queue and we'll make sure everyone is served.'

Totally ignoring her request, the team piled forward. Ivan had positioned himself behind his plate. Several moms stood alongside him, preparing to manage proceedings, but they could only look on helplessly as the first hands lunged out.

'Easy now,' said Ivan, as the assault on the refreshments got under way. As a precaution, he pulled his plate back when the first hand reached out to grab a sandwich, and only relaxed when he looked up and saw Bryce.

'Give me that, new boy!'

'Be my guest.' With his voice close to being drowned out by the chatter, Ivan then switched eye contact to Chad, who snatched the next sandwich from the plate. Once again, he pictured his victims living in blissful ignorance over the coming weeks. A little stomach sensitivity to begin, perhaps, but absolutely nothing that would arouse their suspicions and lead them back to him. Ivan glanced around, looking for the last of the trio. At the same time, he sensed the plate become lighter. With a start he looked back and saw the sandwich leave the plate, but not in Ryan's grasp.

'Thanks, Ivan.'

'*No!*' he yelled, on seeing who had taken it. Crystal had squeezed between the players at the front to grab it, and now stared at the boy defiantly. 'Don't do that. Put it down!'

'Why?' she asked, her voice raised over the chatter and howl of the team. 'What's in it?'

Chad had already ripped away a bite of his sandwich. Ivan saw Bryce lift his to his mouth, but then gasped when Crystal did the same thing.

'Because . . . ' Ivan sighed and bowed his head. 'Because it's poisoned.'

The boy made his confession in a voice so quiet that he was only heard by Crystal and the three bullish young men in front of him. Nevertheless, the way they froze was enough to kill the surrounding babble. It would've left the changing room in complete silence but for the sound of Chad spitting out his mouthful and Bryce dropping his sandwich to the floor. When he dared to look up, having hurriedly collected his bag from the floor, Ivan found the entire team staring at him. He glanced at Crystal, his plan in ruins.

'Run,' she said in a whisper.

Ivan needed no further encouragement. Snatching his plate with the last of the sandwiches, he scrambled over the top of

299

the table, following Crystal as she wheeled around to make her escape. With crockery and curses flying after him, Ivan pushed his way through the scrum, thinking that if he had a ball in his hand right now then this would be a touchdown situation.

'Sorry!' he cried, on rushing past Felicia. Even if she'd heard his admission, frankly she looked more upset by the mess.

'*OK, cool down, fellas!*' he heard her order the team in a voice that sounded more like a battle cry. Glancing over his shoulder, Ivan caught sight of Felicia stepping out to block their path, along with several other football moms. All of them appeared to have summoned some inner warrior queen as they faced down Bryce, Chad and Ryan and the rest of the team behind them. 'Do you know how hard we've worked to lay on this spread?' Felicia screamed. 'Now you three clean up this mess and then return to your refreshments. Nobody leaves until you've finished my flapjacks!'

It was Crystal who led the flight through the corridor, heading away from the pitch before barrelling into the sunshine outside the front of the school. Ivan ran close behind, holding his bag to his chest with the gerbil uppermost in his mind. He could've handled a beating, if that's what it had come to, but there was no way he could let Tinky Dinks suffer, he thought, as they fled through the gates. Crystal led the way to the corner of the block, and only stopped after checking that Ryan, Bryce and Chad weren't in pursuit. Ivan pulled up alongside her, panting as much as she was, and then gasped when she slapped his cheek hard.

'What were you *thinking*?' she yelled at him, and held up the sandwich she had taken. 'I had a bad feeling about these, and when you left the match it fell into place.'

'They deserved it,' said Ivan with a shrug, despite smarting from where he had been struck. 'Who are those guys to stop me from fitting in?'

'Ivan, if you want to be accepted, just be comfortable with who you are. Poisoning people is only going to earn you attention for all the wrong reasons.'

The boy heard what Crystal had to say. It was hard to swallow, but she was right. If he was going to be himself in the one place where that was possible – locked away in the villa with a family that shared his taste for human flesh – then it was important to keep out of trouble. It didn't ease his desire to get even with those boys, but in this instance he recognised that he had been saved from himself. With some humility, Ivan took the sandwich from her and stuffed it into the side pocket of his bag along with the folded plate. Plunging his hands into his trouser pockets, he then kicked at the weeds in the sidewalk cracks.

'It's tough being me sometimes,' he told her. 'I want to do the right thing, but it always ends up wrong.'

'You can change that,' she said, which earned his full attention. Crystal nodded at the bag on the sidewalk. 'Why not start by sending Tinky Dinks back to pre-school?'

Ivan took a step back, scooping up the bag protectively.

'Why would I do that?' he asked.

'To prove to people that you have feelings. That you're not some distant loner, like everyone thinks you are.'

'But I'd just get into trouble.'

'For what?' asked Crystal. 'For looking after a defenceless creature that had escaped from its cage? For feeding and housing

301

him all this time? For showing him you're capable of *love?*'

Ivan responded with a blink of surprise and a little shiver. Nobody had ever used that word around him apart from his mother, and she always did so in a way that meant well but left him feeling suffocated. This time, however, it seemed to make his heart beat with what he could only describe as pride. The boy crouched beside the bag. Gently, he scooped Tinky Dinks into the palm of his hand. The little gerbil sniffed the air, and then sat back to clean his whiskers, looking completely at ease in his care.

'So, you think they'd be grateful?' he asked.

'Overjoyed.' Crystal tucked a bang of hair behind her ear. 'Just think of all the little children who'll be delighted that he's back from the dead. Tinky would have a companion in the gerbil that was supposed to stand in for him, and you'd be a hero, Ivan. Not just to them,' she said to finish, and smiled shyly, 'but also to me.'

The sun was on the slide when Angelica first spotted the boat from the jetty. As it sank away to the west, every ripple on the water appeared to detonate with light. It meant she had to cup her brow against the glare to count the people on board, and then torment herself until she could be sure that Titus was among that number.

'Kat, why don't you run inside?' she said to the little girl clasping her hand. 'Daddy and I need to chat.'

'OK, Mom.'

Before Angelica could make her sigh heard, Katya had turned and skipped back to the villa. It did little to ease Angelica's growing tension headache. Titus had deliberately left his cell phone at home, as he always did on any expedition that might result in a body coming back with him. She understood how important it was that he couldn't be traced to the scene of a crime, but it was torture for her to see the device on the kitchen table throughout the day. As the boat crossed the inlet, Angelica stood with her arms folded and waited. She knew that Titus had seen her, but it was another minute before they held each other's gaze. Judging by his grave expression, it was clear he'd had a challenging day. That Nikolai Zolotov was absent from the boat told her the reason why. As for Lev and Kiril, seated on the bench behind her husband, they just looked shamefaced. Lev also seemed a little sunburned. As Titus slowed the boat and threw the line to Angelica, he simply shook his head at her, as if the pair were badly behaved mongrels who had ignored his whistle on a walk.

'Gentlemen,' he said, turning to address them once he'd shut off the engine, 'I expect your families are wondering where you are. My advice is to head home, give them a hug and let them know you'll be spending more time with them now you're involvement with the café is over. I think today's events calls it quits, no?'

Both men avoided eye contact with Angelica, who stood aside as they left the boat.

'For the record,' said Lev, who had also been badly bitten by mosquitoes, 'we knew the piece was jammed.'

'We just couldn't refuse his request,' Kiril added helplessly. 'The guy eats people alive, man. I didn't see that we had a choice.'

Titus took the key from the ignition. Angelica could tell that he was weighing up the explanation.

'Well, you're off the menu,' he told them, with just a glance at his wife. 'For now.'

Angelica offered Titus a private smile. While Lev and Kiril could have no way of knowing that they were in the presence of the ultimate carnivores, she could tell by her husband's tone that they had come close to not returning from the trip. Lev scratched at a mosquito bite on the back of his neck. Kiril had clearly taken precautions against the bugs and the sun, but that didn't stop him looking equally unsettled in his own skin.

'After you left us,' he said hesitantly, 'what happened between you and Nikolai?'

Titus pocketed the key and shrugged.

'Let me give you guys a lesson in life,' he told him, removing his cap to rub his dome. 'There are times when a bad thing has to happen so that some good can follow.' He paused to step onto the jetty. 'A bad thing happened today. As a result, The Lentil Rebel is a legitimate business. There's no more dirty money to wash, or any need to expand into a chain. I dare say Rolan will be upset that there's no job in it for him, but perhaps he'll learn to stand on his own two feet now his uncle is gone.'

Angelica focused her attention on Lev and Kiril. It was clear they understood that Zolotov was out of the picture and no longer a threat. Even so, they didn't look thrilled.

'But we made a cut of that money,' said Lev. 'What's in this for us?'

'If you want to put food on the table, you have to work hard for it.' Titus narrowed his eyes at the man for a moment before his expression softened. Then he took a step back and Angelica found him addressing her as much as the two expats. 'As it happens, I have a job-share you might be interested in. Having fought to keep the café under our control, I feel I should be more involved in the day-to-day running, alongside my wife and our lodger. As a result, there's a vacancy down at the condo. I'm thinking you'd both make capable property managers.'

Lev and Kiril glanced at one another.

'Maintenance we can handle,' said Lev. 'The tenants? Not so much.'

'Let's just say we lack the sensitivity,' Kiril admitted, and picked at his teeth with his little finger.

Angelica caught her husband's eye. He nodded at her.

'Titus will continue to handle them,' she said, and placed a hand on his shoulder. 'He's a people kind of person.'

40

Amanda Dias floated into the villa with the cell phone pressed to her ear and a smile painted across her face.

'That sounds good,' she purred, having walked home from the café in conversation with the young fitness trainer, who had popped in for lunch and stayed for several hours. Joaquín Mendez had seemed a little jittery when Amanda approached to take his order. Still, he'd settled down by the time she served him a plate of freshly baked mushroom croustades. What's more, he went on to claim to relish every mouthful more than anything he'd ever tasted. Even the breaded veal his mother used to make, he told her, and that was a lifelong favourite. Amanda did wonder whether Titus might've set him up as a challenge, but by then she was finding it hard to resist his shy smile, toasted brown eyes and sense of humility in her presence. By the time it came to ordering coffee, she had dared to take a chair at his table and suggest they swap numbers. 'Then I'll see you tomorrow,' she said down the line just then, clicking the door to the villa shut with her heel. 'I'm looking forward to it already.'

She closed the call just as Katya skipped out of the kitchen with a plastic dolly in one hand. It had been the little girl's favourite toy for years, as was evident from the threadbare dress and chewed limbs.

'Dad is home,' she told the lodger.

'With something to eat?'

Katya shrugged and then shook her head.

'How much longer do we have to wait, Amanda? I'm hungry.'

Amanda knew just what she meant. Ever since experiencing her first feast, the sense of anticipation she carried towards each new one could sometimes feel intolerable.

'Not long,' she assured Kat all the same, and then turned on hearing someone trot down the stairs.

'Zolotov is dead meat.' Ivan was wearing a black cotton hoody and looked strikingly pleased with himself. 'Trust me, I've taken care of things.'

'Really?' Amanda's note of surprise was matched by a sense of relief. 'How?'

Ivan brushed past, heading out to meet his father.

'You know that saying, "The surest way to a man's heart is through his stomach"? Well, you can reach his entire system with the right parasite!'

Amanda looked down at Katya, who seemed equally perplexed. Without word, the pair followed the boy. They only had to venture as far as the kitchen to find him facing Titus and Angelica, who had just closed the back door behind her.

'That sandwich,' said Titus, looking gravely at his son, and crossed the tiles to the island table top. 'Was it intended for Zolotov?'

'Does it matter?' Ivan looked to his feet. 'In a few weeks

from now he's going to realise his days are numbered.'

'I think he realised that a little quicker than you intended, Ivan. Thankfully, he's no longer in a position to hunt you down.'

Ivan looked to his trainers. Thinking back, all that mucking about with the meat over recent days might have left it open to a little bacterial contamination. Had the three jocks eaten their sandwiches, he realised, then within twenty-four hours he might have been a marked man.

'So, maybe it was more potent than I planned,' he said, 'but at least I got the job done.'

'Fortunately for you we'll never know. Nevertheless you still can't turn food into a lethal weapon!' Titus had barely raised his voice, but suddenly it commanded the boy's full attention. Amanda glanced at Angelica, who lifted her shoulders as if to signal that she was none the wiser. 'Are there any more? We could have a public health risk on our hands!'

Ivan responded with a sigh and a shake of his head.

'I binned them,' he admitted. 'Along with my hopes of ever finding a place on the squad. With three players down, I was sure the coach would have to pick me to fill a place.'

Immediately, Amanda identified Ivan's intended targets. He had never talked about it to his family, but only recently she had overheard him in his room; muttering about a trio of tormentors and how he'd like to see them suffer. Given that he spent so much time in his own company, Amanda just assumed he had been acting out some fantasy to an imaginary friend. Even if he was talk.ng to thin air, she realised now, all the promises of payback he had made were clearly for real. That didn't make Ivan some crazed avenger through her eyes, however. Knowing how life had been challenging for him at times, it made him a victim.

'You know, there's only one effective way to deal with bullies,' she said, drawing the attention of Titus as well as his son. 'You just have to tell a teacher.'

'She's right,' said Titus. 'And if that fails to bring results then you come to me.'

Ivan didn't look convinced by his father's offer. That much was evident to Amanda, who shared the boy's misgivings.

'With all due respect,' she said to Titus quietly, 'you've been struggling to bring back a feast for the table lately. All Ivan tried to do here is take care of a situation himself.'

'So, what stopped you?' Angelica asked her son. 'Though may I say how deeply relieved I am that you didn't just take out three members of the team. Your dad and I have gone to great lengths to teach you the values in our family tradition, and that doesn't extend to recklessly *poisoning* people!'

This time it was Angelica's turn to bridle her anger. She took a breath and endeavoured to compose herself by smoothing the sides of her dress. By now, Ivan looked on the verge of tears.

'I've tried so hard to fit in at school,' he said after a moment, 'but it always ends in failure, ridicule or worse – and I'm tired of it. I'm *sick* of people throwing things at my head in the classroom. I'm fed up with the name-calling and the threats. These guys – Bryce, Ryan and Chad – they've made my life a misery ever since we moved here, and I decided it was time to get even. Now, things may not have gone to plan today,' the boy continued, his voice growing in confidence, 'but it's opened my eyes to something in my life that's helping me to see things differently.'

'What?' asked Amanda, just as Katya reached for the comfort of her hand.

'A friend,' said Ivan, who wiped his eyes furiously as they began to gloss. 'I had a friend all along. I just didn't know it until Crystal pointed it out.'

His admission was met by a long pause.

'Isn't Crystal your friend, too?' asked Amanda, in a bid to sound encouraging. 'That makes two, Ivan. You can build on that.'

'But who's the first?' asked Angelica, who sounded astonished to hear her son admit to having any friends at all.

In response, and with some care, Ivan removed his hands from the pouch pocket of his hoody. When he revealed a small but familiar-looking rodent nestling in his gently cupped palms, everyone marked their shock and surprise with a range of gasps and exclamations.

'Mum . . . Katya . . . ' he said hesitantly, addressing them in turn. 'We need to talk about Tinky Dinks.'

Oleg Savage dismounted from his mobility scooter in such a hurry that he dropped his walking stick on the drive.

'Dammit,' he muttered. 'Being old and in a hurry is murder!'

It took him a good minute to drop down on one knee to collect the stick, and only a little less to get back up again. Earlier, he had left Priscilla's bedside after promising her that the restorative meal was imminent. As soon as he had learned from Angelica that Titus was on a boat trip with his Russian visitor, Oleg came to one conclusion. A feast was at hand.

'Just in time,' said Amanda with a smile when she answered the door to him. 'We're about to eat.'

'Already?' Oleg moved her to one side with his stick. 'Then we need to collect Priscilla. We can't do this without her.'

'Not that kind of meal,' Amanda said, to clarify, but already Oleg was making his way into the kitchen.

'So,' he said, on finding the family gathered at the table with bowls of pasta in front of them. 'Where's the dish of the day?'

Titus glanced at Amanda, who returned to her chair, and then at Angelica.

'Oleg, this is just a quick supper. There is no feast this evening, but you're welcome to join us.'

Oleg listened to his daughter-in-law's invitation with his eyes locked on Titus. Despite arriving in a state of some agitation, just then he possessed the unflinching focus of a marksman with his finger on the trigger.

'Did you finish him?'

'Thankfully, yes.' Titus set down his fork. 'But I didn't think he'd sit well in our stomachs.'

Oleg broke his stare to address the ceiling in disbelief.

'You took a life and let him go to waste?'

Titus glanced at Ivan, who suddenly returned to his pasta.

'The man was a little off,' he said. 'Quite bad, as it turns out.

'Very well.' Oleg supported himself with both hands on his stick. 'If my son can't provide for his family then I'll just have to do it myself!'

The way he spoke, his voice rising in volume and rage, brought Titus and Amanda to their feet.

'Come and sit with us,' reasoned Angelica, standing just

311

after them. 'There's plenty to eat.'

'But nothing to make us feel *alive!*' the old man countered, already making his way back to the main door.

'Oleg, we can talk about this.' Amanda was first to reach him, and placed a reassuring hand on his shoulder. The old man shrugged her off, pushing on towards the door.

'Get the oven on, Angelica. Someone has to put proper food on the table! What about the fitness guy?' he asked. 'Wasn't he on the menu at one time? I might be slow on my feet, but he won't outrun me on my scooter!'

'Joaquín?' Amanda frowned. 'Leave him out of this! He's my date tomorrow, not dinner!'

By now, Titus had slipped past Oleg to block the front door.

'Take a breath,' he said to his father, only to receive an upswing from Oleg's walking stick smartly between his legs. Titus let out a yelp.

'Let me show you how it's done,' muttered Oleg, who promptly shoved his son aside and threw open the door. 'In my day, we weren't so choosy about who we ate. We sat to feast and thanked our lucky stars for the privilege!' He turned at the door, his eyes tight with rage, and addressed his whole family. 'All this faddy food fussiness just tells me you've become spoiled. It's high time we went back to basics!' Oleg climbed on board his mobility scooter. 'Not just for your sakes, but also for Priscilla's. You'll thank me for it when we finally sit for a real meal. And nobody leaves the table until I see clean plates!'

'Not too fast!' croaked Titus, but Oleg had given up listening. Ripping away the marker that Titus had applied to the dial, he had every intention of taking it to the maximum as soon as he was on the road.

'What's the point of limits?' he yelled back, his blood still boiling, and pushed the scooter in a brisk semi-circle. 'Aren't we beyond all that as a family?'

It was as he hummed away from the villa that Oleg felt a tug, seemingly from behind. Gasping in surprise, it felt like an embrace so all-consuming it could've come from everyone he had ever loved throughout his life, and even those he'd eaten. The moment caused this man who had lived beyond a century to snap his grip away from the handlebars and clutch at his breastplate.

A second later, as his heart went into arrest, Oleg Savage's scooter veered into the flowerbed and buried its front wheel in the soil.

The back end kicked like a mule, causing the old man to launch into the air. In that split second, tumbling head over heels, he caught sight of his family watching in horror from behind. When the memory of every milestone in his life spooled through his mind, this cannibal elder knew his time had come. His diet might have kept him alive beyond his years, so he continued to believe as he completed a full somersault, but death, it seemed, came to everyone. The moment arrived with a backbreaking thud upon the asphalt. Above all, it opened up a view of the heavens, which Oleg faced with resignation before his gaze went slack.

41

At last, Joaquín Mendez felt as if he had broken the spell. If he thought about Angelica, his heart no longer pumped a sense of yearning through his system. Instead, his thoughts were filled with just one individual, and it seemed she shared his affections.

'Amanda,' he declared the next evening, addressing his reflection in the bathroom mirror as he dressed for his date. 'My fate is in your hands.'

The young fitness trainer had only visited The Lentil Rebel because he was worried about the consequences of ignoring his client's invitation. Titus had been insistent that Joaquín would click with their lodger. She was smart, so he said, quick-witted and boasted strong views about ethical eating. Joaquín considered himself to possess no such qualities. It often took him a second more than most people to laugh at a joke, and while his appetite had returned at last he regarded food as fuel and nothing more. So long as it was low in fat and high in protein, Joaquín didn't much care where it had come from.

'Maybe opposites really do attract,' he told himself, on setting out from his apartment the following evening, as the temperature cooled and stars began to prickle the sky.

Joaquín felt refreshed but slightly strange. A thorough shower had washed away the sweat from another day of working out with his clients. The blazer jacket he had selected afterwards, together with the T-shirt and stonewashed jeans, should've created a look that helped him to relax and be confident. What put a stop to that were the canvas shoes. Ultimately, he just wanted to be himself, but even the young fitness trainer knew that showing up barefoot to collect Amanda for their date would just be weird.

By now, Joaquín knew the way to the inlet community with his eyes closed. Earlier that day, he had picked up a bunch of deep-red carnations, earning himself a mystified frown from the florist when he checked that they were vegan. He had no intention of making a mess of things this time around. Angelica had awakened his capacity to love, but Amanda was surely the one for him. He only had to look at his phone to realise just how deeply he had fallen for her. Scrolling through the messages he had sent, he did wonder why her replies had stopped abruptly the evening before. Still, that hadn't prevented him from thumbing out yet more declarations that she was The One. By the time he reached the loop road, even at walking pace, Joaquín's heart rate had quickened. With no plans as to where they should eat that evening, he hoped that Amanda would recommend some place quiet and intimate. Anywhere they could spend time just getting to know each other. Despite the connection, they were effectively still strangers, after all.

'Joaquín,' he told himself, as the villa came into view, 'this

315

could be the making of you.'

Rolling his blazer sleeves towards the elbow, in a bid to stay cool, the young fitness trainer approached the front door. He noted that the blinds on the ground floor were turned, which seemed a little early. Twilight was settling, but the street lamps had yet to switch on. It was at the porch that he heard a voice inside. Titus was speaking solemnly, but with his voice raised a little, as if addressing a room. It caused Joaquín to hesitate as he reached for the buzzer. The last thing he wanted to do was interrupt.

Then Titus suddenly stopped talking, and Joaquín seized his moment.

He took a step away on hearing a chair scrape back and then footsteps in the lobby. With just a second to spare, Joaquín Mendez smoothed his shirt and prepared for the door to open.

'Yes?'

The pleasant smile Joaquín mustered was at odds with the grave expression on the Savage boy's face. Ivan was wearing a shirt and tie in a way that suggested this was the first time he'd ever had to knot one.

'I'm here for Amanda,' Joaquín shifted his weight from one foot to the other. 'We're going out.'

'I don't think so.'

When Ivan moved to close the door, Joaquín reacted by placing his hand on the other side.

'She's expecting me.' He glanced over the boy's shoulder. With the blinds angled against the setting sun it was gloomy inside the villa. 'Can I speak with her?'

'No.'

As Ivan stood his ground, Amanda herself appeared from the kitchen. She was wearing a black dress and a dark-blue cardigan. As soon as Joaquín saw her, it was clear from her red-rimmed eyes and the way she clutched herself that this wasn't a good time.

'We've suffered a loss,' she told him. 'Ivan's grandfather died yesterday.'

Immediately, Joaquín saw his chances of an evening in her company slip away.

'My condolences,' he said, and crossed himself on instinct. 'I hope it was quick.'

'It was *really* quick,' said Ivan. 'Those scooters aren't safe.'

'I should've called to let you know,' said Amanda, which stopped Joaquín from blundering further into the realms of saying the wrong thing, 'but we've been so busy since he passed.'

'What a terrible loss. I'm so sorry.'

Joaquín glanced back at the boy. If he was in mourning, it barely showed. Ivan simply stared at him, his lips pressed flat.

'We're holding a wake,' he said. 'And now here you are.'

If Ivan intended to make him feel unwelcome, it was working.

'I'll leave you in peace.' Joaquín addressed Amanda. 'Whenever you're ready, just call.'

Amanda looked at him uncomfortably.

'I don't know,' she said. 'Joaquín, all those texts you sent after we spoke on the phone . . . They came as quite a surprise. I'm flattered, but it was all a little –'

'Passionate?' he asked, brightening considerably.

'Intense,' said Amanda, sounding pained. 'I think under the circumstances we should call it a day. I'm sorry, Joaquín.'

317

'You heard the lady,' said Ivan. 'It's over.'

'But . . . it hasn't even begun!'

Ivan rolled his eyes and then gestured at the trainer to remove his hand. It left Joaquín a brief chance to see Amanda smiling fondly at him, though it could've been in pity, before the door shut in his face.

'That went well.' Joaquín sighed to himself and looked to his shoes. It felt as if he had several blisters coming on. 'What a moment this turned out to be.'

It was then he realised that he still had the carnations. Under the circumstances, he thought, Amanda should have them. If not as a romantic gesture then as a mark of sympathy for the family's loss. Once again, the fitness trainer reached for the buzzer, but stopped himself as his fingertip found the button. He really didn't want to summon the boy again, or risk irritating his father. Joaquín turned away from the villa, only to come full circle, having decided to bypass the kid by popping around the side of the villa. Amanda had emerged from the kitchen. As soon as she saw him at the side window, gesturing with the flowers, no doubt she would get to the kitchen door before anyone else. Well aware of the gravity of the event taking place inside, Joaquín headed for the side gate, intending to be quick and respectful. Finding the blinds closed at the kitchen window, just as they were at the front, he crept to the sliding door that led out to the jetty and peeked inside.

Some moments later, without blinking, Joaquín retreated by a step. Having just caught sight of Angelica at the hob, he dropped the bouquet and calmly retreated. This time, it wasn't her powerful presence that claimed possession of his soul, but what she was cooking. Back on the driveway, having stopped for a second to stare into space, he slipped off his shoes and placed them in the family's garbage bin. Without once looking back, he set off for his apartment at a jog and from there booked a taxi. Within hours, he had boarded a flight from Miami to Ministro Pistarini Airport, some fourteen miles southwest of the Argentinian capital of Buenos Aires. Joaquín Mendez never told his mother the real reason for his sudden return home, but she was delighted to have her son back in her embrace. It came as a surprise to her when he found work as a humble cattle hand, but a source of great pride when he went on to buy his own ranch some years later in the remote wilderness of Patagonia. There, the former fitness trainer and committed bachelor devoted himself to raising quality livestock. The welfare of his cows was a priority, and he would go on to secure a reputation as one of the country's benchmark beef producers. Indeed, Joaquín Mendez became as celebrated in the trade for the quality of his meat as he did for his arrival at the abattoir with every laden truck, having clearly wept all the way.

Nobody had seen Joaquín peek into the kitchen and pale visibly. At the time, with Ivan and Amanda back at the table, Angelica had served the first of what would be many dishes. Titus looked on with pride when she set the steaming bread bowl on the table. He smiled at her, and then at their guest beside him.

'It's what Oleg would've wanted,' he told Priscilla, and patted her hand.

Titus had been the one to break the sad news to her, having

personally called round to the Fallen Pine and pulled up a chair by her bedside. Priscilla had reacted to their loss with grace and dignity. She hadn't choked up or shed a tear but simply nodded as Titus explained the circumstances. Then he had leaned in to find her ear and proposed that she join them for the feast Oleg had been so desperate for her to attend.

'A celebration of the dead,' she had said in response, and her face lit up in his eyes. 'He told me it was customary once upon a time.'

Now Priscilla sat at the table with them, tucked in tight in her wheelchair with the oxygen cylinder stowed behind the seat. For someone who was close to following in Oleg's footsteps, he noted, she was a game and spirited old bird. Like the rest of the family, Titus was in a solemn mood. And yet the sense of anticipation that accompanied this, the beginning of a feast, was enough to lift the spirits. In this case, having passed on those too tubby, too sinewy or too fit for Titus, what they had here wasn't just a fitting tribute, but the perfect choice for the table.

'This is a traditional starter with a twist,' said Angelica, as she slipped a serving spoon into the soup.

'A solianka,' observed Amanda, who grinned at their guest. 'It's a kind of soup made with mushrooms, vodka and three different cuts of beef. Only in this case there is no beef.'

'Oh, I understand that,' Priscilla said brightly. 'It contains cuts of Oleg, right?'

Every member of the family beamed at the old lady.

'I think you'll find it unforgettable,' said Angelica, who sat and reached for her glass. 'It means he'll be with you for the rest of your days.'

'And may those days be longer and happier than you ever believed,' said Amanda.

'Wait.' This was Titus, who raised his hand. 'Aren't we forgetting something?'

'Ketchup?' Kat was sitting beside her mother, swinging her feet as she waited to be served.

'Not with a feast,' said Angelica, crinkling her nose. 'You can't have ketchup with everything.'

It was Ivan who caught his father's eye.

'I know,' he said, and held his gaze for a moment. 'May I?'

Titus considered the request and then sat back with a nod. After all the failed attempts to prove himself, it seemed that with this simple gesture his son was set to become a man at last. In the pit of grief, it was a moment that caused Titus's heart to swell with pride. Here he was, surrounded by family, and with the jointed remains of the one they had gathered to commemorate laid out across the kitchen counter. Everything from top to toe had been cooked exquisitely and was now resting to draw back the juices.

'Go ahead,' he told Ivan, and bowed his head.

The boy waited for everyone to follow suit. Then, with great reverence, he rose to his feet.

'For what we are about to receive,' he began, with his eyes squeezed shut and his hands clasped in prayer, 'may God have mercy on us all.'

DIGESTIF

Two days later, on the cusp of spring break, three boys swaggered through the doors of The Lentil Rebel. They had to look around to find a free table, which they promptly filled with elbows spread wide and loud, invasive laughter.

'This is too funny,' said one, and gestured at his friends to look around. 'If these hippies knew we ate meat, they'd freak out!'

Chad, Bryce and Ryan had decided to pay a visit to the café on their way to the beach. The place had fast become a fixture in Jupiter, earning a favourable review in the local paper as 'a refreshing break from all the flesh-heavy rib joints'. As soon as the trio heard about it, they had decided that it should be a target for abuse. On the way, they had come across the Hispanic kid who had just joined the year below and left him on the sidewalk with a grazed elbow and a hot, tearful face. It was the kind of thing the three soccer jocks would've directed at new girl, but ever since the thing with the sandwiches they had come to regard him with a degree of caution. At the table just then, however, as they messed about with the saltshaker, all thoughts of the incident were far from their minds. Ryan, like Bryce and Chad, wore skate shorts, an oversized T-shirt and sunglasses, which he pushed up over his buzz cut when the waitress approached.

'What can I get you?' she asked – a little abruptly for their liking – and handed out menus printed on chlorine-free, recycled card.

The waitress, an English girl, wore her hair in a bob that she seemed to be growing out. She was poised with her notepad to take their order, but looked more like she was ready to write them a ticket for a parking violation.

'Lighten up,' said Bryce, grinning at her. 'We don't bite.'

'You know what would put a smile on your face?' Chad swapped a smirk with Ryan. 'A good serving of pork.'

As the three laughed, none of them noticed the boy at the till who pointed them out to a shaven-headed man before slipping away into the kitchen. It was only when the man cleared his throat, having crossed the floor to stand over the waitress, that they fell quiet.

'Gentlemen,' he said, and nodded at them in turn. 'If nothing on the menu appeals, I can go through the specials.'

'Sure,' said Ryan, who stifled the amusement in his voice, only to share a smirk with his two friends. '*Special* food.'

'I can recommend the vegan chicken Caesar salad,' the man offered, as the waitress left them to serve another table. 'The croutons come fried in chilli oil for that special kick.'

'Dude, can I level with you here?' Bryce was the first to look up from his menu. 'We're not talking about real chicken, are we?'

'It's a flavoured soy product,' said the man patiently. 'But I can assure you it's very . . . chickeny.'

'That's what I don't get about you guys.' Bryce was addressing his friends now, as the grin returned to his face. 'You reject meat and then bust a gut to rustle up something that tastes the same. Why?' He shook his head for their benefit, looking highly amused with himself. 'If you crave chicken that badly, eat chicken. It won't kill you.'

The man considered his point as he waited for them all to stop sniggering, which they did when he rested his hands on the back of Chad's chair and leaned in.

'I think we all know you're not here to enjoy what's on the menu, right? I can practically smell when a carnivore comes through that door, and I'm going to let you into a little secret here. I'm a meat eater myself.'

Bryce, Chad and Ryan exchanged nervous glances.

'You're kidding,' ventured Ryan. 'Do your customers know?'

'Well, I don't make a big song and dance about it!' The man was alone in chuckling at this. 'But that doesn't mean I disrespect their values. In fact, I've come to rate the vegan approach to life. They care about what they consume more than most. Rather than be a part of the herd, they consider every morsel that enters their mouths. It might not be my personal preference, but at least they *think* about what they eat.'

The man tapped his temple as he said this, before standing tall again and folding his arms.

'The Caesar salad,' Bryce enquired hesitantly, if only to break the silence. 'Can that come without the chilli-fried croutons? I'm not good with food that's too spicy.'

Both Ryan and Chad looked at their friend incredulously. The man just beamed at him and then, having looked around, crouched down by the table.

'You know, providing you guys can be trusted, we could rustle up something a little more to your taste.'

'Meat?' Bryce seemed surprised at himself for working this out so quickly.

The man touched a finger to his lips.

'Let's keep this to ourselves,' he said, looking around. 'Fortunately, my wife is cooking in the kitchen today, and you guys can trust her to be discreet.'

'She's a carnivore, too?' Chad seemed amused by the admission. 'I like this place a little more now.'

'What kind of meat?' asked Ryan.

'Something from a blowout we were saving for ourselves, but the last thing I want is for you guys to go hungry. You made an effort to come here, but as there's nothing on the menu that appeals, I'd love for you to taste my wife's home cooking. She's one of a kind.'

Chad glanced at his two friends.

'Does that mean she's a babe?' he asked them quietly, only to receive a dead arm from Ryan.

'Be nice,' he hissed.

Just then, two cops walked through the door. The shaven-headed man nodded to them in greeting, clearly on friendly terms, and then called over to the other waitress serving the tables. The three watched with interest as one sprung forward to welcome the pair.

'Wow,' said Bryce, as the sprightly old lady with the apron led the first cop by the wrist to the front of the bar and offered coffees on the house. 'What's her secret?'

'Priscilla eats wisely,' said the bald guy, who paused to make eye contact with each of the boys in turn. 'As could you.'

It was Bryce who responded first by slapping the table with the palm of his hand.

'OK, you've sold it to us,' he declared. 'So, what have you got, big man?'

'Ribs,' Titus Savage told them matter-of-factly, and rose to relay the order to the kitchen. 'What else is there in this town?'

SINK YOUR TEETH INTO THE SAVAGES ONLINE

Now you've finished the main course,
get more from your dinner at

WWW.MEATTHESAVAGES.COM

Meet the whole family

Find out the history behind the Savages'
unusual taste in people

Download tasty extras

Read Sasha's vegetarian diary

Discover more about Matt Whyman

Acknowledgements

Writing about a family of ordinary, hard-working cannibals certainly raises eyebrows. It's a taboo, after all – something we don't like to discuss – which always draws an author's interest. What I didn't want to create, however, was a novel driven by horror and gore. Above all, what interests me is our relationship with food. To this end, serving up the trials and culinary misadventures of a modern family of people-eaters struck me as a great way to ask questions about what's on our plates.

Contrary to popular belief, I don't belong exclusively to Team Carnivore, Veggie or Vegan. Whatever your preference, I just believe we should all be keenly aware of what we eat and where it comes from. Ultimately, as the Savage family would be first to say, it doesn't cost the earth to make our diets healthy, humane and sustainable. They may be a little extreme in their approach, but you can't beat food served with love.

In cooking this book, I have a whole host of creative chefs to thank, from everyone at Hot Key Books to Philippa Milnes-Smith, Jason Chan and ILA – a team who have shown me boundless energy passion, good humour . . . and taste.

Matt Whyman

Matt Whyman is the author of several critically acclaimed novels, including *The Savages* and *Boy Kills Man*, as well as two comic memoirs, *Pig in the Middle* and *Walking with Sausage Dogs*. He is married and lives with his family in West Sussex.

HOT KEY BOOKS

Thank you for choosing a Hot Key book.

If you want to know more about our authors
and what we publish, you can find us online.

You can start at our website

www.hotkeybooks.com

And you can also find us on:

We hope to see you soon!